Body Shots

Books by Anne Rainey

"Cherry on Top" in *Some Like It Rough*

Naked Games

Pleasure Bound

So Sensitive

"Ruby's Awakening" in *Yes, Master . . .*

Body Rush

Published by Kensington Publishing Corp.

Body Shots

ANNE RAINEY

KENSINGTON BOOKS
www.kensingtonbooks.com

KENSINGTON BOOKS are published by

Kensington Publishing Corp.
119 West 40th Street
New York, NY 10018

All Kensington titles, imprints, and distributed lines are available at special quantity discounts for bulk purchases for sales promotion, premiums, fund-raising, educational, or institutional use.

Special book excerpts or customized printings can also be created to fit specific needs. For details, write or phone the office of the Kensington Sales Manager: Kensington Publishing Corp., 119 West 40th Street, New York, NY 10018. Attn. Sales Department. Phone: 1-800-221-2647.

Kensington and the K logo Reg. U.S. Pat. & TM Off.

eISBN-13: 978-1-61773-352-9
eISBN-10: 1-61773-352-0
First Kensington Electronic Edition: October 2015

ISBN-13: 978-1-61773-351-2
ISBN-10: 1-61773-351-2
First Kensington Trade Paperback Printing: October 2015

10 9 8 7 6 5 4 3 2 1

Printed in the United States of America

Body Shots

1

The dryness in her throat made it hard to breathe. Her bare feet were bloody from the pine needles and broken twigs that covered the forest floor. Excruciating pain shot up both of her legs. None of that mattered, though—Crystal only needed to escape. She had to get as far away from him as possible before she dropped from sheer exhaustion.

Besides, the pain was nothing compared to what he'd do if he caught up to her.

"You're only making it harder on yourself, sweetheart!"

Oh God, Richard. How had he found her so fast? Just the sound of his voice was enough to send shivers up and down her spine. That slick, mesmerizing baritone that had lured her in from the beginning now made her sick to her stomach. She heard his voice in her nightmares. Would hear it in her nightmares for years to come, no doubt.

Crystal ran faster, panicked now with the knowledge her husband was closing in on her. Her sweaty, long brown hair whipped her face in punishment. The belt he'd used on her earlier had left her thighs bloody and her nightgown a shredded mess. Somewhere in the dark recesses of Crystal's tortured mind, she knew she'd never leave the forest of trees that so completely enveloped her now.

"Ah, my sweet wife," Richard called out as he caught her by the arm and yanked, hard, pulling her to a stop. "You ran from me. You'll pay for that, I'm afraid." Then he raised a fist and punched her in the jaw. Her teeth rattled in her head and her vision blurred. The warm trickle of blood from a fresh cut at the side of Crystal's mouth went unchecked. "Please, don't," she shamelessly begged. Her words fell on deaf ears, though, as Richard hit her again.

When had things gone so wrong? She didn't know. One day he'd come home from work and flown into a rage because she hadn't washed the sheets on their king-sized bed. As a result, Crystal had received her first beating. It'd been so violent that it had hurt to sit down the next day.

These days it took so little to rile his temper. After dinner, he'd yanked off his belt and whipped her. Crystal wasn't even sure why this time. When it seemed he had finally finished his tirade, Crystal had tried to stand, but he only started on her again, blow after blow until she'd finally passed out from the pain. When she'd woken, Richard had been gone from the room. Crystal had taken the opportunity to run. Just run. She had no real destination other than away from him. She'd reached her breaking point. But Richard had been quicker than her, and he'd easily caught up to her.

He would make her pay for leaving him. The terrifying knowledge that she might not live through another of his beatings tore at the forefront of her mind. As Richard hit her once more, Crystal felt her body go limp as the black void of unconsciousness stole through her.

Richard wasn't sure why he didn't just leave Crystal there in the woods. She was useless to him. She'd been a huge disappointment practically from the first day, but he'd thought he could teach her how to be a proper wife. But nothing had worked, and he was just about done bothering with her. Still, there was something so tempting about Crystal. His fascination with her baffled even him. Hell, she didn't even take good care of herself. Since their wedding, she'd put on weight and had let herself go. She didn't even take pride in their home. He was constantly reminding her of her household duties. But some softer part of him kept him from abandoning her. As he picked her up and carried her back to the house, Richard knew that their time together had come to an end. He'd wasted enough time and energy on her as it was.

Crystal had been like a lost lamb when he'd met her at a New Year's Eve party two years earlier. She was the sweet to his bitter, and he had known he had no business anywhere near her innocence. But in one thing, they were the same—they both longed to be loved, and in that, they were a kindred spirit. So he'd swooped in, and it hadn't been long before they were married. God, if he'd known what a colossal waste of time she'd be he never would have given her the time of day.

Crystal woke to a splitting headache. As she opened her eyes and tried to focus, the room tilted and the pain intensified. She touched her lip and realized it was swollen. She'd have bruises on top of bruises this time. Richard had outdone himself. The room he'd put her in was dark, but she knew where she was. The guest room. He always put her there after one of their fights. It was where he liked to discipline her. Crystal's stomach knotted as she thought of all the horrors that room held.

As the fuzz in her brain began to ebb, Crystal became aware of a heavy weight across her belly. Tentatively, she took her hand on an exploration to see what it was that kept her immobile. It was as she skated her hand down her body that she felt an arm, strong and firm, holding her in place. Richard. Oh God, would this night never end?

Another hand clamped over her mouth, and Crystal winced at the pain in her already swollen mouth. "Why'd you try to leave? Don't you love me anymore?" When she only lay there, eyes wide in fright, he went on. "Cat got your tongue, sweetheart?"

Still, Crystal didn't move, didn't dare. She knew this was the calm before the storm. Once again, she wondered why Richard didn't just kill her and get it over with.

"If you promise to be good, I'll remove my hand."

After a few moments of debating her options—which were few—she realized she was going to have to obey him if she had any chance at an escape. She nodded her acquiescence. True to his word, Richard removed his hand. He stood, but before she had time to think of her next move, the glow of a single candle lit the room. What did he intend to do with her? Crystal shook her head, not even willing to consider any of that right now. She would not panic, not again. She had to keep her wits about her if she was to get away from him with her life.

Her gaze wandered around the room. When she saw him sitting in a chair on the other side of the room, Crystal took a chance and sat up. Richard stood, then crossed the room. Oh God.

He tilted his head, as if baffled by her actions. "You're terrified of me, aren't you?"

What was he up to? She took a chance and nodded.

He snorted. "You are so pathetic. If I wanted to, I could have you on your knees in front of me, begging."

She kept her breathing at an even tempo, praying she wouldn't do something to send him into a rage again.

"You seem to get under my skin and push all my buttons," Richard said after several beats of silence. "I have no excuse for being so brutal, except that you just never seem to learn," he said.

The only thing Crystal could think to do was nod. He was being strangely kind, but Crystal knew better than to trust his current mood. Until the right opening arose when she would be able to break away from him, for good, Crystal would just have to bide her time. God, she didn't even know how long she'd been knocked out. Had it been just a few hours? Days? Focusing on the one thing she could do without arousing his anger, Crystal said, "My nightgown is mostly shredded. Can I change?" He laughed and Crystal's humiliation intensified. She wished she had the nerve to tell him where he could shove it, but he put an imperious hand in the air and stopped her before she could utter a single syllable.

He smiled. "I'm sorry for losing control earlier." He turned away and walked to the closet. He grabbed some clothes and tossed them at her. "I'll leave you to dress," he said arrogantly. "When you're through, please join me downstairs. We have things to discuss."

Then he turned and walked out of the room, closing the door behind him, leaving her alone. She breathed a sigh of relief. At least he wasn't going to watch her change, and it appeared that he wasn't going to beat her again, either.

Not yet anyway.

Crystal got up from the bed but stopped when the soles of her feet stung. She lifted her foot and saw the scratches from her wild flight through the woods. She shook her head. What had she been thinking to take off barefooted? It was a testament to how scared she'd been. She bent and picked up the white blouse and faded blue jeans he'd tossed at her. She quickly slipped into the silky material. She still had on her underwear, thank God, so it didn't take her long to pull on the jeans. She buttoned the blouse and tucked it into the waist of the jeans, then zipped them up. She felt better immediately. It was stupid, but the clothes made her feel less vulnerable.

After cleaning her face and bandaging her cuts, Crystal headed for the kitchen. Richard stood at the stove, stirring something. Automatically she sniffed the air and her stomach grumbled in eager anticipation. He'd made chicken noodle soup? Her mind started working, turning over various scenarios of death by poisoning. Crazy as it sounded, Crystal wouldn't put anything past her husband. Not after the two years of pure hell he'd put her through.

She crossed the room, barely maintaining her balance. Her head throbbed and her cheek felt swollen. She pulled out the closest chair and sat down. The room stopped spinning at once.

He carried a steaming bowl to the table and placed it in front of her. "Eat," he commanded. Crystal merely stared at him. Richard stared back. Finally, he said, "If I had wanted to kill you, wife, it wouldn't be by poisoning, I assure you."

She thought about that for a second. He was right. Richard would probably just beat her to death. It'd be more fun for him that way. She shrugged and picked up the spoon. As she blew on the steaming liquid and took her first bite, she was surprised to note that it was actually quite good. She didn't even know Richard could cook, considering he'd never done it before. That had been her job. All the household chores had been on her. As she ate, Crystal was having a hard time wrapping her mind around the idea of him doing something as domestic as cooking. And the kindness was so unlike him that it sent chills up and down her spine.

After she emptied the bowl, Crystal picked up a napkin and patted her lips. "That was very good. Thank you."

He nodded, as if addressing a class. "I'm pleased you like it."

Before she could talk herself out of it, Crystal blurted, "I want a divorce."

He leaned forward in his chair and spoke in a menacing tone. "I wondered when you'd get around to that."

She flinched, fear racing up and down her spine, but she

continued, "You've said more than once that I'm a huge disappointment to you."

Without a word, Richard stood and went to the counter. He picked up a stack of papers and handed them to her. "Divorce papers," he explained. "All you need to do is sign them."

Crystal stared down at the neat stack of documents. Could it really be that easy? Suspicious that he had some vicious plan in mind the minute she picked up the pen, she asked, "If you wanted a divorce, then why did you come after me? Why not just let me go?"

He shrugged. "And miss all the fun? Not a chance." He stood and said, "I'm going out for a bit. I expect you to be gone by the time I get back."

"Why?" she asked, just before he walked out of the room. "Why didn't you do this a year and a half ago?"

He turned slowly, a disgusted look on his face. "I had hoped to skip the Q and A part of this, but I can see you're determined to drive me crazy right up to the very last second."

Crystal stood, fear causing her legs to shake uncontrollably. "I'm not trying to drag this out, but I think we can both agree that you don't love me. A lot of time has been wasted."

He shoved his hands in his pockets and let out a frustrated sigh. "I had hoped you'd improve. That discipline and a bit of training would make a difference. I can see now that I was only fooling myself. You'll always be a sad, overweight disappointment."

Before Crystal could digest the hateful words, Richard was gone and the phone was ringing. She forced her feet to move across the room and answered it on the second ring. "Hello?"

"Hi, sweetie."

Crystal's throat clogged with emotion. Her legs gave out and she dropped onto the nearest chair. "Mom."

"What's wrong? And don't say nothing, because I can hear it in your tone."

Her mother would take Richard's side. Crystal had long given up on the notion that her mother would ever fully see the truth. The sad fact of the matter was, her mom thought Richard was a wonderful man and a terrific husband. She didn't understand why Crystal was always antagonizing him. To her way of thinking, marriage was for life, and it didn't much matter whether the man you were wedded to was a monster or not.

"Richard and I, we're getting a divorce." Crystal left out the part about the beating. Her mom wouldn't believe her anyway. Never had. Crystal had tried to tell her before, but her mother always made it seem as if Crystal was only making waves. In her mom's eyes, a woman was supposed to love and support her husband in all things. No matter what. The archaic attitude made Crystal want to vomit.

"What?"

"I'm leaving him." She thought of her friend Mollie in Cincinnati. Mollie had urged her for months to leave Richard. She'd take her in, Crystal was sure of it. "In fact, I might stay with Mollie for a bit." She took a deep breath. "Just until I get back on my feet."

"I see," her mother replied with no small amount of disapproval. "I suppose nothing I say will change your mind."

Please, for once, stand up for me. But Crystal knew better. Her mom's stance toward marriage was as clear as day. She straightened her spine and said, "No, Mom. I'm not living this way anymore. I'm done."

"Honey, this may be hard to hear, but I think you're misjudging Richard. I don't think he's quite as bad as you make him out to be. I mean, are you certain this is what you want?"

Crystal touched her swollen lip and straightened her spine. "Yeah, it's exactly what I want."

"You should come home then," her mother replied. "If only for a few days. It might help to clear your head."

Living under the same roof as her mother and listening to

the woman expound on Richard's many virtues? No way in hell. "Thanks, but I'll be fine." She sniffled and said, "I need to deal with this on my own."

"I understand, dear. Call me when you get settled, okay?"

"Sure," Crystal said, feeling a weight lift off her shoulders for the first time in years. She looked at the clock on the microwave and knew her time was quickly running out. "I need to go before he gets back."

"All right then. Love you, dear."

"I love you, too," she said.

As they ended the call, Crystal looked down at the signed divorce papers. A life without Richard. Without pain and suffering. Without constant ridicule. She sent up a quick thank-you to the heavens for finally answering her prayers, before heading for her bedroom. The sooner she got the hell out of there, the better.

2

Five months later . . .

"Your birthday is coming up and I'm taking you out. That's all there is to it."

Crystal cringed. How pathetic, having her best friend take pity on her on her birthday. It was bad enough that Crystal still lived in Mollie's house after five months of searching for an apartment and coming up empty. Five months working hard as an applications developer had given her a sense of purpose. She'd even taken up self-defense classes and managed to sweat off the extra pounds. The biggest step for Crystal had been making an appointment with a therapist. Opening up about her relationship with Richard had really helped. No doubt there had been a lot of changes in Crystal. Mentally and physically. She was ready to take the final step and get her own place. It would go a long way toward making her feel whole again.

But Lord knew, she didn't want Mollie arranging her nightlife for her. It made her feel like a little lost orphan or something. Even though Mollie didn't mean it that way, Crystal still wanted to crawl under the rug of humiliation. At one time, Mollie had been happily married and well on her way to popping out a baby or two. Three years ago, Alec had come into Mollie's life and the pair had been madly in love. He'd brought life into her friend's eyes. Crystal had been a little envious that Mollie's marriage was such a happy one when hers was such a train wreck. But when Alec had died in a horrible car accident, Mollie had all but given up on love. She hated to see her sweet-natured friend so closed off, even now.

Mollie reached across the table and swatted her hand. "Don't be so difficult. I'm taking you out for your birthday, and that's the end of it. Besides, you know I always enjoy your company."

Crystal forced a smile to her lips as she picked up her mug and sipped her hot coffee. The temperature was in the eighties outside, and it wasn't much cooler in Mollie's kitchen. As she looked around, taking in the nearly fifty-year-old house, Crystal sighed. It'd been Mollie's grandmother's house until she'd passed away and left everything she owned to her only grand-daughter. Crystal knew Mollie wanted to renovate the old two-story, but she couldn't seem to bring herself to change even the color of the paint, much less let some construction crew tromp around getting drywall dust all over everything. No, Crystal thought with fondness, the house would probably never change. Mollie liked it the way it was, well-loved and full of memories.

Crystal took another sip of her coffee and desperately tried to come up with a logical reason why she couldn't spend the evening with Mollie. It wasn't that she dreaded going out with her best friend, but she suspected it would be a pity date. No thanks.

"Have you ever heard of Kinks?"

The question seemed to come out of left field. Crystal shook her head. "Er, what is Kinks?"

"It's a nightclub, but it's not really your average nightclub."

"What do you mean?"

"It's a bondage club," she explained. "A place where you can be a submissive and let a man spank you just for the sheer joy of it."

Mollie was into sex games? "How is it that I didn't know this about you?" They'd been besties for years.

Mollie handed her a business card with the words *Kinks Nightclub* scrawled across it in bold letters. Below that was written, *Get Your Kink On.* "Come on. You'll have a great time, I promise."

Crystal wasn't sure what to say, except, "No way in hell." She dropped the business card on the table, and it sat there like a ticking time bomb. "I do not want to be spanked." She'd never be that vulnerable with a man again.

"Look, you need something to wipe that sad expression off your face. I know Richard's abuse left a lot of emotional scars, but it's time to get back out there, don't you think?" Mollie looked her over, then said, "Besides, you might just like it."

Crystal shook her head. "Am I required to, like, have sex with someone?"

Mollie rolled her eyes. "Of course not, dork. It's not like that. It's like a regular club with music and a lot of people enjoying a common passion. The difference is that their sexual preferences are sort of out there for all to see. It can be shocking when you see a man spanking a woman. And there's a lot of PDA. But all you need to do is watch and enjoy." She shrugged. "Hey, who knows, maybe you'll meet a hot, rich guy."

Crystal covered her face. "Oh God, I can't believe I'm actually considering this."

"You'll have fun, just wait and see." Mollie cocked her head to the side. "And don't worry about an outfit. I think I have something that would fit you. Something sexy."

Crystal's stomach pitched at the idea of putting herself out there again after all the abuse she'd suffered at Richard's hands. "I'm not opposed to hitting the clubs, but bondage and submission? Seriously?"

Mollie bobbed her eyebrows. "How do you know if you don't try it?"

Mollie did have a point. She'd lived in an emotional prison for too long. It was time to step out and have some fun. She smiled and picked up the business card. "Okay, I'll try it."

Mollie patted her on the hand. "That's my girl." She stood and propped her hands on her hips. "Now, let's get dressed and go do some 'therapy' shopping."

Crystal laughed as she got to her feet, feeling better than she had in months. "Sounds great, but I'm buying lunch. It's the least I can do since you've been letting me crash here."

Her friend's arms came around her shoulders and Crystal was suddenly being pulled in for a hug. "That's what friends are for, sweetie."

Crystal knew the truth in that moment. When she'd met Mollie, she'd hit the friend jackpot. She'd be lost without her.

It was Sunday morning and the nightclub that Mac owned with his buddy Trent was closed. They'd taken over the running of the club along with their friend Dane over a year ago, after the previous owner had died of cancer. They'd grown close to Leo, and he had confided in them that he wanted the club to go to someone he knew and trusted. Someone who would take care of it. So they'd stepped in and made it happen. At one time they'd run the club on the side, while handling their law practice during the daytime hours. When the long days became too much, Trent and Mac had both willingly given up their day jobs to run the club full-time. Dane had chosen the lawyer route and sold them his third, giving up the club life entirely. Although that had been more about Lydia, the woman who'd stolen his heart.

Kinks now made them a hefty profit. Still, it was never about the money. It was their home away from home. The only place they could truly be free to explore the darker nature of their souls.

It had been in their college days that they'd realized they shared a common passion for the kinkier side of sex. When the club had practically been dropped into their laps, it'd seemed perfect.

As Mac looked at Trent sitting on a stool at the counter, he knew a sense of rightness about the proposal he was about to make. The nightclub belonged to both of them; it was only right that they both took part in taking it to the next stage. "I have a proposal, but it's a big one. And probably a shit-ton of work, too."

"Make it quick, will ya?" Trent grumbled. "I left a gorgeous woman in my bed and I really want to get back to her."

"I'm sure she'll wait for you." Mac looked closer at Trent and noticed the dark circles under his eyes. "When was the last time you slept?"

Trent sat back in his stool and crossed his arms over his chest. "I was sort of . . . up all night."

Mac glared at his friend, but stayed silent. He'd been doing more and more of that lately. Staying up all night. Drinking too much. Mac was beginning to worry. But Trent was a big boy and if there was something wrong he'd say so. After all, Trent wasn't really known for keeping his thoughts to himself.

Trent yawned. "Why couldn't we just meet at my house? And where the hell is the coffee?"

"Because this is about the nightclub." Mac rolled his eyes at Trent's pissy mood. He'd always hated mornings. Owning a nightclub suited Trent to a tee. Late nights and sleeping in until noon was right up Trent's alley. "You want coffee, sunshine, then make it yourself. I don't work for you, remember?"

"If you did, I'd fire your ass."

"Christ, quit bitching and let me talk, and maybe we'll be able to get through this meeting before dinnertime."

"Fine, talk," he bit out.

Mac started right in, no sense in dancing around it. "I've had a chance to look over the books. The business is doing great. Better than I expected."

"Great, now can I go home?" Trent asked, as he started to turn toward the door.

Mac held up a hand. "No, damn it. The thing is, I've been looking at some property across town. I think it's time to expand. Open a second Kinks."

"That's a hell of a lot of work." Trent rubbed his jaw. "Are you sure it makes sense right now?"

Mac had never been more certain of anything. "I've been over it several times, and it's a good move financially. Since neither of us has a day job any longer, we have the time to make it happen."

Suddenly alert, Trent sat up and placed his elbows on the counter. "That will mean hiring a construction crew and interviewing for a new staff." He shook his head. "I'm sure there's more, but I'm still a little fuzzy here."

Mac waved a hand in the air. "True, but the payoff will be more than worth it."

"Another club would gain us a hell of a lot more customers, for sure. But I don't want to end up bankrupt because we rushed into anything."

Mac was a little worried about that, too. Owning your own business wasn't for lightweights. "I agree. There's a lot to consider."

Trent nodded. "Staff, uniforms, and do we want the new Kinks to have the same BDSM atmosphere or do we go with something entirely different?" Trent shoved a hand through his hair. "This is big."

"No shit," Mac said, as a slight smile appeared. "But I like it. Kinks Two . . . sort of has a nice ring to it," Mac replied.

They spent the rest of the afternoon making plans. When they got ready to leave, Mac asked, "Okay, before we end this meeting, we're for sure doing this, right?"

Trent sent up his agreement. "I'm in."

Mac nodded. "Great, I'll contact the Realtor about the property and we'll go from there."

"Good deal," Trent said as he stood. "Now, I've got a sexy, naked woman in my bed. Later."

"Use protection," Mac called out just as Trent reached the door.

"Always do, Dad," Trent shot back. "Always do."

Mac chuckled, feeling better than he had in months. Excitement about the new club sizzled through his bloodstream, and he was more than ready to get the ball rolling. Hell, the day he'd quit the lawyering gig was the best day of his life.

The week flew by and Friday night came way too fast for Crystal's peace of mind. Now, as she stood reading through the rules and regulations at Kinks nightclub, and then signed on the dotted line, she had to wonder what had possessed her to say yes to Mollie in the first place. When her friend escorted her to the Great Room, which consisted of a large, comfortable sitting area and several high, round tables and stools along the outer edge of the room, Crystal tried not to go all bug-eyed. But who could blame her? There were couples kissing and fondling each other. Out in the open. It was as embarrassing as it was arousing to her.

A pair of redheaded women seated on the floor next to an overstuffed chair caught her attention. They each had a leather collar around their necks with a metal ring in the front, which attached to a leash. The man holding the pair of leashes seemed big and scary, but when he gazed down at both women with affection, Crystal was taken aback. He said something to one of them, who then immediately started to kiss the other woman. The man petted her and continued to carry on a conversation as if it was all so normal. Another man had his submissive seated on the floor between his thighs. Crystal's jaw nearly dropped when she spied the woman's fingers wrapped around his exposed cock. Crystal quickly looked away, but not before she caught the woman slowly stroke the bulbous head with her thumb. Did these club patrons realize they were in a room full of people?

Crystal's breasts tingled and her pussy dampened. She hadn't expected to react so quickly, but as she let her gaze sweep the room, she noticed several men watching her with desire-filled eyes. Suddenly, Crystal was grateful for the low lighting. It gave her just enough courage to keep from bolting out the door. She stayed close to Mollie as they reached one of the round tables along the edge of the room. Mollie pulled out one of the stools and sat down. Crystal followed suit.

Mollie pointed upward and Crystal's gaze followed until she spotted another level. "What's up there?"

"That's what's known as the Upper Dungeon. That's one of the areas where members can play."

"Dungeon? That sounds so . . . medieval."

Mollie nodded. "It sort of is, I guess. There are suspension racks, bondage tables, even a spanking bench. Would you like to go up and see it?"

Crystal shook her head, her heart pounding too fast. "I think I'm good right here."

"Are you having a fun birthday so far?"

She nodded. "It's different, I'll give you that." She cocked her head and asked, "How did you get into this scene?"

"Alec turned me on to it." The light in her gaze dimmed. "It hasn't been the same since he passed away, though."

"But you've dated guys who come here?"

"Yep. But nothing serious." She shrugged. "I guess I'm not ready for serious right now."

Just then two men strode up to Crystal and said hello. Both were gorgeous, tall, and muscular. The one on the left had black hair and silvery-blue eyes that sucked her right in. The other had lighter hair and a grin that would rock any woman's world. The black T-shirts they wore said simply, *Get Your Kink On.* And they looked at her as if she were a shiny new toy. Oh wow.

The one with the sinful smile asked, "Are you new here?"

"Yes, I'm Crystal. My friend Mollie here isn't new."

He nodded toward Mollie. "Ah, I thought I'd seen you here before. It's nice to meet you both."

Mollie blushed and said, "Same here."

Crystal pointed to the men's shirts and asked, "Judging by your shirts, I'm guessing you must work here, huh?"

The hottie with the black hair smiled. "I'm Trent Dailey, and this is Mac Anderson. We own the place."

"Nice to meet you." The music changed and suddenly Crystal wanted to dance. Feeling impulsive for once, she asked, "So, Trent and Mac, which of you is going to dance with me? Don't make me look for someone else."

"It'd be my pleasure," Trent said as he helped her off the stool.

"Mine, too," Mac said, his voice low, a little rough.

"Both of you?" Crystal looked at Trent, then Mac. She couldn't tell whether they were teasing or not. She didn't want to know which was true.

"Come on," Trent said as he led her out to the dance floor. "You can move those sexy hips all you want."

Crystal didn't quite know what to think when Mac followed close behind. Her mind whirled with the possibility that the two men were making a move on her at the same time. Could it be? She glanced back at Molly for reassurance. Her friend winked and nodded, then merely sat back as if content to watch.

Still Crystal started to change her mind about the dance when a third man stepped in front of her. While everyone else was dressed in tight, flesh-baring outfits, this man wore a simple pair of tight, black jeans and a brickred pocket T-shirt. He wasn't necessarily a handsome man—his features were too rugged to be considered handsome—but he wasn't hard on the eyes, either. The *come and get it* smile on his lips made her face go hot.

"I saw you arrive and hoped to get a dance with you." His gaze traveled over her body, giving her the once-over before coming back to her face. "You're awfully damn hard to miss in that pretty dress. A man would have to be blind."

"Thank you, but my dance card is a little full at the moment." Crystal could feel the tension coming off of Trent and Mac beside her, and she could swear they'd both moved closer to her. Heck, their bodies even brushed against hers. It wasn't difficult to figure out that the man hitting on her was stirring Trent's and Mac's ire.

The guy spared Trent a glance and shrugged, as if Trent were nothing more than an annoying insect, then zeroed in on her once more. "Sure I can't change your mind?"

"The lady was clear," Trent said as he wrapped an arm around her waist and pulled her in close to his side. She glanced up and nearly swallowed her tongue at the lethal look on Trent's face. Her gaze darted to Mac and saw a similar expression. Yikes.

"Sorry, but I promised." She smiled, hoping to take some of the sting out of the rejection. "Thanks for the offer, though. It was very sweet."

He nodded, one side of his mouth kicking up as he dared, "Maybe later then."

As he made his way to the other side of the room, Crystal peeked over at Trent. She noticed he stared at the man's back for what seemed like an eternity.

Trent's blue gaze came back to her. "You seem to have quite an effect on me, Crystal. The thought of his hands coming anywhere near you just about caused me to kick his ass out of my club." His eyes narrowed, as if bewildered by his own actions.

"Same goes for me," Mac said from behind her. "He's been here a bunch of times, and he always gets just a little too aggressive with the ladies."

Crystal turned her head and looked up at Mac. His gaze, so cool earlier, blazed hot enough that Crystal felt seared clear to the bone. Suddenly she didn't care about the other guy. All her focus was on Mac and Trent. Two men at once. She frowned. "What exactly is happening right now?"

The men looked at each other, then back at her. Mac was the first to speak. "We're attracted to you, Crystal."

She planted her hands on her hips and narrowed her eyes. "Wait, both of you?"

"Yeah, both of us," Trent murmured. Both of them looked way too satisfied with themselves. It suddenly pissed her off.

Crystal stepped closer and poked Trent in the chest. "I'm here to dance, that's it. So quit with all the chest beating." She looked between the two of them. "I came here to have fun with my friend for my birthday. Not to get mixed up in some convoluted delusion you two are suffering from."

Mac's eyebrows shot up. "You think we're delusional?"

"Well, what else could it be?" Her voice was rising and people were beginning to stare. She took a few deep breaths before continuing in a more reasonable tone, "You're both gorgeous and clearly on the prowl, and for whatever reason you think I should be the lioness for your little lion love triangle."

Mac chuckled. "Lioness, huh? Now that you mention it, I wouldn't be opposed to hearing a certain kitty purr."

Oh God. That should not have her pussy going damp with need, it really shouldn't. Crystal knew beyond a shadow of a doubt that she was way out of her element with Trent and Mac.

An image of the two men naked, pleasuring her, sprang to mind. It was forbidden, and she instantly felt guilty for even allowing the picture to invade her mind at all. Instinctively she knew that Mac and Trent would be nothing like Richard. He'd been easygoing at first, too, though, until she'd married him. Then he'd changed. Mac and Trent were bold, candid, and clearly insatiable when they got their hooks into something . . . or someone. Crystal didn't know what to make of any of it.

"Dance with me," Trent murmured, holding his hand out for her. "I want to get you in my arms, that's all. I want to feel you against me. Just that, Crystal, nothing more."

Hypnotized and unable to resist, Crystal lifted her hand. Trent took it and tenderly kissed her knuckles. Crystal let out her breath and allowed Trent to steer her toward the center of the room where several other couples danced to the beat of some sexy, slow tune. As Trent's arms came around her, Crystal looked to the left and saw Mac watching them, a tender smile on his face.

"I can feel you trembling. Don't think this to death. Just feel. That's all, just feel."

Feel? How could she do any less with Trent's powerful arms surrounding her, embracing her in his masculine warmth? He pulled her up against his hard strength, and Crystal realized that tonight was going to be a night she'd never forget.

Crystal felt at home. It was odd, but there it was. Nothing could ever harm her with Trent's strong arms holding her tight. She twined her arms around his neck, and he pulled her in tighter. She immediately knew what he wanted to show her. The rigid, thickness of his cock was now pressed into her belly. Crystal's knees went weak. Her eyes sought his, searching for confirmation. His wicked smile sent her blood pressure soaring. He rotated his hips, causing heat to pool between her legs and her face to flame.

Leaning down, his hot breath against her ear, Trent whispered, "Don't be embarrassed, baby. You're beautiful. Feeling your sweet curves against me is driving me right out of my mind." He lifted his head, his gaze so dark she barely saw the pupils. "I'm not going to do anything about it. Not unless you want me to. Do you want me to, Crystal?"

"I—I don't know."

"Are you a little turned on?" he whispered against her ear.

"Maybe," she confessed. "But we're strangers, Trent."

"Yes, but I want to change that. Tonight."

Crystal shrugged. "I don't know. I've never done this before."

"Maybe we should find out where this could go."

"Trent's right."

Crystal froze at the deep baritone coming from directly behind her. Turning her head, she saw Mac, and he was close. Close enough she could smell his clean masculine scent and see the tension riding him.

The ramifications of what they were saying hit her at once. "Both of you?" Her nipples hardened, as if begging to be touched, tasted, played with by Mac and Trent both.

Mac cupped the back of her neck. It was a strong, possessive hold. She couldn't move. "You sound surprised, angel."

"Surprised barely covers it," she said, and her voice sounded husky. Damn it, she sounded aroused. "You two must have had too much to drink or something." *Lighten the mood,* she lectured herself.

Mac *tsked.* "Nah, Trent never drinks and I only had a few sips of a light beer earlier."

"Come upstairs with us," Trent whispered. "Where we can be alone. We can talk about this in private."

"Talk?" she asked, turned on despite her suspicions.

"Talk, nothing more. Unless it's what you want," he added. "I promise."

"You have our word, angel," Mac said, adding his two cents to Trent's. "The ball's in your court."

"But you don't deny you want me. Both of you. At once." She said it quietly, but still it felt like all eyes were on her.

"We won't lie to you," Trent said. "Having you beneath us is something we desperately want, Crystal."

Crystal slapped a hand over her eyes. "Oh God. I must be insane to even consider this."

Mac pried her hand away, a tender smile on his face. "Insane because you like the idea?"

She couldn't lie, not about this. "Well, it's not exactly a turnoff," she answered, her voice quivering. From fear or excitement? Both, she suspected.

Trent's arms tightened, and Mac's silver gaze blazed with passion. "Follow me," Mac growled.

Mac gestured to someone. Making arrangements for someone to hold down the fort? Most likely. Heat filled her cheeks when the man's gaze darted her way for a split second. As Mac started out of the room, Trent wrapped a hand around her smaller one, then led her toward the doorway. Her legs shook. She was really doing this. Going upstairs with Trent and Mac. Would they make love to her? Both powerful men? She couldn't even begin to wrap her head around it. Crystal had no experience with the wilder side of life. What would they expect from her, and would she even be able to satisfy them? Suddenly Trent stopped and cupped her chin in his large, gentle grip. "Stop thinking it to death. We only want what you want. We're not going to do anything that makes you uncomfortable."

His gaze dropped to her chest. His nostrils flared as he muttered, "So sweet. So tempting."

"So out of my depth," she muttered.

Trent brought her hand to his lips and kissed it. Without another word, he took her to the stairs. Halfway up he stopped her again, murmuring, "Tell me, baby, are you wet right now? Is your pussy eager for my touch?"

"Trent." She had no idea what she was going to say. She had

no words to describe the feelings rioting inside her in that moment.

"Mac and I are going to make you feel so damn good. Every sexy inch of you, Crystal."

She had to make him understand. He had to know she wasn't this daring. That she'd never been wild or uninhibited in bed. She swiveled on her heel, nearly tumbling right off the step had Trent not reached out and grabbed her around the waist. "I've never . . . this isn't—"

"Shh, it's okay." He reached around and patted her bottom. "Upstairs first."

Crystal hesitated. She could walk away right now. Go back to her friend and forget this ever happened. Oh crap. *Mollie.* Crystal turned around and spotted her friend dancing with a tall, dark-haired man. Crystal didn't recognize him. Was he someone Mollie knew well or had they just met? Crystal stepped away from Mac and Trent and held up a hand. "Uh, give me a sec, okay?"

A beat of silence stretched between them, then they both nodded. She walked away, but quickly peeked back, and a thrill ran up her as she noticed that neither of them had budged an inch. They simply stood by and waited. When Crystal approached Mollie, her friend glanced her way and grinned. "Having a good time?" Mollie asked as she spotted Mac and Trent waiting for her. "Those two are so into you," she whispered into her ear.

Heat stole into her cheeks. "Uh, actually, that's what I wanted to talk to you about."

Mollie held up a hand. "Say no more. I'm going to hitch a ride with Remmington here." She patted the man she'd been dancing with on the chest. "He and I have known each other for years."

Remmington winked as he tweaked Mollie's nose. "I'll take good care of her."

Crystal nodded, then looked back at Mollie. "Are you sure?"

"I'm positive, sweetie, but what about you?" She pointedly glanced over at Trent and Mac. "Do you know what you're doing?"

"No, I really don't," she blurted out. "But for once I don't want to think it to death. I just want to have a good time." She cringed as her own words sank in. "Oh God, is that horrible of me?"

"Of course not." Mollie hugged her close and said, "And just so you know, I think you must be awfully special to catch their eye."

Curious, she said, "Oh?"

"Well, as long as I've been coming here, I've never seen them dance with one of the customers."

A jolt of pleasure shot through her at the knowledge that maybe, just maybe, this was as special for Mac and Trent as it was for her. "I'll call you tomorrow."

"You'd better," she replied with a grin.

As Crystal made her way back to Mac and Trent she saw the warmth in their smiles and the gentleness in the men's gazes. She knew beyond a shadow of a doubt that neither man would hold it against her if she turned them down and chose to go home, alone. But wasn't it about time she did something that gave her pleasure? Her entire marriage had been about pleasing Richard. This was her time. And she was calling the shots. Making the final decision calmed Crystal's racing heart as nothing else could.

When Crystal reached the men, nothing was said as she simply started up the stairs, taking the steps one a time. When she reached the upstairs landing, Mac was beside her, quietly waiting. She let her gaze travel the length of him. As she spied the rigid hardness of his cock beneath the navy slacks, her mouth watered. Trent moved in beside her, both men wearing grins. Crystal shuddered.

* * *

Trent couldn't believe his eyes. The minute he'd spotted her, he'd wanted her. He'd never had such a strong reaction to a woman in his club before. Crystal was different. He was a mere few feet from their private room. Trent licked his lips, anticipation humming along his nerve endings. His cock, already hard enough to drive spikes through cement blocks, strained against the tight confines of his slacks. He looked over at Mac and saw the same hunger, the same wild need. Mac's gaze stayed on Crystal as he stepped backward. Once. Twice. When his back hit the door to their private suite, he said, "Do you trust us, Crystal?"

Trent held his breath. Would she go through that door, or would she tell them both to go to hell? The woman seemed to possess a no-nonsense attitude. He liked it. She said what she meant. She didn't play games like some of the women he'd dated.

"Yes, I trust you. I wouldn't have come up here if I didn't."

Trent exhaled. Mac grinned, then reached behind his back and turned the knob. He pushed it open and stepped aside. "After you, baby."

Crystal looked over at him, her gaze eating him up. Trent easily saw the arousal, but there was a healthy dose of nerves, too. He reached out and cupped her cheek. Damn, she had the softest skin. He'd never touched anything finer. "Easy, baby. We won't hurt you."

"But when I go in there"—she sent a look toward the suite— "we're going to be together. The three of us."

"Is that what you want?" Trent asked, his voice rough with the feelings coursing through him.

"I—I don't know." Crystal pushed a hand through her hair, mussing the shiny brown strands. Trent ached to grab a handful and press it against his face. Crystal's hair smelled like coconuts. He fucking loved coconuts.

As he moved his thumb over Crystal's bottom lip, he smeared

her pink gloss. Christ, he wanted her mouth naked. No paint, just smooth skin. And soon to be wrapped around his cock if he had anything to say about it.

"Would you like to hear what I want?"

She snorted and wrapped her small hand around his wrist, then pulled his hand away from the temptation of her mouth. "I'm pretty sure I already have a good grasp on what you want, Trent."

Trent winked. "In case there's any confusion, allow me to spell it out." He stepped closer, close enough to feel the soft weight of her breasts against his chest. He wondered about the shade of her nipples. Were they a dark mauve or a pretty pink? "I want you to walk through that door," he softly demanded. "I want you to take off that lovely bit of black satin. And I want you to let Mac and me take you to heaven. That's what I want. The question that needs answering now is, is that what *you* want?"

Crystal bit her lip, then turned and stepped over the threshold. He heard Mac curse. Trent fisted his hands at his side, hoping beyond hope to maintain control. *Slow,* he reminded himself. Crystal was intrigued, but she was a far cry from where he and Mac were. They knew exactly what they wanted, and sharing a woman wasn't new for them. But Trent had a feeling that Crystal was a babe compared to them. They would need to be gentle.

Trent entered the room after Crystal. Mac came in behind him, closing the door with a soft *click*. The music from downstairs could barely be heard; the only other sound in the gently lit room was the rapid beat of his own heart. He'd heard the term before, but he'd never truly understood what it meant to hear your own heartbeat. He had a feeling it was beating so hard that Mac and Crystal could probably hear the damn thing.

"Wow," Crystal said as she looked around the room.

"We recently redecorated," Trent said as he glanced around. They'd kept the décor very simple. A butter-cream couch and recliner created a cozy sitting area to one side of the room. A stainless-steel bar with recessed lighting that shone on several bottles of liquor was situated on the other. There was a panel of monitors on the wall that showed different parts of the nightclub so they could keep track of any illegal activity.

"What's in here?" Crystal asked as she walked through a doorway. "Oh," she mumbled.

"The bedroom," Trent replied, knowing it was completely obvious with the king-sized bed.

"I see that." Trent noticed Crystal's gaze land on it and linger. He had to admit, the damn bed looked inviting as hell, with its tufted white headboard and fluffy black satin comforter. Crystal walked toward it. *Can she feel my gaze on her?* Trent's cock hardened as Crystal leaned down and smoothed her palm over the cool material. "Soft. And huge."

"Yep," Mac said, speaking up finally.

Crystal turned around and sat down, her gaze darting back and forth between them. "And now you two are about to share it with me?"

Mac laughed. "Are you always so straight to the point, angel? I have a feeling that's one of the things Trent and I are both going to love about you."

Mac stepped forward and knelt in front of Crystal, his hands wrapping around Crystal's thighs, which the slit in her dress showed off to perfection. Trent stayed silent as he took in the little teasing play in front of him. He liked to watch. It'd been something he'd discovered during his first ménage à trois.

"If that's what you want," Mac murmured as he inched his hands higher on her thighs, "it's what Trent and I want. What do you truly desire, Crystal?"

Crystal stared at Mac, as if unable to pull her gaze away. "I'm not sure, to be honest."

"If you leave right now, would you regret it? Would you always wonder, *what if?*"

Crystal nodded shakily and smiled. "Yes, I would wonder."

Mac stood and backed up. "Then you'll stay?"

Trent could see the arousal in Crystal's warm eyes. He was spellbound when Crystal reached up and fingered a strap on her black dress. Every muscle in his body tensed when Crystal flicked the strap off her shoulder. It fell to her elbow. Trent lost his ability to speak or even breathe.

"I'll stay," she whispered, as she pushed her dress down farther. The material fell to her waist, revealing a black lace bra. Her breasts were barely contained. Damn. If he tugged on the thin material, Trent would get an eyeful of Crystal's perfect full tits.

Trent and Mac both cursed.

Mac cleared his throat. "How'd we get so lucky to have you walk into Kinks tonight? You're like a dream come true," he gritted out as he clutched her around the waist and kissed the side of her neck.

Trent moved up next to Mac, then dipped his head and kissed her left breast, lace and all. "Mm, yeah, definitely our lucky night."

"I'd be ever so pleased if you'd take off that dress, Crystal," Trent murmured as he and Mac stood and stepped away from the bed. "I'd love to see all of you."

Shaking like a leaf on a tree, Crystal got to her feet, before taking hold of the soft rayon fabric and slipping it off. Her black stilettos were difficult to stand in considering her legs were like rubber at the moment. It didn't help her nerves any to have both men watching as she tugged her black panties down her legs. Her bra and shoes went next. She noticed a muscle in Mac's jaw twitch as he yanked his shirt over his head and tossed it away. His strong, muscular chest and ripped ab muscles demanded her full attention. She was about to see both men naked, and she licked her lips in anticipation of the gorgeous show.

When Trent began to shed his clothes, her breath caught in

her throat. As the men stripped out of their clothes without a hint of modesty, it reminded Crystal how far out of her comfort zone she was. Richard's hurtful comments about her weight came back at her full-force. Suddenly Crystal was second-guessing her decision.

Mac's gaze went on a hot journey over every inch of her body. "God, you are so damn beautiful."

A little of her insecurity fell away at Mac's heated praise. Trent smiled as he chimed in, as well. "You truly are magnificent," he said, in a voice as deep and mysterious as the man himself.

The men's words ratcheted up her confidence and kept her from fleeing. Trent's sizzling gaze heated her bloodstream, but it was the gentle understanding that she saw in him that she clung to. Could it be that this night was more than a quick lay for Mac and Trent? She didn't want to go there. Not now. Crystal only wanted to experience pleasure. Nothing more. Still, she did have a sneaking suspicion that she wasn't going to walk away with her heart fully intact once the sun came up.

Pushing those thoughts away, Crystal gave in to temptation and looked at both men. Mac had a few inches on Trent, but that didn't take away from Trent's masculinity. His impressive body was hard, and his long, firm cock jutted away from his body. Her mouth watered. A slow, ornery grin appeared on his face as he caught her eyeballing his erection. Crystal's cheeks burned. Mac shifted to the right, catching her attention. She looked him over, thoroughly, taking in his leaner, taller frame. His solid, swollen cock had her mouth watering. He wrapped a fist around it and squeezed. Crystal stared, dazed. She cleared her throat and spared Trent a quick look. He was so quiet, watching her. She looked down his body and realized he'd hardened further. My God, the man was huge.

"Lie down, baby."

Crystal couldn't possibly disobey Trent in that moment.

What woman could? Sitting on the bed, she moved to do as he bid and positioned herself in the center, then she lay back. The sight of Mac and Trent in all their bronzed glory coming toward her, both men staring at her as if she were a tasty treat, had her pussy weeping with joy. Their well-muscled bodies and naughty grins were enough to have Crystal begging and drooling.

As they slid onto the bed on either side of her, Crystal could do no more than stare. Trent moved closer, his gaze on her face before traveling over her body. She looked down and saw his hand wrapped around his cock. The air in the room turned thick and hot.

Oh God. She was naked in a room with not one gorgeous hunk, but two. Damn if she hadn't just died and gone to heaven.

Mac reached out to her, and wrapped his arm around her shoulders and pulled her onto her side. Her body was as stiff as a two-by-four, every muscle strung tight. "Relax, angel. Leave all those worries behind. For now, we just want you to feel pleasure. Nothing but pleasure tonight," Mac said, his voice rich and smooth, sliding over her skin, firing her blood.

"This is frightening," she admitted. "I've known you both for all of a few minutes, Mac."

Mac cupped her cheek in his large palm. "Shh, there's nothing to be afraid of, sweetheart. We're going to take care of you."

Trent stroked her hair from behind. "Relax, Crystal," he said in a soft command. When she only stiffened further, he wrapped a fist in her hair and tugged hard enough to bring a slight sting to her scalp. "Do as I said, baby."

At Trent's demand, Crystal loosened at once. She reached out and began touching Mac, her right hand smoothed over his pectorals. He was all steel strength. All man. She ran her fingers through the coarse curls that littered his chest. He groaned, and it fueled her to do more than touch. Inching her leg up and over his, Crystal let her pussy slide along the side of his muscular thigh. Her clit throbbed on contact. Her name passed his lips on a growl. Crystal took it as a signal to continue. Encouraged by the hungry sounds coming from both men, she teased her fingers down Mac's rib cage, giving herself free rein. In some dark part of her soul, Crystal enjoyed having Trent at her back, watching her touch Mac.

"So sweet," Mac praised, "so damn gentle and sweet." His rough hands coasted along her overheated skin. One second she lay between the men and the next she was spread out on top of Mac's huge body. He smiled up at her, then brought her head down for a kiss. His lips, so warm and tender, tasted her as if he wanted to spend a good long time pleasuring each and every part of her. Her mouth opened, and their tongues met in a wild mating dance, his hands still massaging and caressing. When his fingers teased over her clitoris, Crystal broke the kiss and opened her eyes, unsure, knowing Trent's stare was on their every move. She felt guilt wash over her. Two men. Both of them wanting her. Both of them watching her. She was so going to hell.

"Let him, Crystal."

Crystal whipped her head around and saw that Trent was still lying on his side, watching. Her mouth watered at the sight of the man. Trent moved closer, aligning his body over top of her, until she was sandwiched between the two. She had a million questions, but Trent wrapped his hand around her neck and angled her head to the side, stopping the torrent of thoughts with a hard kiss to her lips. When he raised his head a mere inch, he ordered, "I'm going to taste you, baby. Every sexy inch of you." He seemed to need no other incentive as he moved down her body. When he stroked the seam between her ass cheeks, she lost her ability to think. Her pussy spasmed as if aching for his mouth, fingers, cock. Thick, long fingers drifted back and forth over her puckered opening. She wanted him there, Crystal realized. While Mac fucked her pussy deep.

Trent kissed the base of her spine. "I want to fuck this tight ass, but first there's this . . ." He pushed her legs wide and stroked a finger over her labia.

"Trent," she moaned, her body already so attuned to his touch.

"Hush, angel," Mac said from beneath her. "Let Trent play."

Trent hummed his approval as she stayed silent. When his tongue slipped inside her opening, Crystal gave in and let him have his way. Clinging to Mac for support, Crystal felt Trent leisurely lick up and down between her swollen folds.

"More, please, Trent," Crystal pleaded, desperate for a deeper touch.

Mac cursed and lifted his head, then wrapped his mouth around one nipple and sucked, hard, while Trent flicked her wet clit with his tongue. Helpless to the onslaught, Crystal threw her head back and spread her legs wider, giving Trent better access to her slick entrance.

"Fuck, you taste like sunshine. So warm and luscious," Trent whispered as he wrapped his arms around her hips and clutched her bottom. Crystal pushed backward in an attempt to force him to move faster.

"Hold still for him."

"I can't, damn it. Please, Trent!"

A gentle swat to her bottom had Crystal freezing. She whipped her head around to see Trent kneeling behind her, a wicked grin on his face. "Need another, or are you going to obey?"

Crystal tried to speak, but the sight of precome dripping from the tip of his cock stilled her words. Once more she did as he asked and forced herself not to move.

Mac reached up and grabbed a handful of her hair, forcing her gaze back to his. The tenderness she saw in his silver eyes relaxed her. This time when his lips covered hers, it wasn't the gentle touch he'd given her earlier. In fact, he all but demanded entrance as he sank his tongue in. He laved at her, hungry, as if starved for the taste of her. Electric sparks shot over her nerve endings as Mac's talented mouth made love to hers. Without warning, Trent's fingers found their way over her clitoris. He teased and flicked her to a fever pitch. When his mouth pressed against her swollen pussy lips, Crystal came undone.

"Yes, Trent. Oh God, yes!" She clutched at the sheets and held tight as an orgasm began to build inside her.

Mac murmured something unintelligible before pressing a hand against one breast and squeezing, his thumb grazing the sensitive tip. Trent clutched her hips in strong fingers, holding her tighter for his loving assault. All at once, Crystal shouted and thrust her pussy into Trent's face. Her orgasm seemed to go on and on.

Several seconds went by before she collapsed on top of Mac.

"Son of a bitch," Trent growled as he cupped her pussy in his palm, prolonging the delicious sensations whipping through her. "You're going to be the death of us." His voice, dark with arousal, took her out of the pleasurable haze he'd wrapped her in.

She turned her head and their gazes locked. "I want your ass, Crystal. Would you like me there? While Mac fucks your wet pussy? Do you think you can handle both our cocks filling you, baby?"

"Trent, please . . . I don't know."

"Yes, you do," he encouraged, as he penetrated her tight pucker with a single finger, little by little, until he was buried deep inside her ass. She shuddered and pushed against him. His finger came in and out, fucking her.

"Raise up so I can play," Mac growled.

She got up on all fours above Mac, Trent behind her, one of his big, warm hands clutching her hips. She felt Mac caressing her clit, squeezing and pumping, and she watched as he lifted his head and suckled her breasts. First one, then the other. He took his time tasting and pleasing her.

"You have the prettiest tits, Crystal," Mac murmured, then went back to suckling.

Trent's finger moved in and out of her bottom, slow at first, then faster. Soon, there were two fingers, and her body went wild. Inhibitions dropped away as need rushed in and took command. She gyrated against Trent, and Mac flicked and toyed with her little nubbin while he bit and sucked her sensitive nipples.

She climaxed a second time, this one deeper, harder than before. She screamed and arched her back, flying apart and breaking into a million pieces. It was fast and unexpected, but she wasn't given time to bask in it.

Trent slipped his fingers free of her and moved to the side until his cock was level with her face. With one hand propped against the headboard and the other wrapped around his glorious erection, he coaxed, "Suck me."

"First, come on up here," Mac murmured as he patted his chest. "I want a taste of that honey."

Crystal looked at Trent and saw him smile and nod his head. She took a deep breath and crawled up Mac's body until she was hovering above his face. He growled in approval, then wrapped his hands around her thighs and pulled her down. His lips closed around her swollen pussy lips. Crystal moaned and pushed against him even more, losing herself in the pleasure.

"Now, come here and wrap those sexy lips around my dick, baby," Trent said, his fist moving up and down the hard length.

While Mac probed her opening with his tongue, Crystal leaned toward Trent, taking the swollen head into her mouth. He cursed and clutched her face in his strong hands. Crystal laved at the tip, tasting his sticky fluid. Trent groaned and began guiding her. He was rougher than she expected. Crystal sucked him deeper and gagged.

"Easy." Trent pushed her head off him to give her a breath, then pulled her forward again. "Relax your throat for me."

Crystal closed her eyes and opened her throat, taking every thick inch of him. As Mac teased her pussy with fingers and tongue, Trent fucked her mouth, his movements alternating between fast and slow. Mac thrust his fingers deep, and it was all she could take. She couldn't concentrate on anything beyond the pleasure both men delivered. Trent slowly fucked her mouth as shocking jolts of heat flooded Crystal's pussy. As she exploded into Mac's mouth, the only thing holding her upright were the arms he had wrapped around her waist.

"Oh yeah," Mac groaned. "Trent's right. You're pure sunshine."

Trent pulled her head off his cock, then praised her with a kiss. She was beginning to come back down to earth when she heard him demand, "Now, Crystal."

Trent moved back into the position he'd been in before, on his knees between Mac's thighs. Crystal allowed him to slide her downward until she was on all fours above Mac, her bottom facing Trent.

Cupping her dripping mound, Trent whispered, "Look at me." She turned her head, already limp and sweating from three glorious orgasms, but when she saw the intensity, the insane yearning etched into his not-so-perfect features, her body went from sated to needy in a moment. She glanced down his body and realized he'd put on a lubricated condom. Mac, too.

"You belong to us, Crystal," Trent explained, his voice rough. "This hot little cunt, this tight ass, is for us alone to fuck. No other."

She didn't have the presense of mind to argue. Later for that. Suddenly, as if on cue, Mac and Trent both entered her. Her inner muscles stretched. Too much.

"I can't!" she cried, her body tensing as panic started to overwhelm her.

Trent pulled out instantly, while Mac stayed seated deep inside her pussy. Holding perfectly still, he waited for Trent's command. They'd done this before, she realized. Enough to establish their own roles. Crystal didn't want to even go down that road.

Lowering his big, powerful body, Trent covered her like a

heavy warm blanket, his arms resting on the mattress on either side of Mac's torso. "You can handle both of us, angel. You're just nervous," Trent murmured as he kissed the nape of her neck. "Let me make love to you. You won't regret it."

He stroked her hair and smoothed a palm down her arm to her hip, where he cupped her bottom and kneaded the plump flesh. She relaxed, giving the men, giving herself, what they needed, craved. Trent seemed to sense her surrender and began a slow glide inside her, filling her. The delicious pressure and friction took her breath away. Oh God, she'd never been so incredibly full, and yet there wasn't any pain. The silky inner walls of her pussy were stroked with the gentle slide of Mac's cock, and her bottom felt every scorching thrust from Trent.

With each inward push from Trent, Mac pulled outward. Her muscles clutched them both in a tight fist. She squeezed her ass, giving Trent a more intense pleasure. Passion soared and their movements turned frenzied as both men took her hard and fast.

"Christ, yeah, baby. Fuck it." Trent grabbed the back of her hair and guided her mouth toward Mac's.

Mac leaned up and covered her mouth with his. He pushed his tongue into her mouth, licking and teasing. He released her and growled, "Damn, you taste like pure sweetness." His large palms cupped her tits and pulled them up. "I need a taste of these, too." He sucked and nibbled on the hard peaks and Crystal moaned, unable to hold back the flood of warmth. Trent took hold of her hips and slammed his cock deep. Dominating her. Claiming her.

Within moments the men exploded. Crystal's body recieved every ounce of Trent's come inside her ass, as well as the hot jets of fluid as Mac erupted inside her pussy. Both men cursed, and her name was a growl on their lips. Crystal felt fingers flicking her clit. She wasn't sure which man touched her, nor did she care because she, too, burst wide open as an orgasm tore through her, shattering her control.

Mac covered her face with tiny kisses. Cheeks, lips, and eyelids recieved special attention. Crystal merely lay there, exhausted, sweaty, and spent. Trent praised her as he came down on top of her, blanketing her body with his larger one. He suckled on her shoulder, leaving a stinging love bite behind, his dick now semierect still embedded deep.

"Happy birthday," Trent whispered against her ear. Mac kissed the top of her head and said, "Yeah, happy birthday, angel."

"T-thanks," Crystal moaned. She wanted to say more, something to show them how completely intoxicated she was with them.

"We aren't done with you yet, Crystal," Trent whispered.

That brought her out of her euphoric afterglow. "What do you mean?"

"You didn't think this was a one-off, did you?" Mac answered as he cupped her chin and forced her to look at him.

"Well, I hadn't gotten that far, I suppose. I've never slept with a guy I just met. Certainly not two guys at once." She groaned and covered her face with her hands. "God, that makes me sound like such a tramp."

Trent pried her hands away and kissed her forehead. "You aren't a tramp. Merely a woman with enough passion to fill all five of the Great Lakes."

She laughed at the absurdity of that statement. "You clearly don't know me if you think that."

"Then let us get to know you. One at a time, if that makes you feel better."

She frowned. "You two would want to take turns dating me?"

Mac shrugged. "It's unusual, but we're not exactly average guys."

"Pfft, hardly," she replied. "You own a BDSM nightclub and you've just given me my first threesome. So not average."

"So, we'll each date you, and we promise not to overwhelm you. Deal?"

As she looked at the pair of them, Crystal knew she was going to say yes. What woman had the power to refuse two such darkly handsome men? "Deal," she said as she moved off of Mac and snuggled against him. Trent sandwiched her in, and both men continued to pet and caress her. Soon her eyelids grew heavy and she fell into a blissful sleep, dreaming erotic dreams of dark-haired men and all the wickedly pleasurable things they were capable of teaching a rather inexperienced, small-town girl.

3

Trent watched Crystal's eyes drift open, as she lazily came awake. Her body stretched like a contented cat after a noontime nap. Crystal fascinated him. He was sure she viewed their night together as a onetime thing, but Trent had other plans. He wasn't ready for her to walk off into the sunset just yet. Her body seemed to respond to him as no other woman's had. He knew Mac felt the same way. He'd said as much before he'd left earlier that morning. Somehow, Trent needed to make Crystal see that this was more than just a single night of fun.

She moved her hand over her face and shifted on the bed. Trent's breathing increased in anticipation of her waking and remembering just how she'd spent her night. When he touched her forehead, Crystal's gaze flew open and landed on him. Awareness showed in their depths and she sighed heavily. He fully expected her to leap out of bed and run from the room. There was something very innocent about Crystal, almost as if she'd lived in a convent her entire life.

"Hi," Crystal said, her smile slowly appearing. Her voice was ragged from all the moaning she'd done the night before.

"Hi," he murmured.

"I, uh, I'm not used to the whole morning-after thing here. I'm not sure what to do, to be honest."

Her blush pleased him to hell and back. He kissed her forehead, then stood. "All you need to do is get dressed and come downstairs so I can feed you."

Her gaze widened. "Are you cooking?"

"Yep. Omelets sound good?"

Crystal hummed. "Sounds amazing." She stared at him, as if quietly evaluating him, almost making him fidget like a boy who'd been caught with his hand in the cookie jar. "Do you do this sort of thing often?"

His heart stuttered at the shy words. "No, I don't. You're special, Crystal." He saw her nod, then he added, "You know, I'm tempted to never let you leave my bed."

She chuckled. "I hog the blankets. You'd get annoyed and kick me out eventually."

"Somehow I doubt that," he said. "Take your time and help yourself to the shower."

Crystal watched Trent leave the room. The events of the previous night ran through her mind. The nightclub. The men. The sex. Oh God, what had she done? She smiled despite the stupidity of her actions and stretched her arms above her head, yawning herself awake.

Crystal pushed the covers aside and started to get up. Only problem with that plan, she was totally naked. Remembering just how she'd ended up that way had her grinning all over again. "I am so going to hell," she mumbled.

Yeah, okay, so meeting two guys in a nightclub and sleeping with them immediately afterward wasn't the smartest thing she'd ever done, but it had been the most adventurous, passionate, and exciting time she'd ever had in her life. God, the sex had been so damn perfect it was scary. But not exactly smart.

Still, wasn't she allowed one stupid act after learning that she was nothing but a punching bag for her now ex-husband? She was entitled to step out of the norm on such an occasion. Right? She knew Mollie would say, "Hell, yes!" to that question.

At the thought of her dearest friend, Crystal grinned from ear to ear. If Mollie could see her now, she'd be floored. Crystal never strayed from the straight and narrow, and yet here she was.

Leaving the warm bed behind, Crystal headed toward her purse, fished out her cell phone, and called her best friend. Mollie answered on the first ring.

"You have a lot of explaining to do, woman," Mollie grumbled.

"Good morning to you, too," Crystal said around a laugh.

Silence from the other end, and then, "Spill."

Crystal gave her friend the nutshell version of events. By the time she was finished, Mollie was lecturing her on the use of condoms and meeting strange men in bars. When Mollie admitted to a twinge of jealousy, they both laughed. Before ending the call, Crystal promised she'd be home later.

Slipping her phone back into her purse, Crystal headed for the closet on the adjacent wall. As she slid the door to the left, she found what she was looking for—a collection of men's t-shirts. Apparently, they liked to keep things simple. Not a lot of colors or styles. Just a boatload of whites and blacks and a few tans. She grabbed a white shirt that sported the Kinks logo, pulled it over her head, and let it fall to mid-thigh, then turned toward the bathroom.

Sometime in the middle of the night, she'd come awake to Trent leisurely washing her with a warm washcloth. It'd been the most intimate thing she'd ever experienced. He'd taken great pleasure in stroking the soft cotton over every inch of her, too. She'd been enraptured.

Now, as she entered the huge bathroom, Crystal gasped. "Wow."

It was by far the largest bathroom she'd ever seen. It simply took her breath away.

The walls were a soft beige, and there were double black sinks and recessed lighting that could be adjusted. The natural slate tile around the tub and inside the shower only added to the character and class of the room. She noticed the warmth of the tiled floor beneath her bare feet and realized it was heated. She'd died and gone to bathroom heaven.

Now, staring longingly at the huge Jacuzzi-style tub, Crystal wished she had more time. She'd love to take a long, hot soak. But she was too anxious to wash her face and find the men who had so thoroughly satisfied her. Would they want to do it all over again? Already considering the possibilities, she felt her body grow warm.

When she saw her reflection in the bathroom mirror, Crystal nearly scared the wits out of herself. Yikes. Her hair was everywhere but where it should be. Her face was totally free of makeup and scraped raw. Trent and Mac's whiskers had abraded her skin when they'd kissed every inch of her face, giving her a rosy-cheeked look—which was not a pretty sight. The juncture between her thighs began to throb at the memory of their sexy mouths all over her body. They'd been so talented. She wanted to experience it again.

Now, if at all possible.

But if something wasn't done with her hair, she would end up scaring the daylights out of the poor men. She never had been one of those women who woke up looking refreshed. No, usually she woke looking like something the dog dragged in.

She turned on the cold water and splashed her face several times. It helped to take some of the redness out of her cheeks, but her hair was beyond repair. She'd need a shower to fix such a pathetic mess, but she didn't want to waste another second. She wanted to find Trent and Mac. Then maybe they could share a really long good-bye kiss. Now that was a pleasant thought.

Crystal was smiling again when she turned off the light in the bathroom and left the bedroom to search and seduce.

She walked downstairs, her curiosity kicking into high gear as she wondered where the guys could have gone. Surely the nightclub was closed this early in the morning. She had no idea what time it was, but she could tell it was before dawn.

As Crystal reached the lower level of the suite, she glanced tentatively around the large room. No one was in sight. She looked to the right and spotted two doors. One, she assumed, led to the kitchen, but the other looked like an office. She went to the second door and gently knocked. No one answered, so she tried the doorknob. Finding it unlocked, Crystal went in. It was so dark she couldn't see her hand in front of her face. She located a light switch and flipped it.

She'd definitely found Trent and Mac's office. It was simple and neat. A large desk, computer, a filing cabinet. Her fingers absently stroked across the surface of the desk as her gaze roamed around the room. It seemed as if she were peeking behind the curtain. She felt naughty. She should turn back around and leave.

But then her gaze came back to the desk and landed on the stack of papers that a paperweight was keeping securely in place. She moved the weight to the side and picked up the first page.

"Find what you were looking for?"

Crystal yelped. "Crap, Trent! You scared me."

Trent, his hard, gorgeous body clad only in a pair of jeans, stood in the doorway to the office, his arms crossed over his bare chest and a frown creasing his sexy brows.

"Hungry?"

"Starving," she replied as she dropped the paper back on the desk and stepped away. "I was looking for you."

Trent's gaze darkened. "Yeah?"

"Mm-hm." Crystal suddenly felt silly because it dawned on her that she was probably supposed to leave. Wasn't that what *one-night stand* meant? One night, then you slip out and forget it ever happened. It occurred to her that she probably wouldn't be seeing Trent and Mac after today. They'd had sex—great sex—but that's all there was to it.

Trent bent down, as if to kiss her, but Crystal stopped him when she heard voices. "Who's here?" Crystal asked, trying not to sound so depressed that they weren't alone.

Trent merely grinned down at her and kissed her lightly, neither confirming nor denying whether he had company. As if he knew that by not telling her, she would only want to know even more.

Who would be at a nightclub at dawn? Workers, maybe?

Crystal walked around him and right out of the office. Trent was hot on her heels. "Uh, baby?"

"I heard voices," she said. It sounded as if they were coming from the kitchen. As she stepped through the swinging doors, Crystal walked smack into an argument that seemed well underway.

A large man leaned against the counter. He looked a lot like Trent, only he was younger and somehow more mischievous-looking with the way his mouth kicked sideways in a roguish grin. Same dark hair, same piercing eyes. Beside him a beautiful dark-haired woman stood ramrod-straight, and another man, but much older, stood next to her with his arm wrapped around her. Crystal stared and listened to the woman berate the Trent look-alike. Whoever they were, it was clear they weren't employees.

The woman was tall and statuesque in her beauty. And even though it was obvious she was older, she'd taken care with her creamy skin, which was smooth and clear. Her hair was her most striking feature. It was still a lustrous shade of brown, despite her age, and it flowed down past her shoulders. She was slim, though shapely. Crystal watched in fascination as Trent moved around her and started talking to the woman in hushed tones. She spoke to him as if he were a child, instead of a grown man.

Who on earth does this woman think she is?

When she heard the woman say something about the atrocious nightclub Trent owned, Crystal decided enough was enough. She cleared her throat and stood a little straighter, her hands firmly planted on her hips. "Excuse me."

Suddenly, all eyes were on her and the room fell deadly silent. The older woman inhaled sharply as if shocked, the man standing beside her frowned disapprovingly, and Trent's look-alike grinned wickedly. Trent's smile wasn't much different, except for the tiny hint of possessiveness lingering there.

Too late, it registered in Crystal's mind exactly why everyone was so silent. She looked down her body and groaned. All she had on was Trent's T-shirt.

Oh hell.

She hurried out, anxious to escape.

When she stepped back into the upstairs apartment, she glanced around the room. The bed looked as if a group of kids had played tag on it. It was a shambles. Hell, her clothes looked even worse than the bed. She went over to the heap and picked up what was supposed to be her dress. It was barely wearable, wrinkles making it obvious that it'd spent the night on the floor. "Yeah, like his guests hadn't already figured that part out for themselves."

Crystal stepped into her bra and panties, then slipped back into her dress. She smoothed out some of the wrinkles as best she could, before moving to the wall mirror. "Crap," she grumbled. Everything about her screamed that she'd just experienced a long night of hot, raunchy sex. Then again, what did she care? She was a grown woman; she could do what she wanted. She didn't need these people's approval.

Crystal closed her eyes and breathed deeply. Opening them slowly, she attempted to keep an open mind as she gazed into the mirror this time. Yep, she was completely steeped in sex. Messy, frantic, lust-filled sex. A three-way, nonetheless. But she refused to feel bad. She hadn't had a night like that in . . . well, ever. And it felt too good to let some unwelcome visitors spoil it for her.

She slipped into her way-too-high shoes and went back out to face whoever had seen it necessary to intrude on her little paradise with Trent and Mac. And just where was Mac? He was nowhere in sight. Would she ever see him again? She sighed, feeling worse and worse by the second.

Now that she was more awake, Crystal saw the scene in the kitchen from fresh eyes.

There was something about the couple. They were made of money. She could spot the type a mile away. Heck, the way she'd been raised, it was hard *not* to spot money. She'd been brought up in a poor household. The church-handout type of poor. Oh, her mother had tried, bless her, but nothing had ever kept them from being food-stamp poor. Her father was nonexistent, since he'd split the day he'd knocked up her mother. As Crystal had grown older, she had learned to be grateful that she'd been an only child. It wasn't that her mother was lazy, but she was a single parent and the entire concept of money seemed to elude her. It disappeared as soon as she earned it. So Crystal practically lived in T-shirts and jeans . . . on a good day.

It was clear in Crystal's mind that whoever was in Trent's kitchen was, to put it mildly, rolling in it. It was in the clothes. The way the woman had held herself, regal and dignified. If that was the case, however, then why were they at Kinks nightclub?

A question that would soon be answered.

This time, when she reached the main floor, Crystal heard the arguing coming from the kitchen. It had increased in volume. She walked through the doors and was again face-to-face with the four of them. Crystal cleared her throat and was immediately the object of attention again. She'd never been a weak-willed woman, but with the four of them staring at her as if she'd suddenly grown three heads and sprouted wings, it was rather disconcerting. This time she was fully clothed, though, and she felt a bit more in control.

She gave Trent a look that said, *Who are these people?* He quickly stepped forward, taking her hand in his, and proceeded to introduce her.

"I'd like you to meet my parents, and the simpleton who cannot stop grinning is my brother, Josh." Then Trent looked at his family and proudly announced, "This is Crystal Shaw."

His mom, dad, and brother? Oh God, it couldn't be. That would be too cruel. She was beyond humiliated. Crystal felt like crawling under a rock and never resurfacing. Her face felt like it was glowing with mortification. Actually, she *knew* it was because she could feel the damn heat rising off it. She could cook an egg on it at that moment. All she could do was look at Trent with pleading eyes. Just so he'd lead her to the nearest hole and let it swallow her up.

Trent winked at her in that roguish way of his and continued with his introductions.

"I met Crystal in the club last night. She and I hit it off rather well."

Crystal was like a woman being led to the guillotine. She turned and looked at Mrs. Dailey, and to her astonishment the woman held out her hand. Crystal shook it with a nervous quickness that only punctuated her humiliation. That's when Trent's mother spoke to her.

"What do you do for a living, Crystal?"

She stuttered and stammered out her answer. "I'm an application developer."

"I'd think that would be quite a demanding job. Quite professional and respected, no doubt." She aimed the last part of her comment toward Trent, who stood frowning and looking very much the unruly child. "Do you enjoy your work?"

"It can get stressful, but I love it. I wouldn't know what to do with myself if I had a boring job that kept my creative juices from flowing freely. Even though at times it can all be very routine, it's still a great feeling when a project is completed, and knowing I had a hand in it is reward enough." She was babbling. God, what must Trent's mother think of her? Crystal definitely hadn't given her a good first impression.

"Well, I can certainly hear the enthusiasm in your voice. We were just talking to Trent about rewarding jobs. Weren't we, Trent?"

"What my mother is trying to say, in her obscure and convoluted way, is that she does not approve of me owning a nightclub."

"Oh, Mrs. Dailey, your son's nightclub isn't exactly a dive. It seems to me that it does pretty well." Crystal wasn't sure if her opinion counted for much, but she couldn't stand there and let Mrs. Dailey berate Trent about his club. He was obviously a good businessman.

It wouldn't do anyone any good to get into an argument with Trent's mother, however, especially the first time out. *The first time? Who said anything about future visits?* Oh Lord, she was in so damn deep.

"I'm sure the nightclub is . . . fine. I just think that Trent's potential lies elsewhere. He belongs back at home and working with his father."

"Mom, don't go into that again. I like this town, I like the nightclub, and I'm quite comfortable right where I am." He looked at Crystal as he finished the rest of his statement, "Anyway, I'm rather addicted to the beautiful people here."

Mrs. Dailey was staring in thoughtful silence at Trent; tension filled the air all at once. And it was Mr. Dailey who broke it by changing the subject.

"Crystal, I'm delighted to meet you." He stuck his hand out for her to shake, and she took it with a smile. She found it warm and inviting, not like Mrs. Dailey's colder, thinner hands.

"It's good to meet you, too. I see Trent gets his good looks from the both of you."

To her joy, his face lit up, and his eyes sparkled. The man was tall, probably over six feet, and had Trent's same broad shoulders. She could also see, even with his now graying hair, the dark raven color woven throughout. It would have been the same color as Trent's in his younger days. His face seemed chiseled right out of a stone block, but when he'd smiled his appearance altered. He looked more approachable, less like the stern father. Still, Trent's mom was going to be one tough nut to crack. The woman's expression had yet to change as she stared over at her son. His arms were crossed over his chest and he stared right back. Trent was definitely a chip off the stubborn block. Mrs. Dailey was clearly determined to have her way, and Trent was every bit as determined to not let her.

Crystal was about to change the subject, to move them onto safer ground, when another voice intruded on the silence.

"I have yet to meet Trent's friend."

Crystal noticed Trent stiffen as if readying for battle when the brother stepped up to the plate and gave her his full attention.

"I'm the better-looking brother, by the way."

"You wish," Trent growled.

Josh didn't even blink; he simply stared at her. Like some old world duke he bent and kissed the back of her hand. Crystal couldn't prevent a smile at the ridiculous gesture.

"It's nice to meet you, Josh."

"Trent asked me to come for a drink here last night, but I had a prior engagement. Now I'm sorely disappointed I didn't cancel."

"Josh, don't start. I'm warning you," Trent bit out.

Crystal could see things quickly deteriorating into a chest-pounding brawl, and as she watched Trent's parents quietly staring in rebuke, it made her feel a bit sorry for Trent. He'd done so well for himself; clearly he could have had it all handed to him, if only he'd agreed to work for his father. Instead, he'd set out on his own.

"You know, I have an idea," Trent said. "How about we all do dinner tonight? The five of us. There's a great place across town that serves a mean streak." Just as Crystal was about to protest, Trent bulldozed right over her. "That way you can get to know Crystal better."

She suddenly felt cornered. "I really don't want to intrude," she replied.

Trent touched her cheek and said, "It's not an intrusion. We can meet at Todd's Steak House at six o'clock."

His mother spoke up, her voice as imposing as any queen's. "That will do fine. Thank you for the invitation. In the meantime, your father and I plan to have Josh drop us off at our condominium. He brought us straight here from the airport, and we are quite exhausted."

She turned at that and strode toward a back door, apparently expecting the four of them to follow along. The funny thing was, just like good little children, they all did follow silently along. Crystal wanted to laugh at the idea of Trent's father submissively trailing behind his wife. Crystal had a feeling Mrs. Dailey was the only person on the planet who would have ever expected Mr. Dailey to obey a command.

Trent's mother turned when she reached the door and kissed Trent's cheek. "We still have things to discuss, son." Without giving Trent a chance to respond, Mrs. Dailey looked over at Crystal and said, "It was very nice to meet you, Crystal. I look forward to getting to know you better."

After they left, Crystal turned toward Trent. "What did you get me into?"

He grinned, totally unrepentant. "Dinner. I'll take any chance I can get to see you again."

"Oh," she said, as her stomach fluttered. "I'd like that very much."

"By the way, Mac says he's sorry he missed you, but he had to get home. He wants you to call him."

Mac wanted to see her again, too? Could it be that both men wanted to continue . . . whatever it was they'd started last night? Trent stepped close and took her chin in his palm. "Last night was only a taste, baby."

She sighed at the realization that she didn't know a single thing about relationships—except pain and lots of it. "I'm in uncharted water here."

"All we want is time to get to know you. We'll let fate handle the rest, okay?"

"Yes, okay." How could she refuse? Two amazing men wanted to spend time with her. It was unconventional, but if she'd learned anything by being married to a tyrant, it was that sometimes going the conventional route wasn't all it was cracked up to be. Might as well try playing outside the sandbox for a change.

4

Later that evening, Crystal arrived early for their dinner date and took advantage of the time to stare at Trent as he made his way around the main room of Kinks. It'd only been a few hours and she was already anxious to see the man. When a customer stepped in front of Trent, vying for his attention, Crystal's line of sight was slightly hindered.

She'd driven past the club several times trying to kill time. She hadn't wanted to arrive too early and appear desperate. As the quick-as-lightning bartender slammed a club soda down in front of her then proceeded to rattle off a price, Crystal was abruptly brought out of her drooling stupor. She grabbed some dollar bills from inside the dark confines of her messy purse and went back to her staring. Only now, Trent had moved a few steps closer to her, and he was staring at her. A slow, sexy smile curved his lips and Crystal knew she'd been made.

God, it should be a sin to have a body as masculine and perfect as Trent's. A deep longing rose from the pit of her stomach. She wanted him. Now. Here. It shocked her that she was responding to him in such an eager way. Then again, any sane woman would want a man like him. He was too gorgeous not to notice.

His black jeans molded to his muscular legs and lean hips as if custom-made. His ass was so solid a girl could bounce a quarter off of it. His simple white T-shirt wasn't anything special, but on him, it looked better than Armani. His wide, solid chest made Crystal want to reach out and touch. With the easy move of his hips and the naughty look in his eyes, Crystal couldn't stop her heart from pounding out of control.

His slate-blue gaze held Crystal captive. An involuntary tremor ran the length of her spine. She realized that he'd probably known all along that she'd been watching him.

Crystal brought the drink to her lips, saluting him, then tipped the contents down her throat. She looked back up and saw Trent's expression turn from teasing to hungry as he skimmed his gaze over her exposed throat. Her body tightened. Seemed all he had to do was look at her and she was ready and aching. She'd never had such a volatile reaction to a man before. She'd also never come across a man so powerful and intoxicating, either.

With no warning, a woman tromped up to Trent and fairly hung on to his shoulder. What the hell? The little tramp plastered her breasts against him in blatant invitation. He turned his head and spoke to her, and Crystal came to her senses. A man like him wouldn't really be interested in a woman like Crystal. He was all about excitement and risks. She was all about work. She was a huge disappointment—hadn't Richard told her that?

For fear of embarrassing them both, Crystal suddenly made the decision to leave. She rose off the hard, cold bar stool and yanked at the hem of her black skirt, wishing for the umpteenth time she hadn't bothered trying to look her best for Trent and his family. Her red, off-the-shoulder blouse, black skirt, and heels made her feel stupid now.

She'd never been one to go to bars and nightclubs. She only

came tonight because Trent had asked her to dinner. She should have done something with Mollie instead. Crystal grabbed her purse. Time to go. It was the only safe and smart thing to do. Unfortunately, that meant leaving Trent behind. A knot formed in her throat at the thought of never seeing him or Mac again.

As she passed the section of the bar where Trent was sitting, his hand snaked out and grabbed on to her arm. Crystal was brought up short. At first, she felt a rush of irritation at his audacity. Not two seconds ago, another woman had been flirting with him. She yanked away from his grasp as a nasty touch of envy crept into her consciousness. After all, the other woman had been daring enough to approach him, while she was all but running out the door.

Crystal jerked her head around to give him a good what-for, but she was left speechless by his narrow-eyed gaze. He had the look of a lion who'd just caught dinner. *Do I want to be dinner? Do I dare give in to him?* If her mind had an answer, it wasn't giving it up. Her body, on the other hand, was screaming at her to surrender.

He bent his head down and she could feel his hot breath against her ear as she inhaled his clean male scent. "Where are you going?" he asked. He got off his own stool and stood in front of her. He was so close she could practically feel the intense sexual heat coming off him. His body was so wide, so muscular, and so very intimidating." I thought we had a dinner date."

"You seem otherwise occupied," she gritted out as she looked at the woman who still stood way too close to Trent.

"Come on," he said, as he took hold of her hand and tugged her along behind him. He was chocolate to Crystal. She wanted him, even though she knew it was wrong. The small hint of amusement in his deep, gravely tone nearly had her purring.

Crystal narrowed her eyes. "Don't you have customers to get back to?"

He turned his head and his eyes darkened. "No. But before you say anything else, I think it'd be best if we continued this discussion in private."

Still, she hesitated. Trent didn't give her a chance to protest. "You haven't taken your pretty eyes off me since you got here."

Crystal caved. Fine, so she was weak. Trent seemed to recognize the instant she succumbed. No more words were uttered from either of them. He simply led her away, twisting his way through the sea of bumping and grinding bodies. People appeared to step aside for him. She was suitably impressed. He took her to the upstairs apartment, and Crystal's thoughts were obliterated as she watched him walk. He was so sexy. So much fluid grace. And he had the most edible ass she'd ever seen. A man's well-muscled tush did it for her every time. Crystal felt the apex of her thighs dampen with arousal.

When he closed the door to the apartment behind him, Crystal started right in. "Why did you bring me here?" she bit out, as anger started to rise.

Trent stepped forward then, taking her head in his large, skillful hands, and gritted out, "I brought you here to tell you that I was turning that woman down. Not taking her number."

Crystal was afraid to believe him. She'd believed Richard's lies in the beginning, hadn't she? "It seemed to me she was getting pretty cozy with you."

"I do own a nightclub," he murmured. "One that caters to people interested in bondage and submission. That brings on a certain amount of flirtatious behavior. Still, since meeting you I'm not interested in other women. Only you, Crystal."

And why did that send her heart fluttering? "You're interested in me?"

"Yes, and I've been dying to do this . . ." Then his mouth

was suddenly crushed against hers, forcing her lips apart, not bothering to wait for her to open them in her own time. He took possession of the soft interior in a way that had her shaking body swaying forward against his rock-hard length, and her arms coming up to wrap around his neck.

Crystal sank against the kiss, giving in to the sweet demands her feminine core was suddenly making on her. Dear Lord, she didn't want to think about her next move. She wanted Trent to take the choice from her altogether. And he seemed all too happy to do so.

He sucked at her lower lip and probed her mouth with his insistent tongue. Apparently not content to leave it there, he deftly bent low and flung her high into his arms, carrying her over to the bed as if she were nothing more than a child. He laid her down on top of the soft, downy blankets with such gentle care that Crystal felt herself melting inside. That such a big man could be so tender was a major *oh my* in her book. He lay down next to her and propped his head up on his elbow, staring down at her with such reverence it shook her.

"Why are you looking at me that way?"

"How am I looking at you?"

She locked eyes with him, her jaw firming as she tried to put into words the way his eyes seemed to see right into her soul. "You stare at me and it's as if you can see my every thought. It's disconcerting."

"I can't help but admire a beautiful creature when I see one."

She squirmed, turning even redder. "See, there you go again, making me all nervous and jittery."

He frowned down at her, as if truly bewildered by her words and actions. "Why don't you know your own worth? From the moment I saw you, I knew I'd not be able to deny my desire for you. You sat at the bar, so alluring and kissable, and my body spun out of control. When your sexy eyes landed on me, it was all I could do to bide my time until I could be alone with you."

All at once, he was there again, taking his lips on a sensual journey over her own. Her cheeks were teased and tantalized by his clever mouth. He caressed his way down her neck, wringing a groan from her. Crystal happily surrendered.

5

Trent had had his fair share of women. Exotic beauties who'd left him gasping and willing to please and be pleased. But there was something about the little brunette; she had tugged at some unfamiliar part of him that he could not quite identify.

She had a vulnerability that called to the masculine predator in him, as if taunting him to swoop down and snatch her up.

The instant she had walked into his nightclub, he had been taken with her. Her shiny brown hair drew his fingers to touch it, and her body had been like a breath of fresh air. All smooth curves, she was built for a man to caress and play with.

Trent had never been drawn to women who were pencil-thin. He liked something to unveil. Something to make his time worthwhile. And Crystal was surely worthwhile. Her body practically screamed at him. She was hungry, and he had scented her arousal as easily as if she had uncorked a bottle. She seemed to only have eyes for him and Trent felt unaccountably pleased.

Now he had her, and he was loath to let her go anytime soon. He knew that she'd wanted a single night with him and Mac. No strings and no recriminations. He'd seen her willful thoughts in the expressive features of her beautiful face. Asking her to accompany him to dinner with his family had given him a chance to see her again. The fact that she'd arrived early pleased the hell out of him.

Using one hand, Trent began unbuttoning the front of her blouse. He looked into her anxious eyes and said, "You look amazing tonight, but I'm impatient to see your sweet body." He lowered his face to within a breath of her lips. "Completely nude, Crystal," he explained. He'd gotten a secret thrill that she cared enough about him to want him all for herself, but he needed to show her that he had eyes only for her. Other women paled in comparison. Trent let his tongue sweep across Crystal's soft ruby lips. She parted them on a sigh, and he knew it was an invitation to taste her deeper.

He slipped his tongue inside, but it wasn't the part of her body he wanted against his mouth. He wanted her nipples, her clit. He ached to taste and tease all of her soft, secret spots and watch her fly over the edge for him. He was hungry for her sweet climax. He wanted her so crazy that she would beg him to take her.

Trent had her blouse half-open, and he could now see that her bra was the same deep shade of red beneath. He dipped his head and licked a fiery path down the valley between her tits. Trent knew a sense of pride when her body arched upward for him. She was so beautiful. So eager. Her hands came up and clutched at his hair, pulling almost painfully, bringing his lips more fully against her flesh in the process. Her skin was as soft as silk and Trent drank her in, swallowing her essence. Soon, her shirt was completely undone, and with a mere flick of his fingers, her bra snapped open, causing her breasts to spill free. He felt as if he'd been given the greatest of gifts when he saw her upper body in the soft light.

"Jesus, you're sexy," Trent gritted out as his eager cock responded to the sight of her. He lowered his head and sucked one perfectly erect nipple into his mouth with ravenous haste.

"Oh," Crystal murmured huskily. The sound sent fire licking through his veins.

Trent nibbled at her precious swell, his need for her uncontrollable. He moved over her, crushing her to the mattress beneath, and used his knee to spread her legs. He pushed his aching erection against her soft little mound, letting her feel what she did to him, then using both his hands, he cuddled and shaped her perfect tits, squeezing one while tasting the other. Crystal writhed shamelessly beneath him. He groaned his approval and released her nipple, leaving a gentle kiss behind. Skating down her body, using his tongue to feel his way, Trent pushed the front of her blouse apart so he could see the softness of her belly. His tongue dipped into the sweet indentation of her belly button, flicking playfully.

"Oh Trent, that feels so good." Her voice quivered. "I need you. So badly."

Trent raised his head at her pleading. "We want this to last, don't we?"

She groaned as if in frustration. "But what about dinner with your parents?"

He chuckled. "We'll be fashionably late," he replied before slipping his hand down her body, committing her curves to memory. When he reached the warm skin of her thigh, it was his turn to groan. He skimmed beneath her skirt and felt his way over a pair of satin panties. She was already so hot and wet, but it wasn't enough. He wanted to feel her with nothing in his way. He wanted her soaked and eager to take his cock.

Trent lifted up so he was kneeling between her widespread thighs, and took no time in getting rid of her clothes. He stared down at the perfection of her luscious, nude body. "I feel like it's Christmas and I've just unwrapped a really great present."

The neatly trimmed tuft of brown curls covering her hidden treasures was the sweetest sight indeed. He wanted to kiss her there, right where he knew she needed his touch most. At once, Trent left the bed, his body going hot with intense arousal when she whimpered unhappily. He was tempted to lie back down between her long, lean legs and sip her honeyed heat, but Trent had a way of doing things, and he would not be denied.

"Stand up for me, baby."

She hesitated for the briefest of seconds, before she rose from the bed, her body as fluid and graceful as a dancer's.

Trent stepped forward, so he was within touching distance, and then murmured, "I want you to undress me."

Crystal's expressive whiskey-colored eyes stared up at him, almost adoringly. She had the look of a shy kitten. The fingers of her right hand reached out and stroked slowly over his chest, back and forth. His muscles jumped beneath his white T-shirt. "A little faster, baby. I'm dying here."

He wanted her.

Yesterday.

Crystal appeared to have no intention of moving more quickly, though. Instead, she seemed intent on massaging his chest and shoulders. Finally, her fingers moved south over his abdomen. Trent threw his head back on a groan. Desire and pain mingled and pushed him precariously close to the edge of control. He was strung as tight as a damn bow.

"Mm, you have the body of a god, Trent."

Trent snorted. "Great, but maybe you'd like my body better buck-naked."

"Yeah, I think I would," Crystal murmured as she licked her lips and drove him that much higher.

Crystal tugged at his T-shirt until she was pulling it free of the waistband of his jeans. She bunched it up as high as she could reach, then Trent took over, all but ripping it over his head and throwing it across the room.

"You really are beautiful, Trent. I thought it the first time we met."

He needed to correct her on the not-so-manly compliment,

but when her fingers finally encountered his skin, Trent lost his voice. Her touch scorched him. He forced himself to remain still, to not fling her to the floor and shove his heavy dick inside her waiting pussy. She leaned forward and placed a small kiss to his left nipple, then nipped it with her teeth. To hell with it. A dark haze came over him.

Trent stepped away from her and swiftly stripped out of his clothes. "You need to learn to move faster," he explained as she frowned at him.

"I was enjoying myself." Her eyes traveled his entire length, then stopped on his swollen erection.

"Yeah?" He watched in predatory delight as her eyes went round and her tempting mouth formed a perfect O. Like any hot-blooded male, Trent imagined his heavy cock sliding between those succulent lips. He wanted to watch her lick and suck, then swallow his hot come. He wanted her a million different ways. It was insane, but he had never felt so out of control for a woman before, not even in his youth. She had put some sort of spell on him, and he was helpless to keep his libido from slamming into overdrive. He bent and kissed her, licking her flesh. He was starved for the unique taste of her. When he lifted his head and noticed Crystal's entire face had gone warm and drowsy with want, he knew he could easily become addicted to seeing such a lovely sight.

She swiped a hand over her lips and seemed to struggle for words when she whispered, "Trent . . ."

The sound of his name on her lips had him swelling with pride. Crystal was so open she wore her feelings for all to see. When her eyes drifted downward once again, her cheeks went rosy.

Trent took no time in lifting her and placing her on the bed. Her cry of surprise had his dick swelling another inch. "Jesus, you try my patience."

Crystal rose to a sitting position and smiled at him temptingly. "Do you know what a turn-on it is when you get so excited? It's very sexy, Trent."

Her hands went to the smooth expanse of her belly. She massaged her own skin and Trent was mesmerized. Slowly she moved upward, sliding over her breasts, kneading and plumping them, and then her head fell back as she pinched the raspberry tips. "This little show you're putting on is like baiting a tiger."

"Yeah?" Crystal slipped her hands around the full orbs and Trent went hard as steel.

"You don't know what you're doing, Crystal. You tempt me beyond reason."

She opened her eyes at his words and smiled saucily, causing his gut to clench. "I don't need you to be tame with me. I want you unrestrained and crazy. And I definitely don't want you holding back. Only please me in the best manner you can. Do you think you can handle that, Trent?"

Trent didn't bother to respond to her little taunt. At once, he was on top of her, pulling her arms above her head and pinning her to the mattress. Wedging his heavily muscled body between her yielding thighs, he shoved her long legs wide and rocked against her wet pussy. Slowly, allowing her to squirm, he lowered his head and sucked one stiff nipple deep. He was rewarded by her groan of need, her eager body shuddering anxiously for him.

He took his sweet time, laving and suckling on one breast then moving to the other. Then he did it all over again. Soon, Trent could feel her lower body lifting, grinding against his hips, seeking fulfillment. He lifted immediately and demanded, "You don't come until I allow it."

While his eyes roamed pleasingly over her bared torso, her body liquid fire against his, Trent growled deep in his throat, enjoying the sight of such a beautiful creature. He got to his knees and held his cock in a tight fist. "Suck it, baby."

He watched her get into position to take him into her

mouth. When her head dipped low, Trent rubbed the bulbous tip over her lips, back and forth. As a pearl of moisture appeared in the slit, he groaned. "Taste it on your tongue. I want my come in your mouth."

As she licked, taking in the sticky liquid, Trent shook with restrained need. "Fuck, I want to shove my cock in deep right now." Crystal's hand grasped his dick and squeezed. Crystal looked up, their gazes locked, and without a second's hesitation she angled her head forward and took him into her hot, eager mouth.

Nothing seemed to matter beyond the feel of her sweet lips wrapped around him so tightly, her tongue stroking him as if he was her tasty treat.

"Crystal." Her name, thickly garbled, was all that emerged from his lips.

She kept her eyes trained on his while he placed one large hand at the back of her head and pulled her further onto him. Trent could feel the head of his dick reach the back of her throat. She moaned in pleasure and the vibrations moved over his entire length, driving him to the very brink. Her hand cupped and squeezed his sac. Trent shut his eyes and concentrated on not embarrassing himself. Crystal's soft hands and mouth played with him, but he was too anxious to be inside of her to let the pleasure continue.

He was equal parts relieved and displeased when she slid her mouth backward, letting her lips give a little love nibble to his tip, before she broke free completely. As she started to draw him in again, Trent stopped her with a hard pull of her hair. "I need you, baby." He wanted to feel the tight clutch of her pussy. He wanted her surrounding him as the night surrounded them. He knew she felt it, too.

Trent grabbed a condom from the bedside table and sheathed himself, then lowered his body to the soft bed beside her. He wrapped his hands around Crystal, easily spanning her waist, and raised her up and over him, impaling her in one smooth stroke. He had wanted to be gentle, but each time she looked at him, he went a little insane, lost another piece of his control.

Crystal took him inside her body with an eagerness that surprised them both. He watched as she rode him, slowly at first, getting used to the feel of him deep inside her body. Trent could and would get rough, this he knew, but for now, he would let her play. They fit together as if God himself had fashioned them that way. One for the other.

Riding on a sea of emotions he did not understand, he let his thoughts drift and decided to just feel. For the first time, he gave himself completely up to another person. He wondered if she was even aware of how powerful she had become.

Moving her hands to his chest for support, she began wiggling her hips in little circles, drawing out their pleasure measure by measure. Aware of each stroke of skin, each time her body clutched around him, Trent moved his hands over her, like a sculptor with a work of art. When he found the tiny nub of her desire, it was her turn to moan. Her need mounted. Her movements became more and more frantic as she drove his cock further into her dripping pussy. Soon there was no separating them. Without warning, Crystal came apart. Her body convulsed. Her fingernails bit into Trent's pectoral muscles as she held on to him for dear life. When her thighs clenched tight and she spurted her juice all around his cock, Trent lost it.

He thrust upward, grasping her hips and pumping faster, harder. Her eyes flew open and he saw the wonder and excitement she was experiencing. The wild desire and need that only he could fulfill. He felt it, too.

"Trent." His name. It was a plea on her lips. But he wanted to push her beyond pleasure, beyond contentment. He wished to show her true rapture.

Wrapping his arms around her bottom, Trent anchored them together and rose to his full height. Standing, in all his crazed and fevered hunger, Trent kept himself deep inside Crystal and continued to thrust into her, harder and harder. He slammed his hips into her, holding her perfect ass in his palms as he fucked her.

He was a breath away from coming. His body flexed, leg muscles steady as he moved her bottom up and down onto his thick shaft, showing her without words how to get the greatest amount of pleasure.

He recognized the instant Crystal began climbing that intoxicating peak again. Soon they were both burning like an out-of-control brush fire. Crystal clutched on to him, digging her nails into his shoulders in a kind of pleasure-pain. He groaned, lowered his head to her neck, and bit down hard, marking her. Crystal slammed her hips into his, then screamed as yet another delicious climax gushed forth. Her smooth inner walls contracted and he joined her this time, her body milking him dry.

It was as natural as breathing. It was euphoria. He knew in that moment that beauty had a name. Crystal Shaw.

Trent vowed she would know him as intimately as he was so eager to know her. If he was moving too fast, too fucking bad. It was not his way to tiptoe, especially not when he saw something he wanted.

Watching the dark fires in her eyes burn bright was as addicting as any drug. When her little pink tongue darted out, licking at his chest, swirling over the dark patch of chest hair, Trent knew a kind of tenderness he had never known with any other woman.

Crystal closed her eyes and rested her head against his chest. Her exotic scent swirled around him, tempting him. He would know her scent anywhere now.

It wasn't until Trent felt her body go limp against his, trusting him to hold them both up, that he shoved back the covers on his bed and lowered her to the cool sheets. He made quick work of disposing the condom and slipped in beside her. When he pulled her atop him, blanketing his body with her silky curves, she sighed, content and replete. Trent kissed her pretty brown head, before pulling the covers up and over them both.

"What about dinner?" she mumbled.

"I'll text Josh and reschedule," he answered as he grabbed his cell phone off the nightstand and sent his brother a quick message.

The last thought that ran through his mind before succumbing to the lethargy of his sated and exhausted body, was that she would not walk away from him come morning. If he had to kidnap her to keep her by his side, Trent was not above doing so. He would happily use everything he had at his disposal. A woman like Crystal came along once in a lifetime, and he was not so stupid as to let her slip through his fingers.

Abruptly he thought of Mac. He knew his friend was every bit as taken with Crystal. Together they would make her see that she belonged to them. And if she wanted only one of them? What would they do, fight over her? Trent tossed the uncomfortable thoughts aside and concentrated on Crystal's lovely curves instead. There would be plenty of time to worry about that later. For now, he had a beautiful woman tucked up close to him and he intended on relishing every moment with her.

6

Mac was miserable. He hadn't seen Crystal since Friday night, and it was now Monday. It'd been two days. Two days of dreaming of Crystal's perfect skin, exotic eyes, tight pussy. They'd talked on the phone. They'd texted each other. But it wasn't the same. He wanted to see her. What was wrong with him? Never had he been so obsessed with a woman before in his life. Now he kept imagining the way she'd looked when she'd come for him and Trent. And just like that, he swelled and hardened. He had to shift around in his seat just so his dick didn't feel strangled. "Fuck," he groaned.

Worse were the feelings of jealousy he harbored for Trent. He'd known that the two of them had shared an intimate evening together. Getting jealous over a woman wasn't like him. Neither was waiting on a woman to call. The night before he'd tried to flirt with another woman at the club in a lame-ass attempt to get over Crystal, to hell if it had worked. He'd only ended up even more frustrated. His dick hadn't wanted the redhead. Only Crystal.

"Goddamn it," he muttered and started to add the numbers

again. Mac loved running the nightclub. He was a night owl by nature, and the fast-paced night life at Kinks suited him to a tee. Still, did there have to be so damn much paperwork involved? He hadn't realized how much elbow grease went into keeping the club afloat, either, staying in the black. Did Trent find it this demanding? Mac doubted it. Because he had a feeling his difficulty today had nothing to do with the hard work and everything to do with Crystal.

Still, as he finished tallying the previous night's profits, he did see the appeal in owning his own business. Mac had always been so involved in being a lawyer. So when he and Trent had given up their legal careers to run the club full-time, it'd been a huge change. Before that time, he'd never considered branching out on his own. Now he couldn't imagine doing anything else. He'd fight tooth and nail to keep Kinks.

A sound outside the office drew his attention away from his thoughts. It was a woman's voice. And not just any woman. He'd know Crystal's voice anywhere.

He rose out of his chair and was in the kitchen before he even realized how eager that would appear. He should have played it cool and stayed in the office. Forced her to come to him.

But she *was* here. Finally. But was she here to see him or Trent? He couldn't wait to find out.

"He knows me. Just tell him it's Crystal and I want to talk to him."

That from Crystal, who, in all her splendor, was staring daggers at his manager, Marcus. Marcus was a big, beefy man, not about to be intimidated.

"Look, lady, he's busy. Come back tonight like all the other women."

"No."

"Is there a problem?" Mac asked, drawing their attention immediately. Marcus was the first to speak.

"I've told her you're busy, but she insists on seeing you."

Crystal stepped around Marcus. "I know I didn't call, but I certainly didn't think it'd be this difficult to see you."

Her eyes were shooting so much fire at him it was a wonder he wasn't burned. Mac crossed his arms over his chest and leaned against the doorjamb. "It's okay, Marcus. She doesn't need an appointment."

Marcus looked at him with a grateful expression on his face and growled, "*Buona fortuna!*"

He didn't know what Marcus was saying, but clearly it wasn't good, and he didn't much care for the way Marcus was acting toward Crystal. "Crystal is very important to me," he stated. "You will show some respect."

Marcus paled visibly, before turning to Crystal and mumbling, "Sorry."

Crystal rolled her eyes. "Yeah, I can see that."

Marcus threw up his hands and started cursing again.

Mac sighed. "Come on, angel." He motioned for her to follow him as he left the kitchen and headed back to his office. No way was he taking her upstairs. Way too much temptation there.

When he entered the small room, he rounded the desk and sat down, then indicated she do the same. He watched her sit, her back ramrod-straight, her purse clutched in her lap. God, she looked good. The dressed-up version was downright edible. But this T-shirt-and-jeans version was just as appealing. With her mass of dark hair tied back in a ponytail and no makeup on, she looked all of eighteen. Holy shit.

He heard Marcus shouting obscenities still and groaned. "I may be forced to defend your honor soon if he doesn't shut up. I can just see me challenging that big bull to a duel at dawn."

He saw Crystal's eyes light with humor. She was so lovely when she smiled. He wanted to see her laugh, even. Christ, what was his deal? He was acting all lovesick or something.

"What brings you here?"

She looked down at her lap. "I just wanted to see you."

"Did you miss me, angel?"

Her gaze darted to his. "Maybe."

In Mac's mind that single word was a victory. He wanted to shout in his triumph, but he had other ways of celebrating. Mac came around the desk and cupped her face in his hand. "I missed you, too. Like crazy."

"You did?"

"Hell, yes," he groaned as he dipped his head and tasted heaven. Oh yeah. The woman was made for loving. Damn, he'd missed her taste. Her scent. Everything about her. No woman had ever gotten to him the way she did. It was as if they'd known each other forever. It pissed him off and turned him on at the same time.

Mac locked his thoughts away and began to devour Crystal's plump lips. He licked, torturing her with ideas of more, then he teased his tongue back and forth over the seam. He was only too glad when she parted them. It was a small sign of surrender, but Mac would take whatever he could get. She twined her arms around his neck and melted against him. He ached to be inside her tight heat. Just as he was about to pull her closer, he had the presence of mind to reach behind him and flip the office door lock into place. He'd been dying for another helping of Crystal's delicious body, and he wasn't taking any chance they'd be interrupted.

Bending at the knees, Mac lifted her up and sat her on the edge of the desk. Without really paying attention, he swept everything off one side of the desk and onto the floor. Crystal's spine went stiff, and she attempted to push him backward. Mac let her, but only so he could taste the delicate skin on her throat. His hand came up and wrapped around the slim column. His cock went hard, and he let loose a low groan of need.

"Mac, wait."

Mac looked into her eyes, seeing the need, but also the fear. "For what?"

"We're not alone here, and I'm not into exhibitionism." She took a deep breath and said, "Besides, I didn't come here for that."

Mac smoothed his palm down her body until he was cupping her buttocks. He squeezed and felt her shudder. "Then why did you come here?"

"I thought we could go to lunch."

"I'm all for that," he replied. "But first a taste. Something to hold me over."

He held himself in check, giving her the ultimate decision. Her answer was pure Crystal.

She bit her lip and said, "I suppose it can't hurt."

"I like my dessert first anyway," he murmured, as he went back to kissing her neck and feeling her lush ass. She had some damn sexy curves. Lush. He thought he heard her say his name, but it was so faint he couldn't be certain. All he really knew was that she still had too many clothes on.

He lifted away from her. Now that he knew she wasn't going to bolt for the door, he was willing to give her a few inches to breathe. He locked the office door, then said, "Take off your clothes for me. I need to see you."

Crystal blushed. She'd been brave enough to seek him out, but apparently that was as far as her bravery went. She had such a soft inner core that had Mac feeling fiercely protective.

She quickly got herself under control and started to undress, her movements uncontrived. She was a beauty, but so untutored, as he'd found out firsthand when they'd had sex. A few straps wrapped around Crystal's smooth hips connected in the center by a vee was all that made up her panties. The vee happened to be blue, and see-through. Mac could see her tempting curls beneath and he could make out the sweet nub of her clitoris. He yearned to lean toward her and give her a good, long lick. He could smell her scent already, a potent combination of dewy arousal and eagerness.

The matching bra she wore was enough to entice him into a horny stupor. And, like a fucking missile, his dick pushed against the zipper of his fly in a lame attempt to get up close and personal with Crystal's hot body. Soon, she was nude and nothing kept him from her creamy perfection.

Mac couldn't sit still and not touch. Reaching out, he grabbed Crystal by the hips and scooted her closer. She let him have his way, a sassy smile playing at the corners of her mouth.

"Are you turned on, angel?"

"Very much. And watching your eyes heat up and your body go all hard for me is making it worse."

"Come here then, and I'll make it all better." He pulled her out of the chair and took the seat himself, then sat her onto his lap.

Mac kissed her as if he had all day to drown himself in her flavor. He wanted her with a wild sort of eagerness that made him almost angry. It wasn't normal to want a woman as badly as he wanted Crystal. She sighed, wrapped her arms around his neck, and opened her mouth for his demanding tongue. Not taking a chance she might disappear like the ethereal being she seemed to be, Mac slipped between her lips and tasted every inch of her dark passion. Crystal moaned and he pushed upward, letting her feel the hard length of his arousal against her bare ass. God, he wanted her. Needed her.

He leaned into her, took one protruding nipple into his mouth, and sucked, hard. Crystal grabbed the back of his head and held him against the fleshy orb. She was every bit as anxious as he was for this. Done with playing it safe, Mac let one hand slip down her body to cup her mound, swiftly sinking two thick fingers all the way into her tight, wet heat.

"Mac!" Crystal shouted. He lifted away from her long enough to see the wide-eyed need on her face. He took her other breast, biting and sucking, while his thumb played over her hard clitoris. Crystal moved against his hand, fucking his fingers until suddenly she was crying out his name, her body squeezing and contracting as she came long and hard.

He let her ride out the feelings before he slipped his fingers free of her and stood. His hands went to his belt, gauging Crystal's reaction as he pulled his cock free. When she licked her lips as if imagining his taste, a drop of fluid appeared at the tip. The sight of her standing there so ready and anxious for him sent Mac over the edge.

He clutched her hips and turned her around so she faced the desk. "Grab hold of the edge, angel," Mac said as he pulled a condom out of his wallet and rolled it on. He took Crystal's ass in his hands and spread her wide, her glistening folds opening, inviting him in. "Now," Mac growled, as he entered her in one smooth stroke, extracting a husky moan from her.

"You and I fit together perfectly. Remember that," Mac said, as he leaned over her, bracing his arms on the desk beside her, caging her in, and bit her shoulder.

Crystal pushed her hips backward, seeking more of him. "Deeper, Mac, please. I need you."

"I've been going crazy for you," he told her. "You have no idea."

"Then stop torturing us both and take me," she said in a rough whisper.

He smiled, a rumble of primal male satisfaction rising. "That's what I wanted to hear."

Then he gave it to her, fucking her hard and fast and with a furious need to leave his mark on her. He wanted every other man to know she belonged to him. His cock swelled as he thrust into her over and over. He reached around to her front and flicked a thumb around her clit, igniting her passion all over again.

Crystal went up in flames, pushing against him. Her hand came to rest over his on her mound as she fragmented and shattered. Mac moved faster, thrusting once, twice, until finally he burst wide and filled her.

He took his other hand off the desk and stroked her hair away from her face. Both of them were sweating and shaky. Crystal tilted her head sideways, giving him her mouth for a kiss. He took it, softly, lingeringly, before releasing her and pulling out of her. Mac fixed his clothes then turned Crystal around and helped her with hers. A soft smile lit her face, making him wonder what she was thinking. "So, lunch?"

She laughed. "I'm famished."

"Good, because I know a great Italian place. Best Alfredo in the world."

"Great," she said. "I don't have a lot of time because I'm supposed to meet Mollie. We're going apartment hunting."

He unlocked the office door, then turned to grab his keys and cell phone off the desk. "Mollie is the woman you were with the night we first met?"

She nodded. "She's been letting me stay with her until I find a place of my own."

As they headed out to his car, Mac leaped at the chance to get to know more about Crystal. "That sounds like a long story."

She shrugged as she got into the passenger side of the car. "Not really," she said after he got in behind the wheel. "I was in a bad relationship. When it ended, I moved here to start fresh. Mollie was nice enough to help me out, but I'm sure she'd like to have her space back. It's been months."

Mac wanted to know more about the "bad relationship," but he didn't want her to feel cornered. Something about Crystal made him think of a wounded cat. Unpredictable and ready to lash out. He needed to be patient with her, and that had never been one of his strong suits. "I'm betting she's enjoyed having you, but I do understand the need for your own place."

"I've never lived on my own, to be honest. I went from living with my mother to living with Richard. So, having my own place to decorate and call my own will be a fun change."

The excitement in her voice was clear, but what sort of guy had had Crystal all to herself and let her go? A dumbass for sure. "Richard? That's the guy you were with?"

"Yeah," she replied, her voice sounding sad and faraway. "Two years."

Did she still care about him? "Are you sorry it's over?"

She snorted. "God, no! Not at all. It wasn't what you'd call a fairy-tale romance."

He suspected that there was a lot more to that answer. "I see. And are you going to invite me over to your new place?"

"Sure. I'm going to need help moving in. Mind if I use you for free labor?"

"Use me all you want, angel. I'm yours."

She was silent a moment before she said, "Mac, I'm not sure what is happening here. With Trent and you, I mean. I'm way out of my depth."

"We both care about you," he answered, hoping she wasn't getting cold feet. "I mean, I know it's a bit unorthodox to be with two men, but I think we can make it work."

"But I was with Trent the other day. And now I'm with you. This goes beyond unorthodox. It's downright crazy."

He chuckled. "When you put it like that, it does sound crazy." He pulled in to the parking lot of the restaurant and snagged a spot near the door. After he cut the engine, Mac turned toward Crystal and said, "Truth is, I've never been satisfied with the norm. It's overrated if you ask me."

She smiled. "I suppose you have a point."

He leaned close and kissed the tip of her nose. "I do. Now, how about some lasagna?"

"The way to my heart," she replied in a shy, whispery voice. "Lead on."

Mac knew a sense of predatory satisfaction when she dipped

close and kissed him. That she was initiating the intimate contact went a long way toward easing the jealousy he'd experienced earlier. Once more he thought of her past relationship and knew there was more to that story that she wasn't sharing. He ached to learn everything about her, but Crystal needed time. He'd give it to her. Hell, Mac would give her the world with a bow wrapped neatly around it if he could.

7

_____

An hour later, Crystal was back at Mollie's apartment, pouring a glass of iced tea. She was floating on a cloud, and each time she thought of her lunch with Mac she ended up grinning like a ninny. He was so sweet and loving, while Trent tended to challenge her. Together they made quite a pair.

The front door opened and Crystal called out, "Mollie?"

"Yeah, sorry I'm late," Mollie replied as she walked into the kitchen and dropped her purse on the table. "Traffic downtown sucked."

"No problem. There's still plenty of time to check out those two apartments," Crystal replied, waving away Mollie's concern. "I was just getting something to drink. Want something?"

"Water would be great, thanks." Mollie sat down at the table and pulled out her cell phone. As she stared at the screen, she said, "I need to take my car in to get it looked at. My brakes are grinding again."

"That's the second time in the last several months. Not to mention the radiator you had fixed recently," Crystal said, frowning. "Have you thought of trading it in for something newer?"

Mollie sighed and pushed a lock of her red hair behind her ear. "Yeah, but I'm not sure I'm ready for that."

Crystal handed her a glass of water. "I understand, but it's still something to think about." She couldn't really blame Mollie for wanting to hold on to the '69 silver Camaro. It had belonged to Alex. After he died Mollie had put quite a few of his things in storage, but the car was special. It'd been Alex's pride and joy. Mollie refused to trade up.

"Enough about my car. How was your day?" Mollie inquired as she reached across the table and grabbed a foil-wrapped piece of chocolate from a candy dish.

Crystal thought of meeting Mac. Both the sex and the lasagna had been amazing. She didn't think Mollie needed to know about the former, though. "I met Mac for lunch. A great little Italian place called Carmine's. Ever been there?"

"No, but a few ladies from the office have mentioned it. I've been meaning to go."

"You should. Their lasagna tasted homemade."

"I have a feeling it wasn't the lasagna that put that glow in your cheeks."

"Maybe," she hedged. God, she never could hold out on Mollie.

Mollie sat up straighter, and suddenly appeared entirely too alert. "And what about Trent?"

"What about him?"

"You had dinner with his parents the other night, right?"

"Well, we didn't quite make it to dinner," she replied, feeling her cheeks heat. Unable to withstand Mollie's scrutiny, Crystal turned and started putting the clean dishes away from the drainer.

"Is that so?" Mollie asked, her voice filled with amusement. "So, does this mean that you're sampling the goods before you decide?"

Mollie's question caused Crystal to fumble and drop a cup. Thankfully the damn thing was plastic. She picked it up and placed it on the counter, then turned to her nosy friend. "I plead the Fifth." She looked at the clock on the microwave and added, "Besides, we're late to meet with the manager of that first apartment we were going to check out."

"No way, sister. You don't get off that easily."

"Fine, then," she bit out, knowing Mollie wasn't going to let it go. "Yes, I suppose you could say I'm sampling the goods." She paused, then added, "There. Happy?" Crystal felt as if she could fry an egg on her face it was so damn hot from mortification.

"Well, those two sure are gorgeous," Mollie replied in a dreamy voice. "So, what's the plan, exactly? Are you supposed to pick one or will there be a duel?"

Crystal rolled her eyes. "You're an idiot."

Mollie laughed. "Maybe you should start upping your vitamins. I have a feeling you're going to need all the energy you can muster."

Crystal shook her head and started out of the kitchen. "This conversation is over. Are you coming or not?"

Mollie stood and grabbed her purse. "All kidding aside, I'm glad you're getting yourself out there. You deserve to have some fun."

Crystal looked back at her friend. "Thanks," she replied. "It's completely warped to date them both, but just for once I don't care. Trent and Mac are both so different from Richard. They're kind and generous and I'm having fun. Does that sound awful?"

"Of course not," Mollie said, her voice softening. "But I do want you to be careful. They seem pretty intense. I don't want you biting off more than you can chew."

Crystal reached out and placed her hand on her friend's shoulder. "I'll be fine, really," Crystal said. "Besides, I have no intention of getting serious. I've been down the marriage road and it sucked, remember?"

Mollie nodded. "Yeah, and I'm glad that part of your life is over."

"Me too," she said. An image of Richard's condescending face sprang to her mind as he'd handed her the divorce papers. She shook away the awful memory. "Now, let's go apartment hunting."

"Works for me," Mollie said as she followed her out. "And maybe afterward you can take me to that Italian place. I've got a craving."

"Great idea," Crystal said, heading to her car. "I'm buying."

"Okay, but I'm picking up the tab next time," Mollie replied, as she got in the passenger side.

"Maybe next time we'll be having dinner at my place." Crystal put the key in the ignition and turned.

"You know you don't have to move, right? I truly love having the company."

Her heart swelled with warmth at Mollie's statement. "I know and I'll never be able to repay you for all that you've done for me. But I need to start the next chapter of my life. Does that make sense?"

"Of course. It's just . . . it's been nice having someone around." Mollie shrugged. "It was hard getting used to the silence after Alex passed away. His laughter and that deep voice of his always filled the place. I still miss it."

Crystal hadn't considered how difficult it must have been for Mollie to live alone after so many happy years of marriage. "Maybe it's time you did a little dating, too," Crystal said, taking her eyes off the road for a brief moment to look at Mollie. "He wouldn't want you to be alone."

"I date," Mollie said, as she stared out the windshield.

"Not much," Crystal said, hoping she wasn't putting her

nose where it didn't belong. "And you don't usually go on a date with a guy more than twice."

"Yeah, you're right." Mollie sighed. "It's time I made some changes of my own, huh?"

Crystal chuckled. "We're quite a pair."

"We might be a mess, but at least we have each other," Mollie said.

"Damn straight," Crystal agreed. No doubt, she never would've survived these last few months without Mollie by her side.

The next morning, Crystal woke feeling tired and sluggish. She thought that just maybe it had something to do with getting practically no sleep. After looking at the two apartments with Mollie and realizing that neither of them were within her budget, she'd taken Mollie out to eat as promised. Once they got back home, they'd stayed up late into the night talking about everything from men to politics. By the time she'd gotten to bed it'd been in the a.m. hours. But as soon as her head hit the pillow, she'd tossed and turned the rest of the night, thinking of Mac, then Trent, then Mac. Around and around. She'd had crazy, erotic dreams and woken sweaty and more tired than ever.

She showered and ate a toasted bagel with strawberry jam for breakfast, then decided it was way too nice outside to sit in the house and work on the computer. Instead, she slipped into her two-piece swimsuit and went out to the back patio to catch some sun for a few hours.

Crystal squirted some sunscreen on and rubbed it in before turning on her stomach on the lounger. Several minutes later, she checked the time on her cell phone and realized she'd been out longer than she'd intended. She turned over and adjusted her bikini top. She smoothed on more of the protective lotion, then lay back down and closed her eyes. Within minutes, Crystal felt a hand pressed against her belly. Startled, she opened her eyes and jerked upright. The face staring down at her belonged to her ex. *Please, God, tell me this is just a nightmare.*

"Hello, wife," Richard said, as if they weren't divorced and he actually still had a right to call her that. "You should've waited on me. I would've massaged the lotion in real good—and in all the right places, too."

"Richard, what are you doing here? Our time together is over. You can't just pop up here as if you have some kind of right to do so, and don't call me 'wife.' I'm not your anything anymore." She was angry that he'd had the audacity to come here unannounced and unwanted. She only hoped the little tremor of fear wasn't detectable.

"Aw, Crystal, don't be upset. I just wanted to see how you were. Of course, I can see you're just fine. Have you lost a few pounds? Whatever you're doing, it's definitely working for you," he said, as he looked her up and down.

"The only thing I've done is get away from you." When he started to protest, Crystal rode right over him. "I'm warning you, Richard, I want nothing more to do with you. Our marriage was a huge disaster. I've moved on. Leave me alone." She swung her legs to the side of the lounger and stood. She needed distance between them, before he decided she should be punished for speaking to him in such a tone.

As Crystal started for the door, she heard another voice chime in, this one deeper and definitely pissed. "You heard the lady, Richard, get lost."

She turned and saw Trent standing next to the patio, his legs spread wide and fists clenched at his sides. He looked very big and very angry. She was so relieved to see him that she could've hugged him.

"Just who the hell are you?" Richard asked, clearly too stupid to realize when he should cut and run.

Trent stepped closer to Richard. "I'm the guy who's going to rearrange your face if you don't leave right now. Crystal asked you nicely, but I won't."

Richard puffed up his chest and pointed toward Trent. "Look, I don't know who you think you are, but I'm her husband so I'm not going anywhere."

Trent's brow arched as he looked over at her. Crystal groaned. It was turning out to be a lousy day. "He's my *ex*-husband. Big emphasis on *ex*." Crystal aimed the last part at Richard, hoping he would just make things easy by simply disappearing into a puff of smoke.

"Go inside and get dressed, Crystal. I'll handle your visitor."

Trent clearly didn't want Richard anywhere near Crystal. Considering the way she shook like a weak little kitten, getting out of Dodge didn't seem like a bad idea. Besides, she was beginning to feel very much like chum in a churning water of sharks. As she turned back around and opened the back screen door, she heard Trent say, "You blew it with her, asshole. She doesn't belong to you anymore. She's mine now, and I don't allow other men to upset her. If I ever find you here again, you'll wish you were dead by the time I'm finished. Do we understand each other?"

The *she's mine* part sent butterflies to flight inside her stomach, but Crystal didn't wait to hear Richard's reply. She let the door close behind her and went upstairs to change into a pair of shorts and a shirt. On the way up the stairs, she thought she heard a car start up and pull away. Was it wrong to feel excitement at Trent's parting words, she wondered? *Mine.* She felt as if she should be upset by his domineering manner, but instead her heart was beating a million miles a second, and her blood was suddenly sizzling. Clearly, she wasn't much of a feminist.

When Crystal came back downstairs, she was wearing a pair of crisp white shorts and a red halter top. Trent groaned. The tiny shirt and shorts weren't any better than the bikini she had on a few minutes ago. At least now, they were alone. He could look his fill and not worry about anyone else doing the same. He decided it was time to get down to explanations. The little hellcat had been married? He felt unaccountably jealous over that thought.

She walked over to her refrigerator and got out a big pitcher of iced tea. Upon retrieving two glasses, she scooped some ice into them and began to pour out the cold liquid. Trent peered down at the table and was struck by how large and strong it appeared. He tested its strength with his hands and recognized that it was as sturdy as it looked. A devilishly kinky thought came to mind. Would the big wooden table hold the two of them? He looked back at Crystal, feeling his temperature rise as he imagined it. Crystal moved with an easy grace and she was such a natural tease, yet she had seemed to have no clue at all. God, Trent was such a goner.

Crystal knew Trent would be curious about Richard, but she didn't want to get into the mess of her marriage. She didn't understand it herself. Still, she knew without a doubt that if he started asking questions, she would end up telling him all the gory details, every nasty little bit that even Mollie wasn't privy to. She was just too lousy at lying, and she had a feeling Trent would see right through any fib she tried to pass off on him.

"Is this table made of oak?" She turned to see him staring at the thing.

Dumbstruck, she said, "Uh, I really don't know what it's made of. It's Mollie's."

Trent moved until he stood directly in front of her. He placed his hands on her shoulders and squeezed. "You're shaking still."

"Sorry about that little scene," she said, enjoying the feel of his hands on her way too much. "Thank you for helping me with Richard. He can be a very stubborn man."

"So can I," Trent bit out as he leaned down and kissed her nape.

Her mouth quirked up into a half smile. "Yeah, I noticed."

"Crystal?"

"Yes?" *Uh-oh, here it comes.* She braced herself for the onslaught of questions to come.

"What do you say we go somewhere and get some lunch?" As he spoke, he slung his arm around her waist and hugged her close.

"L-lunch?" Not the question she was expecting from him, but who was she to complain?

He turned her around, then spoke in her ear in a deep whisper. "Yeah, I'm starved and I thought maybe you'd have lunch with me. That's why I stopped by."

"Oh sure. That sounds lovely."

At that, he left the drinks on the counter and began walking her toward the living room. When he sat down on the couch and pulled her down beside him, Crystal frowned. "I thought—"

"First, tell me about Richard," he said. "How long were you married to that ass and why are you divorced?"

Shoot, she was beginning to think he wasn't going to inquire about Richard. She supposed it was too much to hope for. After all, Trent didn't seem the type of man to let matters like her being married simply go unexplained. She prepared herself to tell him all, every lousy, sordid detail. She wanted nothing to come between them, especially not her ex-husband.

"It's not a very pleasant story. Are you sure you want to hear it?"

He nodded. "Hey, if it makes you feel any better, we've all made mistakes. I've made my fair share. Big mistakes, little mistakes. Even mistakes I'll only share with the big guy upstairs." He smiled then and said, "And I have all the time in the world for you, Crystal." He looked over at her with honesty in his eyes, and it made Crystal feel immensely better.

"Well, he drank a lot, and he cheated on me," she said, hoping Trent wouldn't want details. "It was a wreck of a marriage from day one, and divorcing him was the best thing I've ever done."

"What an ass. If he cheated on you, Crystal, he must be a complete fool. What man would need any other woman, if he already had you?"

Trent frowned as if he wanted to wring Richard's neck. Lord, if Richard's infidelity did this to Trent, Crystal didn't think she could tell him about the abuse. It worried her a little, considering she tended to walk on eggshells around men and their tempers since her ex-husband's abuse. Trent's words warmed her heart somewhat, though.

He must have sensed she was too quiet, because at that moment he reached out and took her hand in his. He pulled her into a tight embrace, murmuring into her hair, "I'm sorry, baby. I just hate that he hurt you, but I promise you, no one else will, ever again." She had a premonition that Trent could hurt her . . . if she allowed him to have her heart. However, she wasn't foolish enough to let that happen. Not ever again.

"Finish telling me what happened. I know there's more to it. I want to know everything, so don't even consider holding back on me, because I will know if you are."

"Isn't that enough? He cheated on me, end of story. I divorced him and moved on with my life. This is the first I've heard from him in five months. I don't know why he's back. He says he wants us to get to know each other again, but I told him not a chance. There's no more to it than that. I didn't invite him over today—he came here unannounced, and unwanted." She was talking too fast, but she was desperate for the conversation to come to an end.

He grasped her around the waist with both hands, spanning her waistline. She was so trim, his fingers almost touched together. She was perfect in every way. She fit his body, the way no other woman had. He watched her eyes heat up. He pulled her close to him, fitting her to him, and kissed her long and deep. With their lips locked together, Trent laid her down, then pulled away just long enough to ask, "Where's your room-mate?"

"She's at work," she answered, her voice a whisper. "She usually gets home around six."

"Good," he murmured, as he began to strip her naked. When her breasts were free, Trent groaned, dipped his head, and sucked one already erect nipple into his mouth. Sweet, soft, pink, and just right. He could feed on her for hours. He hadn't had any breakfast yet, and she was a meal fit for a king.

He flicked his tongue over and around her nipple gently at first, then rougher, demanding her flesh to beg for him. He cupped the round globe and pulled it up higher, kneading the supple skin with skilled fingers. He heard her moan of delight, and felt her writhing beneath him. He took joy in her animated responses to him. He gave in to his primal cravings and bit down. She arched upward compliantly. His hand answered her unspoken pleas: letting go of her breast, he journeyed down until he found her precious mound, shoving aside her shorts. His fingers delved at once, and his nostrils flared to life as he picked up her succulent scent. Anxiously, he searched through her damp curls and found her budding desire. She was swollen and throbbing already. He fondled and toyed with the little nub until the teasing became too much for even him. He lifted off of her, tore at the button fly on his jeans, and freed his erection. In the red haze of his lust, her pleading reached his ears. He looked down and saw her hands outstretched, waiting to take him into her arms, even as her body welcomed him. He went inside both embraces willingly, gladly, plunging into her with a quick kind of force that had them both groaning.

He pumped at her with a furious need that went as far back as time itself, coupling and claiming his mate with a demand that spoke of his passion. She came back at him with her own brand of passion, scoring his back with her fingernails, marking her territory. He reached a hand between their bodies, and touched off the beginning of her orgasm. She screamed and wrapped her legs around him, sending him over the same blissful cliff. He pumped into her one last time and exploded into her eager body.

Only minutes passed, but he lifted off of her, not wanting to crush her beneath his weight, then did up the buttons on his pants. He stood there a moment, transfixed, staring down at her sated body. A pleasant smile was on her face, her hair a mess of waves. Trent thought she'd never looked more beautiful.

Her eyes popped open just then. She stared up at him in awe, that smile never leaving her face, and said, "That was wonderful."

Trent couldn't help the surge of pride that had him puffing up like a proud peacock. He smiled back at her and knelt down. With one arm under her legs and the other supporting her neck he picked her up and cradled her close to his chest. She beamed up at him, her look of sheer pleasure spearing his heart. He shook off the notion and said, "Time to wash, baby, and I plan on taking my time cleaning every inch of you." He felt her tremble and she whispered in his ear, "You wash mine, I'll wash yours." And it was Trent's turn to tremble.

Crystal felt like she was floating on a cloud. They'd shared something profound, and it went beyond hot and heavy sex. There was something about the way Trent looked at her, as if he was seeing her in a different way. Or maybe it wasn't different, but it was as if he was seeing her for the first time. Up until now their relationship had been largely based on mutual desire, chemistry, and sating each other's needs and wants. But with the morning came renewal. She felt fresh and new with Trent. Nothing was the same as it had once been with Richard. There was a comfortable feel about their relationship. She couldn't help the smile that beamed across her face; it seemed permanently affixed there.

Trent stepped into her bedroom and set her on her feet in front of him. Every small inch of her seemed seared by his intense stare. She took her hands to him and removed his shirt, then began with the buttons of his jeans. There was something incredibly intimate about undressing a man. Having her fingers where his usually would be, doing what he did every day, so routine for him, but so sensual to her. She undid the buttons slowly, one at a time, drawing out the anticipation. Trent stood, rigid and waiting. She could tell he wanted to simply rip the buttons away, yet he waited. She adored him all the more for it. She got to the last of them and pushed open his jeans. He had no underwear on. She could see the wavy curls, peeking out at all angles. Licking her lips she touched a finger at the vee opening and swirled her finger in the dense patch. He shuddered, grabbed at the sides of his jeans, drew them down completely, and stepped out of them. They stood in the light of day, naked and eager, both of them devouring the other with their eyes.

Trent was the first to move. He grasped her hand in his own and pulled her to the bathroom, turned on the light, and dropped her hand. He strode toward the shower and turned on the pulsing spray. The steam rose immediately and the bathroom was soon filled with it. She shivered, despite the warmth that seeped into her pores. Stepping in, he turned to her and held out his hand, and she took it and stepped in with him. He turned them so that she was under the massaging spray. First, he stroked his fingers through her hair, taming the curls and letting the water drench her. Her eyes closed, and his fingers continued their ministrations. For a brief moment his hands left her, but then they were back, and soon, the scent of coconuts reached her, giving her dreamy notions of being in the tropics with him. She smiled.

"Such a pleasing smile. What are you thinking of, baby?"

His voice was soft as he spoke in her ear. She was completely entranced.

"I was thinking how nice it'd be if we were on some tropical island together."

He was quiet for a moment, as if considering the idea. She was about to laugh it off as nothing, just a silly notion and nothing more, when he spoke again, his voice as warm as chocolate.

"I'd love to take you away from here, Crystal. Whisk you to some tiny little spot in the Caribbean. Steep you in wild, exotic flowers, play under waterfalls like a couple of children. Mm, yes, that does sound lovely. Think of that while I wash you, Crystal. Think of us dancing under the moon, and strolling along the beach. Making love in the soft sand at night."

Crystal smiled with Trent's words moving through her mind. Then his soapy hands touched her body and her mind went blank. She moaned as he slicked the bubbly softness over her shoulders, over the indentation at her collarbone, down her arms, and finally to her waistline. He moved in swirls, up and down, touching her belly button lightly. A shiver ran through her. She had no idea the belly button was such a pleasurable spot on a woman's body. Though, every inch of her seemed to be one big erogenous zone where Trent was concerned. He traveled his way up her torso, massaging with his fingers till he reached her breasts. He cupped them and moved his hands in circling patterns, working both nipples at the same time, squeezing and plucking. She opened her eyes and, staring at him, silently pleaded with him.

He only stared back at her and shook his head. He was giving her the slow, gentle loving this time. Last night had been so frenzied that he felt she needed gentleness now. She wasn't sure what she needed, but she knew she needed him beyond anything else.

Trent's capable hands left her nipples and traveled south. He wasted no time on her belly this time, but went straight to her cleft instead. He delved into her with such swiftness that she jumped in pleasure, reaching out and grasping on to him for support. Their eyes never left each other. They were locked together. His two fingers were inside her body, his eyes snaring her in their sensual trap. She opened her mouth to protest, wanting him inside of her instead of just his fingers, but then he moved them in circles, like he had with her breasts. He moved slowly inside of her, around and around. Her head fell back and she whimpered. One strong arm went around her for support, while the other kept up the assault inside her body. She fairly melted into him. He released her at once, and slipped his cock inside her wetness. He moved her legs to his waist and she rode him.

"God, yes, Crystal."

He leaned down and sucked at her nipple hard, biting at the turgid bit of flesh. She flung her arms around his back and clutched him to her, digging her nails into his fleshy muscles. He pumped once more, and their climaxes rose and crashed at the same time in perfect unison. He was perfect for her, she thought. They fit together like a supple glove.

They stood, quivering muscles, hot water sluicing their bodies, locked in their loving embrace for a few minutes longer. Trent pulled her into his chest one last time, pulled back, and stared at her flushed face.

He smiled. "Let's go shopping after we grab lunch."

Crystal just stared at him, shocked to silence. Shopping was the last thing on her mind. He was still inside of her. She couldn't think straight with him like that. She doubted any sane woman could. As if he'd read her thoughts, he pulled out of her slowly and set her on her feet—not at all what she wanted. She was wobbly, as if she'd just worked out, though Trent had done all the work really, and he wasn't even breathing hard. She frowned at the thought of shopping.

Trent touched his finger to her chin and tilted her head back. "Why the frown?"

"I don't want to shop. I want to stay here with you. All the rest of the day, making love."

Her pout nearly did him in. She was so damn cute, and she had him wrapped around her little finger so tight. But he was determined to buy her something. He wanted to pleasure her in every way, romance the socks off of her. Maybe if she was plied with enough loving, gifts, and pleasures, she'd be easier to convince that their relationship was special. Hell, he'd try anything, really, but in the end he couldn't imagine life without her.

She was independent enough to give him a fight, but feminine enough to enjoy the romancing. Maybe, just maybe, he could convince her that it was in her best interest to stay with him. "How about a little something to tide you over? Then we'll go to lunch and shopping."

"Works for me," she murmured as she wrapped her arms around his neck and grinned.

Trent moved against her, putting his large arms around her and pulling her into his embrace. She rose immediately and their lips found each other. Home was just a breath away.

She opened her mouth for his invasion, and he took what she offered. Sliding in and tangling with her tongue was delightfully sweet, but he wanted more. His hands met the soft skin of her thighs. Her legs wrapped around his waist and her arms around his neck. His hands gripped and pulled her tight against his erection, and instinctively he undulated against her pubic bone. Still it wasn't enough, not nearly enough.

He pushed his hand between their tightly wrapped bodies and inched himself inside of her. Slowly, tiny fractions at a time, he pushed deeper, dragging out their pleasure. Their lips remained locked, and he took her mouth as slowly and teasingly as he took her body. Crystal groaned and thrust her hips forward, forcing him in to the hilt. He nearly lost his balance, but he swiftly pumped back at her, and the pace was on. They took from each other, forcing and demanding and pushing beyond both of their endurance. He sucked at her tongue, and she pressed her breasts against his chest. They were out of control and lost in some tunnel of need and want. Finally, regretfully, he released himself inside of her, and at once Crystal was screaming into his mouth. His legs shook with exertion and Crystal's chest was rising and falling in fast little pants. They were both thoroughly worked over. Trent figured that should hold him over for at least an hour or so, before he craved her all over again.

He released her thighs and she slowly slid to the floor. Only then did he see the purplish bruises that his fingers had obviously left there. He'd been too rough.

"Damn it," he bit out.

Crystal looked at him with a startled expression. Trent merely knelt down in front of her and kissed the bruises on her thighs. One by one, he touched his lips to each tiny bruise that marred her perfect skin. What kind of man was he, coming at her like a rutting bull? Damn! He should have been more careful. Once he finished with one leg, he moved to the other, kissing the bruises there, as well. He felt Crystal's hands in his hair, caressing him. He looked up at her from his position and she had the sweetest expression in her eyes, a gentle smile on her face. She was so delicate. Trent vowed to never lose control with her again.

He rose back up and took her into his arms, cradling her head to his chest, and whispered, "I'm sorry, baby, I should have been gentler."

"Trent, please don't ever be sorry for needing me as much as I do you. Please don't ever be sorry for making love to me. You are a passionately intense lover, but you're also a gentle man."

"If I were so gentle, I wouldn't have marked you. I came at you like it was rutting season."

She smiled at his analogy, but in all seriousness she said, "I've known ugly bruises before, Trent, and those on my thighs aren't anything remotely close."

Trent stilled visibly. Every muscle went rigid and hard. "What are you talking about, Crystal?" He had horrible visions of her being beaten. Who, though? Her father? Her ex? They'd pay dearly, no matter who it was.

Crystal wedged herself out of Trent's crushing embrace and said, "Well, remember when you said you thought there was more to the divorce than what I told you?" As she spoke she got dressed. She watched Trent as she did, and he nodded his head. "You were right, there was more to it."

"Go on."

"Richard was very sweet in the beginning of the marriage really, but as time went on, he began drinking, began getting increasingly more jealous and possessive of me. Anytime I was late coming home from work, he'd be upset and toss things around, cursing and accusing me of messing around on him."

Crystal walked to the couch and sat, and Trent did the same, sitting next to her. She continued, "One night I came home from work and he was especially drunk, worse than I'd ever seen him before. He shouted and was in a mad fit. His face frightened me, Trent. The way it turned so red, like he could simply explode at any given time. I knew this time was different. He'd had enough time to work himself up to an aggressive rage. So I stayed silent, listening to him rant, but then he started slinging accusations at me. Telling me that he knew I was 'whoring around.' I got angry myself then. I'd always been faithful to Richard. So I spoke up and told him I wasn't messing around, there was only ever him."

Crystal took a breath before finishing the rest, but she did need to finish, as much for herself as for Trent. "That seemed to be the final straw. Having me talking back was too much for his ego, I suppose. His fist came out of nowhere. It knocked me out cold. You've seen Richard—he's not a huge guy—but still, his punch was enough to put me out for about an hour or so.

When I came to, he was crying over me, and so sorry. I remember he kept saying he was sorry, over and over again."

Oddly enough, she actually felt better, getting it out, telling someone the whole story. She felt immediate relief. Trent was so quiet, though, just staring at the floor, not saying a word. Finally Crystal couldn't stand the silence so she broke it and said, "Trent?"

Trent looked up at Crystal, stared for a few more seconds, and then said, "I'll kill him for this."

There was something in Trent's set expression, the look in his eyes that told her he meant every word he said. She pleaded with him, "Trent, please don't take that attitude. Don't make me regret I told you this. Richard is no longer a part of my life. The past is the past."

"Were there other times that he hit you, Crystal? Other times when you were knocked unconscious?"

She thought about lying to him for a second, but decided she'd come this far. "Yes. Times when he pushed me down or grabbed at me really hard. Bruises and scrapes."

"I should have killed him when he was here. I could see that it bothered you having him near. It wasn't normal the way you seemed wary of him. Irritation over an ex, yes, but not fear. If I ever see him again, I'll—"

Trent stopped in mid-sentence and got up to pace around the room. He seemed to be waging a private battle with himself. At last he grumbled, "Crystal, I can't promise that I won't put my fist in his face if I ever see him again, but I won't go looking for him. For you, I'll leave him be."

She knew how much it cost him to give her this. She rose off the couch and slung her arms around him. "Thank you. Richard is history, and that's the way I want him to stay." Then she kissed him. He held her, kissing and touching her face, as if the bruises were still there, gently soothing away the long-forgotten pain. "You'd better go get ready for our shopping trip, baby. Because if we keep this up, I'm liable to skip the whole damn thing and take you again."

Crystal did as she was told, leaving Trent alone while she got ready. Something in her gut was telling her that he needed a few moments to himself to work through his feelings about Richard and calm himself down. She reached her bedroom and went to her closet. The sleeveless yellow dress with the low-dipping back caught her eye. It was a gorgeous silk material, and when she'd tried it on at the store she'd loved the way it had molded perfectly to her curves. She hadn't gotten a chance to wear it until now.

She unzipped the dress and stepped into it. She put on a pair of strappy sandals and made quick work of her hair and makeup. She bunched and brushed her tangle of curls and squeezed them into a quick bun. When she was through, she stepped back and stared at herself in the mirror above the dresser. Well, it wasn't movie-star quality, but it would do.

As ready as she would ever be, Crystal left the room and made her way back to the living room where Trent waited. When his eyes caught sight of her, he groaned. "Damn, you look good."

The dress showed off her amazing figure to perfection. Damn. He didn't need that picture in his head right now. If he was going to walk around a shopping mall filled with people, he would need a clear head and not a freaking boner. That wasn't about to happen if he kept watching her ass twitch back and forth in the sunshine-yellow dress.

Great, now he was hard as iron and it would be hours before he would get a chance to have her again.

"Trent?"

His voice was hoarse when he answered, "Yeah?"

"I feel like I've revealed all my skeletons, but you've barely shared your life with me."

Oh boy, now it was his turn to be questioned. It was only

fair, after all, but he hated the trip down memory lane. It wasn't exactly the good old days. "Her name was Jill, and we were married for a year and a half."

Crystal was quiet for a moment, then she said, "What does she look like?"

Trent went to the couch and sat down. Crystal sat down next to him, then quietly waited for him to continue.

He sighed and gave in to the inevitable. "When I first saw her, I thought there could never be anyone more beautiful. Long pale-blond hair, eyes as blue as the sky, and a body that was just made for sex. God, I was so wrong. I only saw what I wanted to see, her surface beauty. Inside was a selfish and spoiled little girl." He paused before saying, "Right after she got the shiny ring on her finger, she cut her hair and slept in a separate room. She was determined to have a baby, so if she was ovulating I was welcome in her bed. I finally realized that was the only reason she'd married me. That and my family's money."

"She sounds very materialistic."

He nodded. "She was only nice when it benefited her future plans. She had wanted to be Mrs. Dailey, the socialite. She was so different, so cold and callous. And I was a blind idiot."

"I'm sorry," she said, her voice soft and full of kindness.

"It wasn't long before I was filing for a divorce." He rolled his eyes. "You can imagine how well that went over with my parents."

"They weren't supportive?"

He snorted. "Mother had a fit. She'd hit it off with Jill right off. I should have known right then that Jill was the wrong woman for me."

"How did Jill react?"

"I don't think she'd ever been tossed over before. She was devastated, more because it damaged her pristine reputation, not to mention her gigantic ego. She fought damn hard, but when it was all said and done, the judge decided in favor of the divorce and split everything right down the middle. Hell, I think he felt sorry for me."

Trent stopped and thought about it all over again. Funny, it didn't hurt like it used to. Then he thought of Crystal and knew she was the reason. She was so different from his mother, from Jill. She was kind and compassionate, sensual and loving, filled with life. She'd give as much as she got in any relationship. If he wasn't careful, this woman was going to sneak into his heart. It shook him for a minute, but he couldn't stop the smile that crossed his face as he thought of how much he enjoyed being with her. It hit him then that he'd forgotten to wear a condom earlier. Shit. "Crystal, I know this is not the time to ask, but are you on birth control pills?"

Crystal looked anxious at the change in conversation. "Actually, yes, I am. I started taking them when I was very young to control the flow of my monthly."

Trent digested that news. "That's good news. Still, I should have been taking better care with you. I think I let my emotions rule my actions." Crystal worried her bottom lip with her teeth. Trent touched her there with his finger, effectively stopping her actions. "Ready?"

Crystal appeared to search his face; what she was looking for he didn't know. Finally she said, "Whenever you are."

He kissed her, keeping it light on purpose. They'd never leave the apartment if he let it get too hot. He rose from the couch and held out his hand. She took it easily, sending a shock of heat clear to his core.

"You are without a doubt the most handsome, caring man. Jill was an idiot. That's all I can think about a woman who would let you get away."

He chuckled. "Pretty much how I feel about your ex."

"Good riddance to them both," Crystal declared.

"Exactly," he groaned. "Now, let's go before I change my mind, woman."

As they left the apartment, Trent thought back over their conversation. Richard had a lot to answer for. If he ever saw that son of a bitch again, he'd beat the shit out of him. Trent thought about Mac and wondered if he should fill him in, then quickly nixed the idea. It seemed like that should be for Crystal to do. Whether she felt comfortable sharing that part of her life or not, it was her choice to make, not his.

8

On Wednesday afternoon, Crystal sat across the table at a little bistro with Mollie and her friends. She was beginning to wish she hadn't agreed to meet with them, though, because they all kept asking her about the mysterious men of Kinks that she was currently dating. Darn Mollie for letting that particular cat out of the bag. They pumped her for information about Trent, then Mac. She'd been very good at keeping the questions at bay, so far. She felt cornered, and there was no escape.

"Okay, spill the goods, sister," Trina prodded.

Mollie worked with Trina. The heavyset woman with the blond bob seemed nice, but Crystal didn't know her well enough to go into details about her sex life. "I don't know what you mean," she hedged.

"Just what's happened between you and those two hotties?" she pushed a little more. "And what's with the rosy glow you've got?"

Crystal choked on her ice water and laughed. "Rosy glow?"

"*Pfft*, we know you got laid, but we still want details," Mollie's other friend Sherry said, adding her own two cents. Her usually stern expression was lit up now with a curious gleam in her eye.

Crystal had only hung out with these ladies a handful of times, but Mollie knew the bunch from the administrative office where she worked. Still, two things were clear. First, the candid discussion was obviously one they were used to engaging in, because none of the ladies had even the slightest hint of a blush. Second, she wasn't getting out of the restaurant without telling them at least a little of her private life. Crystal knew they would never give up on her. Not until she gave them all something to gossip about.

Crystal took a long drink of her water and said, "Well, I went to a club with Mollie and I ended up meeting the owners. Since that night I've gone out with them a few times. End of story."

"Them? As in plural?" Sherry probed.

Crystal rolled her eyes. "You guys are way too curious about my sex life. Really, there's not that much to tell." For some reason she didn't want to share Trent and Mac with them. What she had with the two guys was no one else's business.

"Hey, I've seen those two," Trina said as she wagged her eyebrows. "They're delish. If you're taking them for test drives, you are one lucky lady."

"Fine, you want the truth? Their names are Trent and Mac, and they're absolutely the hottest, sexiest, nicest, most caring men I've ever met." Crystal let out a frustrated breath. "I swear, you ladies are nosy."

Everyone went quiet for a moment, then Mollie spoke up finally. "They are seriously amazing. And if anyone deserves amazing, you do."

"You know, once Richard was out of the picture for good, I wasn't sure I ever wanted to date again. Much less date two guys at the same time. Finding Mr. Right didn't seem like something that was ever going to happen to me." She pushed her plate away and leaned back in her chair. "I guess I didn't know if I was ready to take that next step until I met Trent and Mac."

"Then why do you seem sad?"

"It feels like I just got away from one mess and now I'm riding this emotional roller coaster. Still, with them . . ." Crystal hesitated, attempting to put into words how she felt about two men she'd known only a few days. "I don't know. They're different. Other men pale in comparison." Crystal shook her head. "Still, I'm not the naïve girl I once was. I'm a big girl now, and I'm not going to let a man dictate my life."

"What about two men?" Sherry asked as she attempted to stifle a laugh behind her napkin.

Mollie reached across the table and patted the back of Crystal's hand. "You need to have a little faith. Not all guys are like Richard."

Sherry and Trina were both silent. Finally Trina spoke up and added her weight to Mollie's. "Don't give up on finding Mr. Right. Hell, sometimes it's necessary to run across a few Mr. Wrongs, just so you'll know the difference."

"I know. Really I do. But what if they're both just more Mr. Wrongs?"

"Then you move on," Sherry said. "From what I hear, that nightclub has plenty to choose from."

The women were right. Mac and Trent might not be perfect. Being with the two of them might be wrong on every level, but they definitely weren't like Richard. She had to have a little faith.

Several hours later, Crystal called Trent to see if he wanted to have dinner. She'd missed him and when he'd invited her over to his apartment, Crystal hadn't hesitated to say yes. As she arrived and knocked on the door, her hands shook. The anticipation of seeing Trent sent her head spinning.

Mac answered the door instead and Crystal's entire body

heated up. When she caught sight of his sexy, sideways smile, she lost her ability to breathe for second. He was dressed in a pair of faded jeans and a plain navy T-shirt. His dark hair was a mess, as if he'd been combing his fingers through it, and he had on a pair of black boots. Staring at the man sent her temperature into the danger zone.

"Hi," Mac said as he reached for her hand.

"I didn't know you were going to be here."

"A good surprise, I hope," he said with a wink.

Crystal looked around him to find Trent leaning against the doorway to the kitchen. Mac pulled her into the apartment, then kicked the door shut behind her. Crystal started to say something, but Mac merely dragged her into his arms and kissed her witless. Crystal's mind went blank, and she melted against him as every nerve ending fired to life.

When he pulled back, they were both breathing heavily, and the predatory gleam in his eyes sent a pool of heat to the apex of her thighs. "H-hi," she stuttered out.

"Mm, I needed that," he murmured.

"Me too," she admitted, wishing she was bold enough to lean in and kiss him harder and longer.

Trent moved around Mac and said, "Hey, I didn't get to say hello." He groaned as he swooped in and took her mouth in a heated mating of lips. Crystal's arms went around his neck as she sank into the kiss. Trent tasted and teased until she was utterly breathless by the time he pulled back.

"I made pizza and margaritas. Hungry?"

"Starved," she said, but it wasn't her stomach she wanted satisfied.

"Trent makes the best pizza," Mac said, rubbing his stomach. "You'll love it."

"I thought maybe later we could watch a movie," Trent said.

"He rented a chick flick," Mac muttered as he plopped onto one end of the couch. After Trent retrieved their pizza, he sat at the other end, putting her smack in the center. Not a bad place to be, all in all.

After a few slices of pizza, Crystal took a fortifying sip of her margarita, then leaned back to enjoy the movie. She felt Mac pull her in close to his side. He wrapped an arm around her while Trent pushed PLAY on the remote. As the movie started, Trent flipped off the table lamp and they all fell silent.

Partway into the movie, Crystal knew it was futile. She hadn't paid a bit of attention to the screen. All she wanted to concentrate on were the men at her sides. Mac kept touching her thigh and rubbing her through her jeans, while Trent massaged her nape. She looked over at Trent and realized he wasn't watching the movie any more than she was. He was watching her. Mac's fingers inched higher, nearly grazing her mound.

"Mac," she moaned.

Trent stood. "Come on. We need more room than what this couch provides."

Within minutes they were in Trent's bedroom, and the three of them were nude. Trent got up on his knees on the bed. "Here, baby," he urged, as he helped her into the center of the bed. He moved behind her, then stroked the seam between her ass cheeks. She quivered and he let his finger drift back and forth over her puckered opening. She wanted him there and she knew he wanted to be there just as bad. He leaned over her and kissed the base of her spine. "I want to fuck this tight ass."

"Yes, Trent. Oh God, yes." Her voice had gone hoarse with need long ago.

"Would you like me there now? While Mac fucks your wet pussy? Do you think you can handle the two of us fucking you?"

"Trent, please . . . you know I want it."

"Yes, you do," Trent encouraged, and then he let his finger penetrate her, little by little, until he was buried deep inside her ass. She shuddered and pushed against him. His finger came in and out, fucking her.

"Raise up so I can play, angel," Mac growled.

She got up on all fours above Mac, Trent behind her, one of his big, warm hands clutching her hips. She felt Mac casing her clit, then watched with anticipation as he lifted his head and suckled her breasts. First one, then the other. He took his time, tasting and pleasing her.

"You have great tits, Crystal," Mac murmured, then went back to suckling.

Trent's finger moved in and out of her bottom, slow at first, then faster. Soon there were two, and her body went wild. Inhibitions dropped away as need rushed in and took command. She gyrated against Trent, Mac flicked and toyed with her little nubbin, while he bit and sucked her sensitive nipples.

Her climax came from somewhere deep inside as Crystal screamed hard and loud. She arched her back and flew apart. It was so fast and unexpected, but she wasn't given time to relish in it.

"You have pretty lips. I'd love to feel them closing around my dick."

Trent spoke up before she had a chance to digest Mac's words. "Next time, Mac."

Mac's mischievious grin said it all. "I'm looking forward to it."

Trent slipped his fingers free of her, stood on top of the mattress, then walked until he was standing next to them. With one hand propped against the wall, and the other wrapped around his glorious erection, he coaxed, "Let him taste you, Crystal, while you suck me."

"I don't know, Trent." She didn't know whether Trent could truly handle watching that.

"It's okay. Let him," Trent murmured, then Mac lent his weight to the idea.

"Come on up here, angel. I don't bite."

Crystal wanted to laugh and cry at the same time. In her head this had all gone so smoothly. The reality was quite a bit different. She looked back at Trent and saw him smile and nod his head. She took a deep breath and crawled up Mac's body until she was hovering above his face. He growled in approval and wrapped his hands around her thighs and pulled her down. His lips closed around swollen pussy lips. Crystal moaned and pushed against him further, losing herself in the pleasure.

"Suck me," Trent hissed.

Crystal was beyond denying him.

While Mac probed her opening with his tongue, Crystal leaned in and took Trent's pulsing cock into her mouth. She tasted his sticky fluid and lapped it up. He groaned and wrapped both hands in her hair to guide her. He was rougher than usual, his arousal more intense. She sucked him down her throat and gagged. He pushed her head off him to give her a breath, then pulled her forward again. This time she was ready for his wild thrusts. She opened her throat and took him deep. Trent fucked her mouth, his movements alternating between fast and out of control, and slow and gentle. As Mac flicked over her clit, she felt his fingers dipping into her pussy from behind. It was all she could take. The throbs turned to shocking jolts of heat. She exploded. Mac licked up every last drop of her fluid passion.

Trent pulled her head off his cock, then praised her with a kiss. She was beginning to come back down to earth when she heard him demand, "I want this ass, baby. Will you give it to me?" He was back into the position he'd been before, on his knees between Mac's thighs. He wrapped strong fingers around her hips and slid her downward until she was on all fours above Mac, her bottom facing Trent.

Cupping her dripping mound, Trent whispered, "Look at me." She turned her head, already limp and sweating from two beautiful orgasms, but when she saw the intensity, the insane yearning etched into his not-so-perfect features, her body went from sated to needy all over again.

"Mac and I are here for your pleasure tonight," Trent explained. "But I hope you know that we don't share well with others."

Then, as if choreographed, Mac and Trent both entered her and her inner muscles stretched. It was too much, too soon.

"Trent," she cried, her body tensing as she began to panic at the fullness of it all.

Trent pulled out instantly, while Mac stayed seated deep inside her womb, holding perfectly still and waiting for Trent's command.

Lowering his oversized body, Trent covered her like a heavy, warm blanket, his arms resting on the mattress on either side of Mac's torso.

"You can take us. You only need to stop tensing up," Trent pleaded. "Let me in and I swear you won't regret it."

He never waited for a reply, only began stroking her hair and smoothing a palm down her arm to her hip, where he cupped her bottom and kneaded the plump flesh. She relaxed against Mac, giving them all what they needed in that moment. Trent felt it instantly and began a slow glide into her, filling her. She felt a delicious sort of pressure and friction. Fullness. Oh God, so full, but not so much that it hurt. In fact, it was like nothing she'd ever experienced. The silky inner walls of her vagina were caressed with sweet strokes from Mac, and the tight channel of her bottom felt every slide and thrust from Trent. Suddenly, all the worries, all the questions and fears fell away.

With each inward push from Trent, Mac pulled outward. Her muscles held them both tight. She squeezed her ass, giving Trent the pleasure/pain that they both craved. Pleasure spiked and their movements turned frantic as both men fucked her hard and fast. Trent grabbed the back of her hair and pushed her face toward Mac. Mac leaned up and kissed her hard, thrusting his tongue into her mouth, then his hands cupped her tits and pulled them up so he could suck and nibble on the hard peaks. Trent grabbed her hips and slammed into her, fucking her from behind in a way he'd never done before. Dominating her. Claiming her, body and soul.

Within moments they all three exploded.

Trent spilled his seed deep, and Crystal felt every spasm. Mac was right behind him, shouting her name and pumping her full of hot come. Crystal felt fingers flicking her clit and then she, too, burst wide open as an orgasm tore through her.

"Oh yes!"

Mac sprinkled her face with gentle kisses. Her cheeks and lips and eyelids recieved attention. Trent came down on top of her, blanketed her body, and sucked on her shoulder, biting and leaving his mark. His dick was still embedded deep. She sighed and collapsed against Mac.

"Hot damn," Trent whispered against her ear. Mac kissed the top of her head and said, "I do believe I can die a happy man now."

"You two will be the death of me," she mumbled as she cozied up next to Mac.

Both men chuckled. "But it'll be a great way to go," Trent added as he lay down beside her and covered them with the blanket.

She didn't have the strength to respond. The last thought on her mind was that she really needed to do something about their odd relationship. They simply couldn't go on like this forever. Surely it wasn't humanly possible. Someone would eventually cry uncle. Crystal had a feeling it was going to be her.

9

The next day, Crystal was busy putting the dishes away. She'd worked a long day, and it hadn't been easy considering her lack of sleep the previous night. Mac and Trent were wearing her out. Not that she was really complaining. Every second she spent with them was better than the last. Which left her more confused than ever. Dating them both meant picking one of them eventually, right? Mac and Trent seemed content to share her. And she had to admit, their little trio seemed to work. Better than her relationship with Richard, for damn sure. Still, loving two men? That wasn't something a person did for always and forever. That sort of thing was temporary. Eventually one of them was going to get jealous or want out. And where would that leave Mac and Trent's friendship? She didn't want to come between them. She cared too much for them to do that.

As she put the last dish in the cupboard and dried her hands on the dish towel, Crystal poured a cold glass of iced tea. When she heard a knock on the door, she frowned. She wasn't expecting anyone, unless it was someone for Mollie. When a second knock came, Crystal sprinted across the apartment and pulled the door open, then stopped dead in her tracks. "Mom?"

Her mom smiled. "Surprise!" she said as she tugged her close for a hug.

"I didn't know you were coming," she said, trying to hide her suspicion. Her mom was here for only one reason: Richard. Had to be something to do with that blasted man.

"Of course you didn't, that's what a surprise is." Her mother pushed her bangs off her forehead. "Are you going to invite me in or what?"

Crystal quickly stepped back. "Of course, sorry."

"It's entirely too hot out for my liking." She tossed her purse on the chair closest to the door and asked, "Got anything cold to drink?"

"Sure, come on back to the kitchen," Crystal said. Once her mom was seated at the kitchen table, Crystal got her a glass of tea. "What brings you here?"

"Can't a mother visit her daughter without there being an agenda?"

Crystal frowned, not about to let her mom off the hook that easily. "You hate to drive, and it took a good three hours to get here. So, what gives?"

Her mom let out a deep sigh. "I needed to talk to you about something, and though I don't want you to be upset, it still needs to be said."

Crystal's defenses went on high alert. "If this is about Richard, you can forget it. I'm not going back to him. It's over and I've moved on with my life."

"It is about him, but not in the way you think," her mom said. She looked down at the table. "Mollie called me. She . . . she told me everything you went through with Richard." Her mom's lower lip quivered. "I swear I never would've encouraged you to stay with him if I'd know what that beast was capable of."

Crystal looked at her mother for a long moment, unsure how to respond. "You came all this way to tell me that?"

Her mother's head shot up. "Yes. I wanted to apologize in person."

Crystal shook her head. "All the times I tried to talk to you about him and you never wanted to hear it. You never wanted to know the truth."

Her mother frowned at her as if Crystal was being ungrateful. "I thought you'd be a little more pleased about this visit."

Crystal reached across the table and took her mom's hand in her own. "I love you, but it would've been nice if you'd listened to me. I'm your daughter. You should've been on my side."

Crystal's voice had slowly taken on a pleading note, and finally her mom seemed to realize how much she'd messed up. "You're right. I don't really have an excuse for the way I acted, but if you'll let me explain, it might help you to see where I was coming from."

"I'm listening," Crystal said, taking advantage of the rare open moment with her mom.

"The thing is, love is fleeting. Just as quickly as you find it, it could be yanked away. Your father was a wonderful man when I met him. He swept me off my feet, and I loved every second of it."

Considering the man had split after her mother got pregnant, Crystal asked, "What happened?"

"When I found out I was pregnant with you, it was the happiest day of my life. I thought he'd be happy, too. We'd get married and have more children." She shook her head. "I was a fool. The minute he found out about the baby, he was gone. Wanted nothing to do with either of us."

Crystal could hear the pain in her mom's voice even after all these years. "I'm sorry," she said, wishing she could take her pain away.

"I'm not. He would've been a horrible father. You and I were better off without him." She patted Crystal's hand. "I suppose that's why I wanted your marriage to work so badly. I wanted you to have what I never did. A man who was willing to go the extra mile. For richer or poorer and all that."

"Richard wanted a puppy. Something to train to be obedient and well-behaved. That was never going to be me."

"He's a horrible man and I'm glad you're far away from him."

Crystal didn't bother to tell her about Richard's latest visit. "Me too," she replied. As she thought of Trent and Mac, she added, "I do believe there's someone out there for me, though."

She smiled at Crystal and said, "From what I hear, you're already seeing someone. A couple of someones, in fact."

Crystal was shocked, to say the least. She hadn't expected Mollie to tell her mother about Trent and Mac. What's more, she never dreamed her mother would have approved. "Uh, well, yeah. I suppose I am."

Her mom smiled and asked, "So, when do I get to meet them?"

Mortified at the idea, Crystal blushed a bright pink. "Soon," she said, not willing to commit to anything.

"Take a leap, daughter. You're only young once, take it from me." Her mom winked over at her. "Besides, the good ones get snatched up fast. Best grab 'em while you can."

A laugh burst out and soon her mom was joining in. They sat talking for hours. After Mollie came home, the three of them went out to eat. As her mom was getting ready to head home, she took Crystal in her arms and said, "I love you with all my heart. I hope you'll forgive my foolishness."

Crystal hugged her back and let the tears flow. "Already done," she replied in a shaky voice. "I love you, too, Mom."

A chirping sound woke Crystal. "What the hell?" She glanced at her phone and realized someone was calling. "Hello?"

"Crystal?"

She was tired and wanted badly to sleep, but Mac's voice had the effect of a strong cup of coffee. "Mac, is something wrong?"

"No, just wanted to hear your voice. Did I wake you?"

She chuckled. "Um, it's three in the morning. Yes, you woke me."

"Sorry," he said.

"You don't sound sorry," she replied.

"I'm not really," he admitted, his voice rough. "I was lying here all lonely. You wouldn't want that, would you?"

"I ought to hang up on you."

"You won't, though."

"Don't push your luck, Mac."

Mac relaxed the instant he heard her voice. He wasn't sure what was up with himself lately. It was like he couldn't get his mind off Crystal. "I could just come over there. Slip inside your room and kiss every inch of your body. Would you kick me out, Crystal?"

"I wouldn't have the energy," she said, her voice sounding breathless.

Mac was gentle and warm in his response. "I'll love you real slow, angel, then tuck you in next to me. We'd both be able to sleep then."

"You are a tempting man, for sure."

Mac could hear the rising desire in her tone, and he was pleased. He wanted her to always feel desire for him. It would finally put them on even footing. "So, you're in bed. What are you wearing?"

She laughed. "I'm so not answering that."

"Come on, angel. It's just me." Mac held his breath at her answer. Already he could picture her there, all sleepy-eyed and sexy. His body heated instantly.

"Fine, I'm wearing a T-shirt and panties." Crystal laughed. "This is so weird. You are the most voracious man I know."

"Only for you." He heard her shifting around, as if she was attempting to get more comfortable. "Are you hot, Crystal?"

Crystal went silent a moment before saying, "Maybe."

He forced himself to take this slow. The last thing he wanted was for her to back away from him, just when he was beginning to make some headway with her. "Never hide your sexual desire from me."

Crystal *tsked*. "That's not what I was doing. And you shouldn't make assumptions."

"Yeah, but I know you. You're shy, and this kind of conversation is new for you, isn't it?"

"You mean this dirty phone call in the middle of the night? Yes, it's new." Again she laughed. "You're outrageous."

He loved to hear the sound of her laughter; it filled him as nothing else could. "Laugh all you want, but I could just come over there."

That quickly caused her laughter to die. "No. If you come over, I'll end up letting you make love to me and I need to work tomorrow."

He grinned at that confession. "You mean, you wouldn't be able to tell me no?"

"You know it's impossible to deny you. I get around you and I lose myself. It's like you're a wizard and you put a spell on me or something."

"Hey, if I had that sort of power, I'd just use my magic wand and bring you over here."

She snickered. "Magic wand? Really?"

Mac laughed. Crystal was an ever-changing bundle of emotions, and he loved it. He wondered if she was there alone. "Is Mollie in for the night, too?"

"Yes, we're both in bed. Did I mention that it's three in the morning?"

"I'm glad you don't live there by yourself. Makes me worry less that your friend is there."

"You worry about me? That's so sweet."

Mac groaned. "I'm not sweet. Puppies are sweet."

She laughed outright, making him crazy. "Sorry."

She was the only woman who had ever been brazen enough to laugh at him. Tenderness welled up unexpectedly. "Since you're already in bed, and you're nearly naked, then I think it would be a pity to waste such an opportunity, don't you?"

"You stay right where you are, pal."

"Ah, but I can do plenty from right where I am." She was so quiet he wasn't sure what had happened. "Crystal?"

"So, this is a dirty phone call."

Mac rolled his eyes. "You're obsessed with the concept, aren't you?"

"A little, considering this is my first."

"We should definitely do something about that." He gave her a few moments to think about that before he let a picture come to his mind. "If I were there, I'd pull you on top of me, let you ride me. I can picture you now. Your head thrown back, your hair all down your back in beautiful waves."

"Oh God, that . . . that's hot."

He liked that her voice was less coherent now. He was getting to her, and he could feel her mounting desire. "Earlier I said that if I were there then I would make love to you. The part I left off is that I'd love you so slow and sweet that the sun would come up before I left you alone. I'd want to hear you come, over and over again for me. Do you like that, angel?"

"Yes, you're turning me on, Mac. You know you are."

Her voice sounded husky and low, turning Mac on even more. "I'd also want to fuck you quick and hard. I'm aching to sink into you so deep. I want to pound my cock into your soft pussy until you're calling my name." Mac gave her a few moments. He could feel her body heating up, her heart pounding hard and erratic. "You'll have to tell me what you like, or I can't continue. I don't want to do anything that would make you un-comfortable."

"I like everything you're saying right now."

It was Mac's turn to chuckle. Crystal obviously did not want him to stop, as she was so quick to answer. Still, he wanted to know in detail what it was she wanted, not just a quick few words from her.

"Not so fast. I want to know what you're agreeing to. To be sure we're thinking the same things." His voice was deep and fervent. "Tell me, do you want me right now? Do you want me to make love to you? Slow and soft, so it takes all night? Or do you want to be fucked first? Hard and fast? So damn deep that it's unclear where you leave off and I begin?"

"Please, Mac, there's no way I can make a decision like that."

Restless now, he demanded, "Touch yourself for me then. Stroke your nipples and play with your clit. Do it for me, Crystal. If I can't be there, then touch yourself for me."

"Yes, Mac."

"What are you doing?" He had a feeling, but he wanted to hear her tell him. He didn't think she even knew how transparent she was when she was anxious like this. Her voice gave away so much. It was making him insane with lust.

He reached down and took himself in hand. He wanted her so badly it hurt, and if he had to wait until tomorrow night to truly have her underneath him, then his own hand would have to suffice for now.

"I'm playing with myself." Her breathless reply had him going ramrod stiff. He waited to see if she would say more and he wasn't disappointed. "I'm doing what you said, I've got my breasts in my hands, and I'm . . . massaging."

"Such amazing tits, too. I love touching you there, because you are so sensitive." He stroked himself, thinking of what she was doing to herself. Imagining the creamy swell of her breasts, her delicate fingers kneading and stroking. Her dark pink nipples would be puckered and erect, begging him. "Can you feel my mouth on your nipples? I can almost taste your succulent flavor." He heard her breathing grow rapid, and he continued his onslaught. "I would suck you first, and then bite you. Just tiny bites, enough to make you grab at my hair the way you do when you get all wild."

"Oh God, Mac. I need you so bad."

His voice turned hoarse with his own need. "I know, angel. Touch your clit now for me. I need to make you come. I want that pussy well-sated before you slip off to sleep."

"I am touching myself there. Since you mentioned biting my nipples, I've been fondling my clitoris."

He loved to hear her say the words, because he knew that she'd have to be mad with lust before she could. "Mmm, that's what I wanted to hear. Now, tell me how hard you want me to fuck you. Do you want it slow? Or would you plead for me to go faster?"

"Yes, I want it fast."

"I want you to say it, Crystal. Tell me. Give me what I crave."

His voice was a whip of demand, and she was helpless to defy him. "Damn you, Mac. I want you. Please, I need you to fuck me!"

"Christ, yeah. Anything for you, love, anything." Mac pumped his dick harder, all the while sending her the exact image she had just requested.

He saw her in his mind on her hands and knees. His strong hands holding her hips still for his powerful thrusts. Her pussy squeezing him, milking him dry.

Suddenly, she cried out and Mac knew she was coming. "That's it. Fuck, yeah." Mac pumped his cock once, twice, then soared over the edge with her. Christ, he needed her to be physically with him. He was desperate for her in that moment. He hoped she was imagining him there, in her bed, in her body.

"N-never have I felt anything like that," Crystal admitted, her voice hoarse from her cries. "That was amazing."

"I concur."

"Did you come?" she asked, as if needing to know she wasn't alone.

"I was right there with you, angel," he murmured.

Crystal lay atop her sheets, totally spent and relaxed. It was only as the afterglow from her mind-numbing orgasm started to subside that she noticed how quiet Mac had suddenly gotten. "Mac?"

"I'm here, angel."

His answer seemed solemn, and she didn't like that, not after what they'd just shared. "Where did you go just now?"

"Just . . . thinking."

Crystal was beginning to worry at his calm mood. "What about?"

"I was thinking that it never seems to matter what form our sexual games take, it always ends up the same way."

"And what way is that?"

"I always end up wanting more. No matter what, I always end up craving you like a drug."

"I hope you know it's the same for me," she said as her eyelids began to get heavy.

"I've kept you awake long enough," he said. "Sleep, angel. Call me when you wake up so I can have a good day."

No way, not so fast, Crystal thought. She did need at least one small thing confirmed before she let him go. "I loved what we just shared, Mac."

"Good, because there's more to come. Now, rest up for me. You will need it for what I have planned for you."

She sighed. "Sweet dreams, Mac."

"Always sweet dreams of you, angel," Mac replied as he waited for her to hang up. Just as the line died, Mac was smiling. He rose up out of bed and pulled on his clothing, then left his bedroom. He headed for his home office to get some work done. Because sure as hell he wouldn't be getting any sleep. Not in a cold, empty bed. He'd only lie there all night wishing Crystal was there.

Two days had gone by and all she'd gotten from Trent was text messages. When they did pin each other down long enough to talk on the phone, they'd chatted for hours. Before they hung up, Trent had wriggled a date out of her for the following Friday.

Now that the night had arrived, though, Crystal was a freaking nervous wreck. She paced her living room waiting for Trent. She was the kind of shaky, sweaty-palms nervous that she had never felt before. It had snuck up on her and she'd not even recognized what it was at first. But now here she was, worried and anxious about seeing Trent. She seriously couldn't remember a time when she'd felt this way. It made her defensive, and that was never good. A defensive woman was the equivalent of a cornered mountain lion.

When Mac had called her in the middle of the night, Crystal had let herself go, and it had been wonderful. She had *so* completely lost control and Mac had loved her so thoroughly that she was still feeling the vibrations from it. Her entire body felt alive tonight. He was an amazing lover, and the fact that they'd only been talking on the phone didn't seem to dampen it one bit, although it had left her wishing she'd said yes to him when he'd offered to come to her apartment. He had managed to charm her, to weave a kind of magic between them, binding her irrevocably to him. The frightening part was that she liked feeling bound to him.

Now she couldn't help wondering if he'd done it before like that with other women. She really, really didn't like that idea. As a matter of fact, just thinking of him doing that with another woman made her feel sad. She wanted that to be reserved for her alone. But she again had the nagging feeling that she was fooling herself into believing she was special to him and Trent. *Don't go there,* she told herself for the millionth time. She couldn't go down that road. She needed to keep a clear head.

Looking at the outfit she had chosen, however, made her cringe. Her mind might want to remain detached, but her body—and, more importantly, her heart—were telling her other things. The tight blue skirt was designed to send a man's libido into overdrive in six-point-zero seconds. Of course the silver "do me" pumps were the icing on the cake. Did she want answers, or did she just want him to ravish her?

"Okay, don't answer that one."

"Talking to yourself, baby?"

Crystal spun around at the deep velvet sound of Trent's voice. How did he do that? He was the one and only man who had the ability to sneak up on her like that. It was eerie how silent he could be. She stood there, not speaking, and allowed him to look at her. He was his usual bold self, she thought, hiding her smile. His eyes moved like a lover's touch as they drifted slowly over her from head to toe. Obviously, Trent hadn't been the only man to look at her with heat in his eyes. There had been other interested looks from the opposite sex. She knew she wasn't horrible to look at, but there was something different about the way Trent stared. It made her feel beautiful.

From the very start, Crystal had wanted to please him. She knew he liked what he saw, but she had wanted more than physical pleasure with him. The easy teasing between them had vanished now. They both seemed to want something more tonight. He seemed to be the only man besides Mac who could see beyond her face. Something in his expression, his possessiveness, told her he knew it, too. He knew that what she felt for him was different.

With him standing so handsome in the doorway to her apartment, staring at her as if he had a right to her, what did she do? She melted. Like ice cream in the summer, she felt like she was quickly reduced to a mere puddle at his feet.

"Damn, you look good enough to eat, Crystal."

His voice was a low growl, filled with aching desire. Crystal could see as well as hear the intensity in him. Everything in her screamed to tell him to come and sate his hunger, but she had to get them on track or the night would quickly disintegrate into an orgy of orgasms. She knew that look he got whenever he was aroused, and he had that look now, which only served to arouse her in turn. Enough was enough.

"Wait, I thought we were going on a date. What happened to that?"

Trent groaned, "And we will, I promise." He moved closer and closed the door behind him. "But I see no reason to deny ourselves dessert first, do you?"

His smile was predatory. The man was lethal, that was all there was to it. She backed up a step, but kept her voice firm. "Do not come any closer." Then she smiled up at him despite her resolve.

"God, you are so beautiful, baby."

Her mouth parted to say something, anything, but he stole the words with a kiss.

He was so careful and restrained. As if he was afraid she would bolt if he let his passion have free rein. But she wasn't going anywhere. She wanted his excitement and his heat. She wanted all of it. She wanted him wild and untamed, the way she knew he could be.

With that in mind, she took control of the kiss, sliding her tongue into his mouth, tasting and licking at the wet warmth she found there. He groaned and slipped his own tongue between her soft pink lips, and she surprised him by sucking on it. Crystal felt the exact moment when his willpower evaporated. He pushed her backward and away from him. He stood stock-still, staring down at her, dark desire etched into the rugged features of his face. He looked untamed and dangerous, and Crystal felt a shiver run the length of her spine.

"You're playing with fire."

She loved the gravelly tone of his voice; it gave her a hint of how turned on he was. She had done that to him. The thought enticed her further. "Good," she said, a sexy siren's smile curving her lips.

"Don't tease me, woman. I want you too bad right now to be easy with you." He looked around the room and asked, "Are we alone?"

She reached out and flattened her palm on his chest, directly over his heart. Feeling the fast, frantic rhythm made her own heart speed up, matching his beat for beat. "Yes. Mollie had a prior engagement. And I don't want you to be easy with me. I won't break, Trent."

Crystal crossed her arms and grasped at the hem of her shirt, yanking it up and over her head. She watched as his eyes landed on her lace-covered breasts. His stare prompted her nipples to tingle and pull into tight peaks beneath the see-through fabric. Trent's eyes widened and darkened further, as if mesmerized by the sight.

Her hands went to her skirt next. She pulled the button free and slid down the zipper. He watched, unmoving, unblinking at her impromptu striptease, and it fueled her own internal blaze. She felt wanton and uninhibited. "Yeah, later we can eat. For now there are more important appetites to nourish."

She let the blue skirt fall to the floor, then stepped out of it and away from him. He started forward, but she held him off by putting a hand between them. He frowned, pinning her in place with his questioning gaze.

"I want you, but not if you're going to hold back on me."

She unsnapped the front hook of her bra and let the cups drift open. Her breasts spilled free and she cupped them both, but her own small hands weren't adequate to hold the plump globes. "What's it to be?" she asked, even while she kneaded the soft flesh. "The real you or some tame façade you think I need?"

Trent moved forward, stalking her. She was breathtaking, standing before him in nothing but her lacy panties and high-heeled shoes. Her dark, shiny hair spilled down her back, caressing her ass as she moved. His hands flexed, aching to grab hold of her curvy backside.

His eyes continued to feast even as he gave her his answer. "I have no choice now. I'm beyond reason, Crystal." Her eyes widened when he seized her hips and pulled her forward. She lost her balance and tipped forward, landing against him. "I want you so bad it hurts."

Crystal wanted to shout out her triumph at his words. She flung her arms around his neck and nestled her pelvis into his growing erection. "I want you even more, I'll bet."

Her words were husky, and it made Trent want to rip off his pants and drive himself into her. He held himself in check—just barely. He didn't want to come at her like some wild animal. He wanted to please her first. He wanted to hear her come apart, just for him. Shout out a climax, just for him.

"You have no idea what I want to do to you right *now*. You're on dangerous ground, little girl, and there's no going back." His face was a harsh mask of need as he murmured, "First things first, though."

Then he dropped to his knees in front of her and rubbed his face against her soft, firm belly. He loved her belly; the skin there was as soft as a baby's, and it made him acutely aware of the difference between them. Where she was soft and supple, he was hard and immovable.

Trent wrapped his arms around her and cupped her ass in his hands, squeezing just as he'd wanted to. He effectively held her still while he played with various other parts of her precious body. "You're so goddamn sexy, baby." He reached between them and pinched her nipple. At her whimper he growled, "I could come in my pants just staring at you."

He looked up at her and saw the blush that stole into her cheeks. "You knew I'd go nuts over those fuck-me pumps, didn't you?"

She nodded shyly at his crude words, and he smiled wickedly up at her. Trent slipped his fingers under the waistband of her panties and said, "Most of all, I love these delicate little panties, red being my favorite color and all. But they're in my way."

Not wasting another second, he gripped the lacy material in his hands and ripped. Crystal's startled intake of breath prompted Trent to demand, "You wanted the real me, Crystal. This *is* the real me. Still think you want it?" He held himself rigid as he waited for her to answer. If she denied him he would stop, but it would kill him.

Crystal wasn't sure if she knew what she was doing. But she did know that she trusted Trent. She couldn't lie to herself anymore about that. "I do want you."

Trent released a breath he hadn't even known he was holding. His voice was harsh when he said, "Spread your legs for me, then. Show me how much you want me, Crystal."

She did as he commanded. There was no possible way she could deny him. Trent touched a finger to the dark spirals at her cleft and she nearly exploded.

"That's it." Trent's throat felt raw as emotions rose up. "You are hot for me, aren't you? So wet and tight and all mine." He looked deep into her eyes, desperate for her to submit to him entirely. "You want me to fuck you, don't you? You want my cock inside you?"

She nodded.

He smiled. "You aren't ready yet. Close, but not close enough to satisfy me."

She nearly begged him then, but his fingers searched and parted her. He was watching her face closely when he slipped a finger inside her wet heat and she flung her head back and cried out, helpless to the craving this man provoked in her. She abandoned all sense of modesty, dug her fingers deep into Trent's hair, and pulled him closer still.

"Now, that's what I like. I want you quivering. I want you all hot and eager for me."

Trent was merciless in his ministrations. He held her still with one powerful arm while the other palmed her mound possessively. He loved the way she responded to him. But what excited him most was the way she totally lost control of herself. It was all or nothing with Crystal.

He knew damn well it had been that very quality that had drawn him to her in the first place. When she made love, she did it with every ounce of her being. It was with all her heart, and it was everlasting. He knew of no other that would be so giving or love with so much energy. Any man would be lucky to have her, and Trent was selfish enough to want her for himself. He didn't deserve even a scrap of her goodness, but he wanted it anyway. Screw it, he was probably going to hell when he died; he might as well enjoy it while he could.

He felt Crystal pull his head toward her in a silent plea for his mouth to replace his fingers. Not good enough, Trent thought—she was going to have to tell him what she wanted. He wanted her to give in and let go.

"If you want my tongue inside you, baby, you're going to have to ask me for it." She whimpered and pulled at his hair again, but he would not be swayed. "I want to kiss your swollen lips, angel. I want to taste your sweet juices so bad I think I'm going to explode from it. But I want to hear the lovely words from you first. That's not so much to ask, is it?"

He only had to wait a second before she raised her head back up and looked down at him. Her face flushed and her eyes were made more vivid by her arousal. When she spoke, it was all Trent could do not to throw her to the floor and delve in.

"You want me to tell you exactly what I want?" At his nod, she decided to go for broke. She had nothing to lose anyway, as she'd already given him her heart. "I want you to suck on my clit." She took his dark, fiery look as a good sign so she continued, "I want your tongue thrusting inside me, and I desperately want you to push me to the floor and take me as hard and as fast as you want, for as long as you want, until we're both limp and sweating. I want you, and I'm not going to stop wanting you. Pretty please . . . fuck me." She smiled sweetly and then whispered, "Is that what you wanted to hear?"

Silence gathered between them for several heartbeats and then, "Jesus, woman." Trent was amazed. She did it to him every time, turned him inside out and upside down until *he* was the quivering mass of need. It prompted him to say the first thing that came to mind. "You're like a drug to me, and I'm so gloriously fucking addicted." Then he dipped into her and did as she'd asked so prettily. He parted her and sucked her swollen nub into his mouth. Her gasp was the most satisfying thing he'd ever heard. Never would he get enough of this woman. He knew that now. They could share eternity together and he would always want more of her.

He felt her hands in his hair once more, her fingers yanking until he felt the slightest amount of pain. The sting of her slender fingers pulling at his hair was sweet torture, and he knew she was close to coming. His tongue thrust inside her at last, just as she'd wanted, and he was the one to moan when he felt her climax building. He gave himself up to the pulsing vibrations of her tender flesh as his tongue mimicked what his cock wanted so badly to do, inching in and out of her tight opening, lapping at Crystal's creamy heat.

Her legs shook slightly around him, and Trent could feel her struggle to stay standing as she screamed out her pleasure. He gripped her harder with his arm, holding her in place. Not all women could come standing up, and he loved having this one particular woman in just such a place, he on his knees with her beautifully naked body all but draped around his face. The heels put her at just the right level, too. He'd have to remember that for their next time.

She was just so uninhibited and free with herself, it thrilled and humbled him that he was the one to see her in such a state of total abandon. He vowed no other man save for Mac would ever see her this way. He got angry just thinking of such a thing. She was his and Mac's. They'd do anything to keep her.

Trent mentally backed away from the intense, unfamiliar feelings and gave one last lingering kiss to her clitoris. She moaned and loosened her hold on his head. He leaned back on his haunches and stared up at her. Her face was flushed, with tendrils of sweat-soaked hair sticking to her cheeks. Her breasts, heaving with her rapid breathing, implored his mouth to suck and lick and taste. She had a serene smile on her face that kept Trent pinned in place.

How could he be so lucky to have such a woman as Crystal?

It scared him that she was rapidly becoming a very important part of his life. He wasn't about relationships or love-everlasting. Trent was about the here and now, doing what he had to do to survive. But as he looked at the woman who stood brazenly naked in his arms, Trent became aware of just how empty his existence was. Somewhere along the line, he had started yearning for more than just surviving. He wanted laughter and joy. He wanted it all.

Crystal was shaken to the core. She'd only ever been able to have such explosive orgasms with Trent and Mac. They'd been the only men over so many years who knew just where to touch her, just the right amount of pressure to exert, and when to give her the finish she craved.

Trent rose up to his full height and swept her into his arms. "Bedroom."

Crystal sighed. She knew that look as well as that tone. He wouldn't be spilling any more truths for a while.

"To the right, and at the end of the hall," she said, and then she proceeded to settle back against his hard chest.

Trent's lips kicked up at the corners. "I know." He felt like smiling. She was the most enchanting woman he'd ever known. Damn, if she didn't appear to be made for him, too, as she quieted and relaxed in his arms. She was content with silence, knowing when questions were necessary and when to let their bodies do all the talking. Trent couldn't have asked for a better lover than Crystal.

He went down the hall she'd indicated and walked into her bedroom. He'd ignored her bedroom before, and even her apartment, for that matter. But seeing the intimate surroundings had him seeing her in a different light. She had a whimsical side to her, that much was obvious.

While Mollie's taste ran toward dramatic colors of blacks, whites, and reds, with modern-styled furnishings, Crystal's bedroom was just the opposite. It was like stepping right into the pages of a fairy tale. Unicorns, fairies, princesses, wizards, and even dragons were everywhere.

The king-sized bed was covered by a huge, fluffy comforter with a picture of a powerful white unicorn, the sky as its backdrop. Her bedside table lamp was shaped like an ominous green and purple dragon. There was a large, overstuffed chair that looked plenty big enough for the both of them—which gave him all sorts of interesting ideas for later. But its upholstery left much to be desired. There were fairies of all shapes, sizes and colors adorning it. Even the wallpaper had gotten into the act. It had all of the creatures mixed together. He felt as out of place as ever. Suddenly, Trent wasn't so sure of himself. It was a new and rather unpleasant feeling for him.

"This room makes me feel like an evil lord debauching the virgin maiden."

Crystal sensed his hesitation and was quick to explain the odd motif. "You're no more an evil lord than I am a virgin." She shifted awkwardly. "It's just that I've always loved fairy tales. Happily ever after and all that really does it for me. Of course, if you tell anyone I'll have to kill you."

That drew his attention. Was she telling him what he thought she was telling him? "Are you saying no other man has ever been in your bedroom, baby?"

Crystal tried to be casual about it, but having Trent in the apartment, in her bedroom, was not at all a small matter. She'd never wanted to get close to a man. It hadn't been hard to keep her sex life separate from the rest of her life, until now.

Tonight was a night for truths, and she wasn't about to taint that by lying. "I've never wanted anyone in here, until now. Until you."

Trent's heart swelled and his blood heated at hearing her bravely spoken declaration of love. And that was exactly what it was, too. She was telling him how much he meant to her.

"You make me want things with you that I've never wanted with any other woman," he mumbled. He cringed at his inade-quate words. When it came to speaking his feelings aloud, he was lost.

Crystal reached up and cupped his cheek. "I'm very glad I do."

Neither of them spoke again as he walked them over to the bed. He laid her down in the center of it, tenderness engulfing him as her body was slowly surrounded by cottony softness. He began taking off his own clothes then. He wanted to rip away at them, but since she'd taken such strides to strip for him, he felt she was owed the same favor.

He started with the shirt, as she'd done. He undid one but-ton at a time until it was hanging open, revealing a well-defined chest. He shifted his shoulders, and the shirt fell to the floor. She never took her eyes from him, and when he got to his pants, he was all but bursting with need. Her anticipation of what was to come driving him on. He unsnapped and unzipped and his erection happily sprang free.

Still, Trent made no move to join her on the bed. First, he wanted something from her. "Touch yourself for me. The way you did with Mac." She looked puzzled and he explained, "Mac told me about the phone call. I pictured every move you made. I knew exactly what you looked like, but it drove me mad wishing I could be here, in this very room, watching you."

She gave him that sexy, cat-that-ate-the-canary smile and then did as he'd proposed, one hand moving to her breast, the other to her mound. She arched her back and closed her eyes, fondling herself for his viewing pleasure. She was stunningly candid, and Trent could take only so much.

He went to her, moving over her aroused body, pinning her beneath his larger frame. Using his knee, Trent pushed her legs open wide and settled himself between them. Keeping himself from sinking into the cradle of her warmth was by far the hardest thing he'd ever done. But he wanted this to last a little longer. He didn't want it to end just yet. If he was being honest with himself, he'd admit that he also wanted to be the only man who could bring her such a wealth of pleasure. He wanted to be etched into her memory forever.

He took her hands and raised her arms above her head until she was stretched out under him like an offering. He held her in place by wrapping his hand around both her tiny wrists. Once he was satisfied that he truly had her right where he wanted her, he let his other hand have free rein. Stroking her wet folds open, he sank his finger inside. Crystal moaned and thrashed about. Seeing her breasts sway back and forth in her struggle for completion was the ultimate temptation to him. He took one round breast into his mouth and suckled the sensitive tip, when suddenly she screamed his name and came yet again.

Once her contractions subsided, Trent took his finger out of her and rubbed her juices over her other nipple. He licked and suckled it, lavishing it with the same amount of attention that he had the first. Once he was sure that both breasts were glistening and rosy from his ministrations, he pressed a gentle kiss to her mouth, then lifted his head up and away from her altogether. He let go of her hands and lifted off of her only long enough to flip her over and onto her stomach. He came back down atop her, caging her in with his arms at either side of her head, and drove his throbbing cock into her with one quick movement.

"Christ, you feel good," he whispered into her ear. "So wet and tight and all mine." The possessive words tumbled out of him, and he was pleased when he felt Crystal gasp and nod her head in agreement.

He held her still as he pumped into her from behind. He felt his own orgasm building, but he wasn't through with her, not just yet. He moved his hand beneath her hips and seized her clit between his index finger and thumb. Trent rolled the swollen nub, pinching and caressing, even as he impaled her tight sheath. When he felt Crystal's pleasure mounting, cresting, he moved his hips even faster, harder, until he was buried so deep he didn't ever want to leave the safe haven of her body. This time, when Crystal soared over the edge, she took Trent with her.

Trent became aware of two things at once. The first was that he was most assuredly crushing Crystal, and the second was that she wasn't protesting his heavy weight. He rolled off her and stared down at her prone body.

"Crystal?" His voice held a note of worry. Perhaps he'd been too eager, too rough. She was so small and delicate. Then she mumbled something and Trent reached out and grabbed her by the waist. He laid her out on top of him and then asked, "Are you okay?"

"Yes, just exhausted. Happy, but exhausted."

Crystal's sleepy mumble was music to his ears. "You've not eaten yet. Once you have, you'll feel better."

She gave a contented sigh, slipped down his body, and rested her cheek against his chest. He wrapped his arms around her, holding her to him, desperate to keep her with him now that their loving had come to an end. He wanted to bind her to him somehow, never let her go.

When they went to dinner later, Trent had no doubt that other men would check her out. But he couldn't be so selfish as to keep her hidden away. He would just have to trust that she wouldn't let anyone else sway her feelings toward him.

"The thought of sharing you with anyone but Mac makes me see red," he blurted out.

Crystal stared suspiciously at him, and said, "Is this some macho thing?"

His voice was so low she almost didn't hear him when he said, "You smiled at my brother. He smiled at you. He flirted."

Crystal blinked in astonishment. That Trent could possibly be jealous after what they'd just shared together, well, it was ridiculous. Jealous of a smile when he'd managed to make her scream in ecstasy? She couldn't help it; she giggled.

"What the hell is so funny?"

Crystal quieted and settled against him more comfortably. She wiggled her hips to press more firmly into his groin for emphasis as she said, "After you gave me not one, but three deliciously satisfying orgasms, you're jealous over a mere smile?"

Put that way, he did seem unreasonable. He moved his hand down her back and cupped her bottom firmly. "Where you are concerned, I can't seem to help my caveman tendencies, baby. I hate to even think of another man looking at you, much less coaxing a cute little smile out of you."

Her eyes darkened and heated, and Trent was once again struck by her unusual beauty. "Trent, no other man has ever made me feel the way you do." She smoothed his brow with a fingertip and said, "Mac and you are the only guys for me. Josh is nice, but he isn't you."

"I'm glad to hear that, baby." He started to get up. "Want to go to dinner?"

Crystal got up and went to her closet. "Just give me a minute to find a new outfit. The one I started out in got a bit wrinkled."

Trent watched her get out fresh clothes. As she bent at the waist and inched a beige skirt up her calves, he had the perfect view of her ass. "Mm, I could get used to this."

Crystal gasped. "Hey, quit eyeballing me. I'm hungry and you're going to feed me."

Trent laughed as he left the bed and got back into his own clothes. "I was in the mood for Greek, you?"

She moaned. "Sounds perfect."

He crossed the room and kissed the back of her head. "You're perfect, baby."

She smiled and turned in his arms, then pressed her hands against his chest. "You keep saying things like that, and I might just fall in love with you."

Trent went still. The thought of having Crystal's love made his chest tight with emotion. "I fail to see why that's a bad thing."

10

It'd been a week of not seeing Mac or Trent. She'd been too busy with work, and they'd been busy finalizing plans to open a new nightclub. When Saturday night finally arrived, Crystal was all but bursting with excitement. Mac had told her that he wasn't about to wait another minute to see her, so they'd made plans to go to dinner and a movie. She wanted it to be special. She sifted through her closet and found a turquoise sundress that she hadn't gotten the chance to wear yet. She slipped it on, letting the soft cotton glide down her body. It felt pleasantly cool to her heated skin. It had been an oddly hot summer so far, which was what made her opt to go braless. After all, she wasn't what anyone would term chesty, and so going without a bra was neither obscene nor even obvious, much to her dismay. She walked to her bed, sat on the edge, then slipped into her white strappy sandals before heading to the bathroom to apply her makeup. She never wore much, just a pale peach lipstick and mascara to enhance her eyes. She hoped to make tonight memorable so she applied a light dusting of blush and some smoky gray eye shadow. She decided to leave her hair down so it swept her shoulders in waves. Right on time she heard the knock on the door announcing Mac's arrival. Her stomach suddenly filled with butterflies, and her legs felt weak and shaky.

She left the bathroom, turned off the light, then walked on wobbly legs. *Get a hold of yourself. You are going to be fine, and you are not going to make a fool of yourself.* Maybe if she told herself that enough times, she would start to believe it. She was now wishing she had gone out on a few dates in the months since her divorce; maybe then she wouldn't be so nervous. Although she had a feeling that a big part of her anxiety had to do with *the man* she was going out with. Mac simply made her insides turn to jelly. She reached the living room and walked to the front door. She glanced one last time in the mirror that hung above the table there, and realized she had a "deer caught in the headlights" expression. She groaned, straightened her spine, placed a smile on her face, and asked, "Who is it?"

"The man of your dreams," Mac said, in a deep, sexy voice that curled her toes.

She swung open the door and with a startled look said, "Johnny Depp is here! Where?" She stood on tiptoes to peek over Mac's shoulder, pretending to search for her dream man.

"Very funny, angel." He laughed.

"Who's kidding?" She smiled hugely. She looked at him this time, really looked. He was wearing black trousers and a black V-neck T-shirt, and he had his hair combed so that it swept the tops of his shoulders in neat ebony waves. Lord, this man was lethal! "Come in, Mac. I'm just about ready to go. Just give me one more minute."

She turned to retrieve her purse, but his hand snaked out, capturing her arm and pulling her up against his firm frame. He muttered, "You look good enough to eat." His mouth came so close to her own that she could smell his sweet breath. Peppermint—she loved peppermint.

He whispered, "I wonder, do you taste as sweet as you look?" Then he tilted his head and gently touched his tongue to her bottom lip, inhaling her sweetness, the scent of her still managing to elude him. He lifted his mouth away, grudgingly, and growled, "Go. Finish whatever you need to do, or we'll never get the hell out of here tonight."

"You're always doing that," she managed to say at last.

"What?" Confusion clouded Mac's dark eyes.

"Throwing me off balance." She planted one hand on her hip and smiled.

He bent at the waist so that he was staring directly into her eyes and exclaimed, "In one more second I'm going to throw you over my shoulder, carry you to your bedroom, and quench my appetite with your sweet body." His hand reached around and smacked her lightly on the rear.

"You wouldn't dare," she retorted, completely stunned that he'd just swatted her bottom.

"Try me, angel . . . please." His voice was hoarse from desire, and his eyes were swirling with passion.

She turned from his heated stare and headed for the hall closet where her purse hung. She didn't want to take the chance that he was serious, yet she wondered all the same what he'd do if he followed through with his decadent threat.

Damn, Mac thought, this woman was turning him into a Neanderthal. He raked his hand through his hair in an effort to gain some modicum of control. He paced the living room, trying to distract himself, but the phone rang.

"Mac, can you answer that please?" Crystal called from the hallway.

Mac quickly looked around the living room for the phone and located it on the table beside the couch. In two strides, he was picking it up and saying, "Hello?" He sounded harsher than he had intended, though. Silence. Mac said "Hello?" louder and with more strength this time.

"She's not for you. One day real soon she'll see what a mistake she made leaving me," the shadowy voice on the other end growled.

"Look, asshole, I don't know who the hell you think you are, but be warned if you come near her. I will personally take you apart with my bare hands. Do I make myself clear?" Mac's entire body tensed with rage.

He was met with insane laughter. "Ah, that's just it, Mac. You don't know me, but I do know you. She's my wife, and one way or the other she'll come back to me. And when she does, I will have to teach her what happens to whores." There was a pause, then: "By the way, what a lovely turquoise dress she's wearing. I so enjoy when she goes without a bra. Great tits she has, don't you agree?"

Then came the most depraved laughter Mac had ever heard before the line went dead in his hand. Mac quietly replaced the receiver and turned around. Crystal was standing there, her eyes wide and frightened. She had heard enough of his end of the conversation to determine the call was from her ex-husband. He didn't say a word. He walked to the stairs and ascended them two at a time. When he reached the top, he paused at her bedroom door, turned on the light, and saw what he had already suspected. Her curtains were tied back and the shade was pulled up. He walked over to the window and peered out. He didn't see anything suspicious, but he hadn't really expected to. The caller was probably long gone by now. How the hell had the caller known who he was? He made a mental note to call Trent tomorrow. He pulled the shade down and then heard a faint voice say, "Mac, what's going on?"

He turned around and spoke in a no-nonsense tone, "I want this shade pulled down from now on. Do you understand me, Crystal?"

She nodded. "But why?" She felt numb, for she feared she already knew the answer.

Mac walked to where she stood, took her soft hand in his, led her over to the bed, and sat her down on the edge of it. Crouching between her legs, he spoke in a comforting tone, "Your ex-husband just called. And he said something on the phone just now that leads me to believe he's been watching you through there." He paused and pointed to the window. He went on, biting out each word, "This guy is a sick bastard, and I don't want you taking any chances, okay? Keep this shade drawn."

She simply couldn't speak past the lump of fear in her throat, so she nodded instead. Her ex-husband had been watching her? How many times had he seen her walk into her private bedroom to go to bed or change clothes? She shivered, and when she glanced over at the window, abruptly her entire body shook with chills. She rubbed at her arms, but to no avail. The fear was stealing all the warmth from her body. She felt an invasion of privacy that she'd never known before. Worse yet, she'd inadvertently put Mollie at risk. She looked back at Mac, who was still crouched in front of her, and said the first thing that came to mind, "What did he say?"

"Angel, listen to me carefully. He only said something to indicate to me that he's been watching you. I don't know for how long." He stopped and looked at her hard. "He did say one other thing . . ."

His voice trailed off and he looked at her more thoughtfully, as if debating whether she could handle the rest. Crystal straightened her spine and spoke in a calm voice, "Mac, whatever he said, I have a right to know."

He remained silent. However, he seemed to give in to the inevitable because he responded, "He said he intends to show you what happens to a whore. He intends to teach you a lesson."

"Oh God!" Her hand flew to her mouth. She felt sick. She spoke in a quivery voice, "I feel like I'm going to throw up."

Mac placed his palm on the back of her head and gently

pushed. "Angel, put your head down and take deep breaths. Can you do that for me?" She nodded and did as he said. He was stroking her hair in a soothing motion. She felt some relief from the rising panic immediately. When she had herself back under control, she said in a stronger voice, "I'm okay." He pulled his hand away slowly, as if reluctant to do so. She rose up and came face-to-face with him. He looked so concerned for her that without thinking she leaned forward and kissed his angular cheek. Lifting away from him, she said, "Thanks for being here."

He nodded. "Do you want to call Mollie and warn her?"

"Good idea," she replied as she pulled her cell phone out of her purse. "She's staying with a friend tonight, but I'll fill her in so she can take precautions."

Several minutes later, Crystal hung up and smiled over at Mac. "She wants to make sure I'm not alone tonight, either."

"No way in hell am I leaving you tonight," he said as he stood. "Now, let's go see that movie. I am not letting that asshole ruin my evening with the prettiest girl in town. Besides, I am very much looking forward to sitting in a darkened movie theater with you." He rose to his full height, took her hand, and pulled her up off the bed. Like any handsome Prince Charming, he said, "Will you accompany me this evening, my lady?" he asked, in a Prince Charming sort of way.

She quickly responded, "Indeed I will, kind sir." And she curtsied.

They both laughed, dispelling the tension, and left the bedroom arm in arm.

Crystal was having the time of her life with Mac. They had gone to see a movie, and much to her surprise, he had picked a comedy. They laughed themselves silly. She hadn't laughed and had such a good time with a man in . . . well, ever. They were back in his black Blazer and on their way home, but he turned down a different road.

"Mac, where are we going? Aren't we going back home?" She looked over at him in puzzlement.

"Oh, angel, the evening is not yet finished. After all, Cinderella, it's not midnight, is it?"

He looked over at her for a brief moment, not wanting to take his eyes off the road, but she saw mystery in his and something else pooling in their depths . . . hunger? But for what? Crystal wondered, or perhaps the correct word was, for *whom?*

She finally said, "Well, my debonair prince, where are you taking me on such a lovely evening as this?"

"Now that would certainly spoil my lady's surprise, would it not?" The corner of his lips quirked up along with one eyebrow questioningly.

"Yes, I suppose it would, and I certainly wouldn't want to spoil it. Shall I close my eyes, too, so your surprise will be complete and untainted?" She laughed, fully expecting him to laugh, too. However, he only whispered lustfully, "Yes, close your eyes. Trust in me to tell you when. Will you trust me, Crystal?"

She spoke breathlessly, "Yes, Mac, I trust you." And she continued to show him how much by closing her eyes.

Mac hadn't expected the conversation to take such a turn. Nevertheless, he couldn't let the opportunity to observe Crystal in such a way go by. She was beautiful, especially when she laughed. She made him feel like the luckiest man on earth when the smiles were directed toward him. He had taken her to a comedy for two reasons. He wanted to take her mind off the jerk who had called earlier, and he wanted to see her laugh. Who would have thought that laughter from a woman could make a man hard as granite? Well, not any woman . . . only his Crystal. Hearing her in the movie theater made him glad that it was dark; he would've made a spectacle of himself if it wasn't.

Hell, he was so horny by the time they had left that he knew if he took her straight home, he'd have her stripped down and on the floor and been inside of her within seconds. So the thought struck to take her to Gibby's bar. As appealing as it was to take Crystal in such an abandoned way, he didn't want her to think he had no finesse at all, that he was no more than a rutting bull, even though that was damn close to the way he felt at the moment.

As they turned the next corner and were traveling down the street where the bar was located, he glanced over at Crystal to see if her eyes were, indeed, still closed. They were, and she was now resting her head on the back of the seat. Her hair fell down past her shoulders, giving him a perfect view of her slender, delicate neck. He might well have been a vampire in some other life, because the need to taste her pulsing vein with his tongue and bite her pale ivory skin there, marking her as his, was almost overpowering.

He pulled into the parking lot to the bar and drove around to the back, so they could enter through the private entrance. He stopped the SUV and put it in Park, but he did not turn off the engine. He looked over at Crystal again; this time a slight smile curved her peach-colored lips. He leaned over her to murmur seductively, "You turn my insides to jelly and my outside to iron, angel."

He wanted to soothe her, mesmerize her into doing as he wished. She started to open her eyes, but he touched each lid with his forefinger and said, "You trusted me to say when, and I have yet to do so."

She remained quiet and kept her eyes closed. He caressed her hair with his fingers, stroking her silky tresses. "So soft and baby fine." He trailed his hand down her hair to smooth one finger over her neck. He touched the pulse beating in her throat; it seemed to quicken under his fingertips. He leaned in to her closer still, breathing in her scent. "Your smell drives me mad at night. It's as if you're lying right next to me, and I dream hot, erotic dreams of you." His voice grew raspier with the fever that was running through his veins, a fever only she could cool.

He bent his lips to her pulse and licked the length of her protruding vein. "Do you want more? Would you trust me with your body?" She nodded her acceptance. "Mm, yes, I want more of you, too, so much more. I want to know all your secret spots, the ones that cause your blood to pound hot in your veins and have you quivering with need. I want you begging beneath me . . . for me."

With that he bent and tasted her sweet ivory neck, arched up toward him like an offering to a god. He tasted her soft skin and sucked her into his mouth. Then he bit her, lightly, branding her as his woman. He lifted his head, looking down at her pliant body, and groaned, "Open your eyes, angel. If we stay out here much longer, I will have you beneath me, where you belong, which would bring me infinite amounts of pleasure, but having sex in my truck isn't how this night is supposed to go."

She did then, as he bid. She looked at him finally, her body burning with need. Her chest was heaving like she had just run a marathon. She looked into his eyes and saw that it was the same for him. It pleased her and she wanted more. More of him, more of his touch, she wanted him to appease the hunger that he had created. Instead she said, "Mac, the things you do to me, it's positively not becoming of a lady." She tried for lightness, but it seemed to fall flat.

"Angel, I want you any way I can get you." He did smile then, albeit lecherously, but it was a smile nonetheless. "Having you completely willing and quivering underneath me will suffice . . . for now." He turned the engine off and opened the door. "Come on, we're here."

As he came around to her side to open her door, she asked, "Where is *here?*"

"Gibby's Bar and Grill." He took her hand at that, helped her down out of the Blazer, and closed her door. "I hope you like it. It can be a bit loud at times, but I thought we could grab a bite to eat and I could check to see how everything is going."

"I'm sure I'll love it. Thank you for bringing me." She leaned up on tiptoe and kissed his rigid jaw, then smiled.

Mac groaned. "Crystal, have mercy. I told you no kisses unless you are prepared to take more."

"Mm, I can't wait," she said naughtily.

Mac only grunted his reply and led her to the door where he could hopefully get himself back under control, but he could have sworn he heard a faint giggle from the woman at his side.

Wow, what more could a girl ask for anyway? A great movie, wonderful food, stimulating conversation, and all from a devilishly handsome man. She figured she would have to come down from her perch soon enough, but for now she was content to enjoy herself.

Gibby's was much better than she'd expected. Everyone seemed to know each other. The music was a mix of top-forty hits and songs by the top country artists of today. There was something to please every ear. The place had a woodsy, rustic appearance to it. The walls were done in a kind of barn siding wood, which in the end would save money on paint and upkeep. There were wooden wagon wheels hanging from the ceiling with colored lights attached to them. Even the dance floor was made of hardwood, meant to remind customers of the old-time barn dances, when they put it all together. Everything was decorated with taste. The owner obviously wanted the patrons to feel at home, able to kick their heels up and just let loose for the time they were there.

Everyone who walked by their booth greeted Mac with a friendly hello and a handshake. A few of the men who stopped by gave her the once-over, but they were met with a steely look from Mac, completely obliterating any interest they may have shown in her. All waiters and waitresses wore a simple clean white T-shirt and jeans. That way they could be comfortable for the long hours they were on their feet and also blend in with the country décor. She had met Gibby, the owner. He was an extremely large African American. He was a few inches taller than Mac was and much broader. He had a wonderful smile and was as sweet as a teddy bear, but Crystal got the feeling that he could be very mean if provoked. He looked at Mac with the kind of respect that was born from a long and firm friendship.

She looked at Mac and spoke over the music, "Where did you meet Gibby?"

Mac looked at her and waited a beat, as if debating what to tell her. At last, he said, "I met Gibby in somewhat odd circumstances." He paused. "He was in a bit of trouble when we first encountered each other. He apparently owed some rather nasty people some money, and when I came here for dinner one night, the men were attempting to beat the dollar bills out of him. That's about the time I decided to intervene."

"What did you do?" Her eyes grew large and she leaned forward, completely riveted to the story.

"I very calmly explained to the men that they were going about getting paid the wrong way." Mac took a drink from his Pepsi then went on, "Then I paid them the money myself."

"You actually gave them the money? I mean, you didn't even know Gibby at the time. Why would you do that?" She was dumbfounded.

"Yes, I gave them the money, but Gibby has paid me back every single cent since then. He's a very proud man and he refused to let the matter drop. So we worked out a deal, and here we are today. Hell, I've gotten more than my fair share from our relationship and I gained a very loyal friend to boot. What more can a guy ask for?"

"And it seems he has gained a loyal friend, as well. You're very kind underneath that gruff exterior," she said in admiration.

"Underneath this gruff exterior lurks a very lusty man, eager for your hot body, angel." His eyes grew darker with passion and bore straight into hers.

Just then, a waiter came to their table and asked if they wanted anything else.

They both declined, then he said, "I'll be right back. I need to hit the restroom." He winked, then rose from the booth and went to the far end of the room.

Crystal resumed eating her fries. She had ordered a simple burger and fries, figuring they would be a safe bet. However, she hadn't expected them to taste so good. Gibby's obviously had a wonderful chef tucked back in the kitchen. A shadow covered her table, and she thought it was Mac returning, so she looked up smiling. However, it wasn't. Instead it was a man she didn't recognize. He was tall and blond, very muscular and tanned, as if he worked outside, perhaps in construction or something similar.

"I've noticed you tonight. You're awful hard to miss. A man would have to be blind not to see you, sweetheart. You're very beautiful," he spoke in a rough voice.

"Thank you." She never knew quite what to say when a man complimented her.

"My name is Dale." He extended his hand for her to shake, then said, "And yours is?"

"Her name is Crystal, and she's with me." Mac spoke from behind the stranger. The look in his eyes was deadly.

"You have a beautiful name, Crystal. Would you care to dance?"

He never took his eyes from her, completely ignoring Mac. She looked at Mac and saw his anger that was barely leashed. Crystal calmly said to the stranger, "I'm sorry, Dale, I'm here with Mac. Thank you for the offer." She smiled brightly.

"No worries." He smiled and walked away.

Mac stared at the man's back until he was well away from them; only then did he sit back down. He didn't say a word, just stared at her.

"Now that he's gone, I'd love to dance with you."

Her eyes brightened at the prospect of being in Mac's strong arms. "You would?"

"I'm anxious to get you in my arms and have *my* hands on you." He stood and smiled down at her. "May I have this dance?" He bent over her hand as he spoke.

She laughed and said, "Why, of course."

Mac took her hand in his and led her to the middle of the crowded dance floor. Once there, he put his arms around her and pulled her into his hard length.

Crystal felt at home at last. With Mac's strong arms surrounding her, she felt like nothing could ever harm her. She twined her arms around his neck, and he pulled her even closer still. She immediately felt what he was trying to show her. His rigid length pressed into her belly. She looked up into his eyes as if looking for confirmation; he smiled down at her and rotated his hips, just once. Immediately she felt heat pool between her legs, and her face flamed.

Mac leaned down to whisper in her ear, "Don't be embarrassed. You're beautiful, and feeling your sweet curves against me drives me nuts, but I wouldn't have it any other way." He rose up and smiled devilishly at her, then once again bent to whisper, "Except if we were both naked, that would be better. Of course, if we were naked, then dancing would be the furthest thing from my mind."

"You are *so* bad!" She giggled.

"Later I will show you just how good I can be." He winked.

They finished their dance in quiet, content to hold each other and sway to the beat of the music.

"Thank you for a wonderful time, Mac." They stood at Mollie's front door in that awkward moment when women were often left wondering, *Is he going to kiss me? Should I invite him in? Will he think I'm being too forward if I do? Will he think I'm a prude if I don't?* She hadn't a clue as to the answers. When she and Richard had dated, it all seemed so fast and he took all the control while she was left following his lead. This whole thing with Mac was new ground for her, and he was not Richard, thank God. She could tell he was leaving it up to her to decide whether things proceeded or not. She quickly acted on impulse and went for the plunge, saying, "Won't you come in for a drink, Mac?" She held her breath.

"I thought you'd never ask." His mouth quirked up in a devilish grin. She opened the door, and Mac followed her into the house. After their dance together, they had walked out of the bar and grill hand in hand without speaking to each other or anyone else. The drive home was made in silence, as well. It seemed that neither of them wanted to chance breaking the magical spell that had been woven around them. The whole night seemed special somehow, despite the events earlier in the evening. Maybe, just maybe, it was *because* of those events, as if God had granted them this enchanted evening as a reprieve. Whatever the reason, Mac was glad he was the man who was lucky enough to spend it with Crystal.

They walked into the living room, and Mac had the oddest feeling come over him. It was as if he was home. How strange for him to feel this way after all this time of never really feeling at home no matter where he was. He'd never felt this way before, even growing up. His father had always made him feel like he was a burden rather than a gift. His mother seemed to barely be there, like a shadow to his father. She was always in the background, quiet and content to bend to her husband's rule. Still, he didn't want thoughts of his less-than-ideal childhood to interfere with his night with the sexy woman at his side.

"Crystal, it's a cool evening. Why don't we take our drinks out to the porch? We could sit and watch the stars. What do you say?" While he was strolling down memory lane, she had already prepared a serving tray with iced tea and cookies.

"That sounds like a great idea." Her eyes lit up like a child's in a candy store.

"Here, I'll carry the tray. You just get the door." He picked up the laden tray and proceeded out the door.

"You just don't want tea all over you." She snorted as she held the door open for him.

"Well, you may have a point there, angel." He waggled his eyebrows.

They sat down on the cushioned porch swing, and Mac put the tray on the table in front of them, then handed her a glass of tea. After taking a long swallow of his own, he remarked, "Mm, tastes good."

"Thanks. I didn't know if you took sugar in yours or not, but sweet tea is all I drink. I can get you something else if you want, though. I'm sure we have something in there." She paused, then said, "I'm rambling, aren't I? Sorry." She took a deep fortifying breath and went on, "I'm just nervous."

"Don't be." He leaned back into the swing, put his arm around her shoulders, and pulled her into the crook of one arm. "Just enjoy the night, Crystal."

Crystal leaned her head on Mac's shoulder and let out a contented sigh. "If time could just stand still right now."

"No way, angel. I've got way too much in store for you

later," he murmured. "For now, just relax and look at the beautiful clear sky." He smiled down at her and kissed the top of her head in a loving caress.

She closed her eyes and knew a sense of belonging in Mac's arms. He was everything a woman could want. Now she just had to figure out a way to hold on to it. That would be the biggest challenge of all.

"Penny for your thoughts?" he said, his voice low and intimate.

"Just thinking what a wonderful night I had."

"Ah, but the best is yet to come, angel," he murmured.

She was about to ask what he meant by that, but he hushed her. "Let your fears go for now. Just feel me next to you, Crystal. Just me. Nothing else exists."

"Oh Mac," she breathed out. "The things you say . . . you make me want to let myself go and trust you to catch me."

"I *will* catch you," he replied emphatically. "You should have no fear when I'm with you. I won't let anything happen to you."

"Make love to me, Mac."

He leaned near her ear and whispered, "That's been the only thing on my mind since the first moment I saw you."

After that stark confession, the only sounds were of Crystal and Mac touching and kissing. It was the single most beautiful experience of her life. When Crystal's cell phone rang, breaking the spell, she heard Mac groan. A perfect moment ruined by technology. What else was new?

Crystal stirred at the familiar tinkling sound. She looked over at Mac and saw his frustration. "This will just take a minute, I promise," she said as she reached for the phone on the table. "Hello?" The voice on the other end of the line sent chills down her spine. "What do you want, Richard?" Crystal tried to force a measure of calm into her voice, but found she was sorely lacking.

"Now is that any way to talk to your ex-husband, sweet-heart?" Richard said, laughing.

"Don't ever call me sweetheart again. You lost that right." Now she was beginning to feel her temper. How dare he simply phone her after all this time and attempt to sweet-talk her? He was in for a rude awakening if he thought that tack was going to work. She was no longer a young innocent girl.

"I miss you. I've changed a lot since you left," Richard said earnestly. "I know I made lots of mistakes by you, but just hear what I have to say, and then I will leave you alone. Okay?"

Crystal sighed and decided to let him say his peace and then hang up on the jerk. She turned and saw Mac looking at her with worry etched on his face. In her anxiety over hearing Richard's voice, she'd forgotten Mac was still there. She leaned over to him and placed her hand on his shoulder in a gesture meant to say, *I'm alright*.

"Very well, get on with it, then," Crystal said, getting more perturbed with every second she spent on the phone.

"I just wanted you to know that I'm in town. I thought it'd be real nice if we got together and talked about old times. What do you say? We could go to dinner and talk things through, fig-ure out what went wrong."

"I'm going to say this once, and then I'm hanging up the phone. I won't go anywhere with you ever again. Our marriage is over, and I have moved on with my life. I suggest you do the same. Don't attempt to call me again." Crystal spoke with calm authority in her voice and then hung up the phone. After taking a deep breath, she once again turned to look at Mac's worried face.

"What did he want?" Mac asked, his voice dripping icy venom.

"He says he's back in town and wants to get together for old times' sake." Crystal went on with vehemence, "Can you believe the nerve of him to call and expect to just pick right up where we left off!" She was angry now just thinking of the whole thing. "What an idiot." She scooted up next to Mac, pleased when his arm went around her in a protective embrace.

"I don't like him calling you. Maybe you should change your number."

Crystal stiffened and peered up at him. "I won't hide and cower. Not again."

Mac stared at her a few seconds before kissing the top of her head. "Okay, but if he calls again, you'll let me know, right?"

"Yes," she replied, loving that he cared so much. It was such a new experience for her. It was just the thing she needed to send her into a deep sleep.

Mac had no intention of sleeping. Whether Crystal would admit it or not, the phone call from her ex had shaken her up. She was so sturdy and determined, Mac didn't think anything could bring Crystal down. But now, seeing her so fragile, he knew different. Richard. That son of a bitch had no rights to her. She belonged to him and Trent now. Richard was out of the picture. One way or another, Mac would keep it that way.

He carried her inside and locked the door behind him, then took her to her bedroom. He stood her on the floor and murmured, "Come on, sleepyhead. Let's get you tucked in."

She yawned and started to shuck her clothes. "I'm so sorry. I don't know why I'm so tired."

"Because Trent and I have been keeping you up late, probably," he said as he kissed the top of her head. Once she was nude, he slipped his T-shirt over her head and laid her on the bed. He quickly stripped and got in beside her, then closed his eyes. It was several hours later when Mac woke to the gentle feel of Crystal stroking his chest with her fingers. "Is it morning already?" he asked. The room was semi-dark with the shades drawn, and he couldn't tell the time of day.

"Not quite." She glanced at the clock at the side of the bed. "Three in the morning," she said as she flicked his nipple with a fingernail. The little sting brought him around instantly.

"Keep that up and you're going to be in trouble."

Crystal pulled her hand away. "I really love waking up to you. Thank you for staying."

He tipped her chin up and kissed her lips. "I could get used to it, too."

"Tell me something about yourself," she stated. "What are your parents like? I really want to know more about you, Mac."

He shifted, uncomfortable with this conversation already. His parents weren't exactly the Cleavers. "Well, my dad was very rigid. He insisted his only son toe the line, and if I screwed up, there was hell to pay. Mom followed whatever Dad said. His orders were akin to the law with her."

Her hand came back to his chest, and Mac relaxed. "I'm sorry. I never knew my dad. My mom did her best to raise me, but I know it wasn't easy," she said.

He tucked an arm behind his head. "Parents make a huge impact on our lives. I remember my dad telling me once that I was too stupid to amount to anything."

"God, that's awful."

Mac shrugged. "When I graduated from law school, he had to eat his words."

Her head shot up and she stared at him. "You're a lawyer?"

"Yes, but I'm no longer practicing. Trent and I both got out of the business when Kinks began to do so well."

"That takes a lot of schooling. Do you regret walking away from it all?"

"Not one bit. It was a high-stress job. Besides, Kinks makes a ton more money for me."

Her palm continued to massage him, and her fingers toyed with his chest hair. Was she trying to comfort him? Probably.

And damn, he loved every bit of her efforts. She was gentle and nurturing without even realizing it.

Her finger dipped into his belly button and he had to bite back a curse. "Do you get along with your parents now? And what do they think of the nightclub?"

"They don't know much about Kinks. Just that it's a nightclub. Mom would have a coronary if she knew the deets. Dad and I are civil. I see him on holidays and birthdays. It's not ideal, but it's more than what a lot of kids have."

Her palm moved a few inches lower, then stopped. "You're right. It's good that you don't hold a grudge. Some kids wouldn't be so forgiving."

Mac cleared his throat, unable to grasp on to the thread of the conversation with her touching him. "Huh?"

"I'm sorry, Mac. I'm sorry you didn't have the type of parents you deserved."

Her voice sounded shaky, and he didn't like it one bit. "No, don't be sorry. It wasn't as bad as all that. I'm a grown man, and I make my own way in life. I'm happy with that."

She smoothed her palm over him. "Yes, you are a grown man," she murmured.

Without giving her any warning, Mac sat up and flipped Crystal over to her stomach. "Mac!"

"Hush, angel," he murmured as he straddled her legs. "I did as you asked and talked about myself. Now it's time I get what I want." He swatted her upturned ass and Crystal yelped.

"You did not just spank me, Mac Anderson!"

"Yep. Now, are you going to give me what I want?" He rubbed away the sting, then swatted her again two more times. She stopped struggling and started moaning. "Damn, you're fucking sexy like this," Mac gritted out as he cupped both of her ass cheeks in his palms. "Yum."

She moaned. "Mac, you're driving me wild here."

"Ah, but it's only fair, since you've been driving me wild from the moment I first saw you." When she shifted around to get more comfortable, Mac's cock hardened.

"Let me up," she pleaded. "I want to see you."

Now they were getting somewhere. "I suppose I can allow that." He moved to the side, and before he could take his next breath, she was on her knees in front of him. Jesus, she tore him up. So pretty and sweet. One minute he was taking a stroll down memory lane, and the next she was teasing him into a horny frenzy.

"Ah, that's better," she whispered.

"I'm all yours."

With her silky mass of tangled brown hair drifting down her back and those big eyes smiling up at him as she descended on his cock, Mac forgot all about distant parents and his lonely childhood. With the first tentative touch of her lips to the bulbous tip, Mac lost all reason. Her touches and kisses pulled a primitive response from him. He put his hands on either side of her head and directed her onto his pulsing shaft.

"Damn, that's nice. I love that sweet tongue of yours, Crystal."

Her eyelids drifted downward, and Mac felt the gentle sigh she let out all the way down the length of his dick. With one hand, Crystal guided him inside the wet heat of her mouth, then farther still until he was nearly down her throat. She licked and teased, the tiny movements of her tongue and lips drawing his balls up tight. Mac clutched a fistful of her hair and pulled her mouth onto him tighter. She gagged and Mac immediately pulled out. Crystal whimpered and quickly took over, sucking him deep all over again. This time his balls were smashed against her chin.

"Goddamn," he growled.

He watched as she threw herself into the task. Seeing her so anxious to please him and enjoying his taste had Mac close to coming already. Crystal pulled his rigid length all the way out and placed a gentle kiss to his tip before sweeping her tongue down the underside of his cock. She appeared to be in no hurry, as if she had all day to kneel in front of him and lick his dick. When she cupped his balls in her other hand and squeezed, every thought fled his mind. Only Crystal existed. Crystal and her talented mouth and fingers.

Mac groaned her name as her movements turned rapid, her own excitement growing. Crystal sucked, hard, once more. "Fuck!" He grabbed the back of her head and held her still while he shot over the edge, his come spurting into her mouth and down her throat.

Long seconds passed, with Crystal still on her knees, Mac's cock buried between her lips. He slid out of her and lifted her onto his lap. "I love you," he admitted, "and I figured it was about time you knew it."

She froze and stared at him. "Y-you love me? Seriously?"

He chuckled. "That's not exactly what I was hoping you'd say, angel."

She blushed and looked away. "I'm sorry. It's just . . . I need time to think about all this. Between you and Trent, I mean."

He tugged a lock of her hair until she was looking at him once more. "Are you worried that you're in love with us both, Crystal? Or is it that maybe you only care for one and not the other?"

She slapped a hand over her face and groaned. "I don't know. You are both so wonderful. I can't imagine not being with the both of you. Saying that makes me feel guilty. Isn't love supposed to be one-on-one?"

Mac shook his head. "Hell, sometimes it feels as if Trent and I are one person." He winked and added, "We sure fell for the same woman, at any rate."

Crystal placed her hand on his cheek and said, "Give me time to figure this out, okay?"

"I think I can handle that," he murmured.

Crystal kissed him lightly and replied, "Thank you."

"I've got other ways for you to thank me," he groaned, as he took her mouth as if it were for the last time. Shit, for all he knew, it just might be.

11

Two days later, Crystal shook with stress as Trent stood in the bedroom of her apartment, watching her freak out over just the right outfit to wear around people with more money than she would ever see in a lifetime. And every time she told herself it shouldn't matter whether they were rich, she realized she was only deluding herself. Of course it mattered! It wasn't as if she could go to a dinner with Trent's parents wearing shorts and a T-shirt.

"Pick something!" Trent shouted.

Crystal looked at the slate-gray slacks and cream-colored silk blouse, her current choice, in the mirror, standing this way and that, then she asked, "What do you think of this one?"

"I think that one looks as nice as the last thirty you tried. You're much too worried about this dinner."

Crystal snorted and whirled around to glare at him. "Your mother saw me in your T-shirt and nothing else, Trent. They all three saw me kiss the daylights out of you. It was one heck of a first impression!"

Trent's eyes turned a deeper shade of blue as they roamed

over her body from head to toe. "I liked you in my T-shirt, baby, and I truly enjoyed the kiss."

Crystal wasn't touching that with a ten-foot pole. She whipped back around and looked once more into the mirror. "This will just have to do. I don't really have anything much better without looking overdressed. My wardrobe needs some work, I'm afraid."

Trent crossed the minefield that used to be her bedroom, and pulled her back against the hard length of him. "My mother will see you as a beautiful woman who has managed to enrapture her son. Stop worrying, Crystal. You don't need to make yourself into anything you're not, simply to please my family."

Was she so transparent? How was it possible a man she'd only just met could see her so clearly? The entire time she'd been married to Richard he'd never been able to figure her out.

Still, she wasn't quite ready to be so easily read, so she lied. "It's not that. Your mother is clearly more refined than I am, and I don't want her to think I'm some floozy who would go to bed with any Tom, Dick, or Harry."

In the mirror, she watched with fascination as Trent's sexy mouth tilted sideways. "I'm quite glad you're no . . . floozy. As I remember it, you were rather willful. Not to worry, though. I'm quite confident I will soon make you more . . . biddable."

Crystal wanted to smack him, and if he wasn't currently palming her breast through her silk blouse, she would have. As it was, she was forced to make a small verbal protest.

"Look, you domineering control freak, your accent makes it sound like you said 'beddable,' and whether you said 'biddable' or 'beddable,' neither is going to happen if you don't quit with the attitude."

"Domineering control freak?" he asked, his mouth kicking up at one corner, making him look entirely too devilish.

"Yes. You're most certainly that."

"I see." Still standing behind her, his gaze wandered the

length of her in the mirror, and Crystal's flesh tingled to life. "In that case, I'd have you. Now."

Have her? He wanted to make love? "We can't, Trent, we'll be late," she protested, only half-caring.

"Do as you're told, Crystal, and turn around."

In a flash, her body went up in flames at the sudden command in his voice. Geez, she loved hearing that tone from him, so aggressive and so male. It was hot.

She hesitated a moment too long, and apparently Trent decided to punish her for her lack of speed with a swat to her bottom. Instinct had her crying out, surprised by the act. "Trent!"

Without even an ounce of remorse, he crossed his arms over his impressive chest and stared at her. "I'm a domineering control freak, remember? Turn around."

This time she didn't dither. Crystal turned until she was no longer facing the mirror. Now she was looking directly into the bluest eyes of the most gorgeous man she'd ever seen.

"That's better. I like when you do as you're told. Now, off with the blouse and bra. I want to see the soft pink of your succulent nipples."

Again, Crystal was surprising herself by doing Trent's bidding. She stripped out of the clothing and stood in front of him with only her slacks on.

She saw Trent's right hand move, and then the left, until he was cupping and massaging both of her breasts. He flicked his thumbs over the hardened buds, and then pulled them upward for a long, lazy lick.

His tongue swept back and forth over one tight nipple, while his fingers played with the other. As he pulled back, she watched through half-opened eyes as his tongue moved downward to her belly button. He growled something unintelligible, then his tongue darted out and licked. Crystal pushed against him, on fire already.

Oh God, she was suddenly aching with need. Her entire body yearned. "That feels so good, Trent."

"I will give you more, much more, but first I want you on your knees."

Her body quivered, then quivered even more at the idea of purposely disobeying him. Would he smack her bottom again? Only one way to find out.

"I think I'd rather stand, thanks anyway," she replied, intentionally sounding haughty to wind him up.

"You're too willful, Crystal Shaw. You need to learn obedience," he whispered, the words a sensual promise to her overactive sex drive.

Trent moved away from her then and looked around the room. His gaze stopped on something, she couldn't tell what, as the room was in total chaos. But when he walked toward her bed and picked up a long black silk scarf, her pussy dampened with the idea of being blindfolded again. She hadn't realized she could enjoy such a thing, but she had. A lot.

When he came back to her, she was taken by surprise as Trent moved behind her and clasped one wrist in his calloused hand. He wrapped the black silk around it, then grabbed the other and did the same. Her hands were securely tied behind her back, and Crystal was now completely at his mercy.

"Mm, I like you this way. You're mine now, to do with as I please. If you're a very good girl, I will let you come. If you're naughty, I won't. Would you like me to tongue-fuck your sweet cunt, Crystal? Would that please you?"

His guttural voice was the single most stimulating thing she had ever heard. There was, of course, only one answer to give.

"Yes."

"Ah, so compliant all of a sudden."

She didn't speak. She couldn't. Her blood was liquid fire coursing through her veins.

"I like it when you do as I say. I will reward you for it in a while, but for now, get down on your knees. I have a need to see you that way."

This time Crystal started to lower herself, but Trent had to help her, and she felt awkward with her hands tied. She couldn't look at him; she was too embarrassed and excited and so many other things all at once.

He cupped her chin in his hand and lifted her face upward. Her eyes connected with his, and she saw the wild frenzy of sexual hunger there. He was as turned on by what they were doing as she was. It was enough to have her loosening up, if just a little.

"Do you know what you look like in this position, Crystal?"

She shook her head, still staring into his eyes.

"You look like my sex slave. A concubine."

"No." Her independent streak reared its feminist head at the notion.

"Yes. And you're mine to use," Trent growled.

"To use?"

He touched her breast, then flicked her nipple as if the action was boring him. "Will you let me?" he asked, his eyes staring at her naked torso.

"I don't know if I can."

"Stop thinking so hard. Let me take you somewhere you've never been. I want to be the first man to draw pleasure from the very depths of your soul. Let me."

She was beyond telling him no. The moment she'd let him tie her hands behind her back she had been his to use. Who was she kidding?

"Okay. Yes."

Not a single sound came from Trent at her acceptance of the game he was playing. He didn't even appear to be breathing hard. He seemed totally at ease. As he moved his finger away from her breast and began unbuttoning his black slacks, she nearly whimpered. Crystal licked her lips, anticipating what was about to come. She wanted him in her mouth, the taste of his sticky fluid on her tongue.

Slowly, as if he had all the time in the world, Trent unzipped and freed his cock, and finally Crystal could see him in all his magnificence. He was hard and pulsing with life, the bulbous head darkly engorged. Jesus, he looked delicious. It was crazy how eager she was.

His cock held firmly in his hand, Trent stepped forward, bent slightly at the knees, and demanded, "Open those sexy lips, baby."

Crystal tilted her head upward and opened, but just as she would have sucked him in, he stopped her with a hand to the back of her head, pulling at a fistful of her hair just hard enough to bring the slightest sting to her scalp.

"What?"

"Not your mouth, just your tongue. Lick my cock. I want it nice and wet for what I'm about to do to you."

Crystal didn't know what he could possibly do that they hadn't already done, but if he wanted to be licked, then she was just the woman for the job.

Opening wide and slipping her tongue out, Crystal let her eyes close and tasted the sensitive tip of him. She took the small bead of moisture that had appeared there into her mouth, then she let her tongue roam freely over and down, slowly moving to the underside, and then finally to his balls. She swiped her tongue back and forth, craving their unique flavor and wishing she could take them both into her mouth and suck. But, knowing her orders, she held back and moved her wet tongue over the rest of him instead, giving his cock the thorough licking he demanded.

She felt his hand pulling once more at her hair, and Crystal eased away, leaning back on her heels and opening her eyes. But what she saw was the most feral look on a man's face she'd ever seen. He looked ready to explode. To throw her on the bed a few feet away and fuck her brains out. Had she pushed him too far?

"At times, you tempt me beyond reason," he growled, then he dipped down, put an arm beneath her, and swung her into his arms. He carried her to the bed, but he didn't throw her down, as she'd feared. Instead, he placed her, ever so gently, in the center of it. She adjusted her hands slightly, trying for a more comfortable position, but when he began stripping off his clothes, Crystal went still.

He could always make her go pliant and mute with the mere sight of his body. He was just too good-looking for her peace of mind. His wild mane of black hair tossed all over his head and just the slightest hint of stubble on his chin, lent to the notion of how incredibly rugged and masculine he was. Trent put one knee on the bed and turned to the task of unfastening her slacks and ridding her of the rest of her clothing. Soon, nothing stood between them and sexual heaven.

He pushed her legs wide, and before she could protest, he descended between them and licked her. She arched up and tried to get him closer, to get his tongue inside her as he'd said he would earlier, but he seemed in no hurry.

"Trent, quit playing and get to it!"

He chuckled and murmured, "You're in no position to be giving me orders, *slave*."

She glared down at him and muttered, "Don't make me regret letting you tie me down, damn it."

"Once I'm done with you, you will crave being tied down. Your mouth will water and your pussy will drip with need any time I mention this black silk scarf," Trent whispered, the heat of his breath stroking her clit, causing her femininity to throb to life.

"So confident of yourself, are you?" She had to struggle to say the words coherently.

"No. So confident of you. You're a woman with great passion deep in your soul, and I intend to suck you dry."

Now, that sounded promising. "Then quit talking and get to work. You've barely scratched the surface," she dared.

"Ah, just what I love, a challenge." Then his tongue delved deep and she whimpered.

He was right about one thing; she would crave him after this. There was no denying it.

Trent was exactly where he wanted to be: between the widespread thighs of the woman he loved. He had realized it when he watched her get down on her knees in front of him. Her supplicant position had pulled feelings out of him that he'd never felt before. He had fallen in love with a woman who saw him as a moment of fun and excitement.

He had always thought himself free of entanglements of the heart. His father had warned him once that, when a Dailey man falls in love, it was for life. There would be no going back. Somehow, he was going to have to convince Crystal Shaw, independent go-getter, that they were meant to be together.

It had been fate when she walked into his nightclub. He did not laugh at such things as fate and destiny. Nor did he balk at the idea of a challenge, and making Crystal see that there was more to their relationship than sex would indeed be a challenge.

As he tasted and teased her, feeling the quiver of Crystal's supple body, he knew that if any other man besides Mac ever touched her in such a way, he'd see red. She was theirs. Her desire was for them to play with and nurture to life, no other.

He lifted up and stared up the length of her nude body. Her eyes were closed, her hands behind her back, securely tied, and best of all, she was already in the beginnings of a climax. She looked magnificent and so damn hot he felt singed.

Trent used his thumbs to part her delicate folds, exposing her swollen clit as he did, and then he dipped his head once more and sucked the tiny bit of flesh into his mouth, flicking back and forth with his tongue.

Crystal came undone, screaming his name and arching high off the bed, but he held her firm as he swallowed every last drop of her tangy flow.

This time when he lifted his head, she was staring at him through half-raised lashes, the sexy hint of a smile on her face. Trent spoke, uncaring how his words affected her.

"I'm a selfish bastard, Crystal. If it were within my power, I'd make the world fall away and keep you here forever." His throat felt like raw barbed wire had scored his throat.

She only stared at him. Unmoving. Her eyes seemed to look straight into his very soul. No woman had ever been able to do that to him. Trent didn't want to think too hard on such serious issues, however.

To take his mind off the out-of-control freight train of his thoughts, he slipped his hands beneath her hips, cupped her ass cheeks in his palms, and squeezed. She clenched up on him, drawing a grin from him.

"Before Mac and I came along, had you ever had a man's cock in your tight little ass, Crystal?"

Her face turned red. *I think not,* Trent thought with masculine delight.

"Good, I'm glad we're the only ones to touch you so intimately."

That pushed her out of her delirium, and she began to shift and wiggle atop the bed, as if by doing so she could free herself. He knew better; the knot he had tied was secure.

"Trent, this is all becoming too much," she said, her voice unsteady."

"Shh, you trust me with your body, Crystal, I know you do. I won't hurt you. I will never do anything you don't wish. Just relax and let me show you how good you can feel, if only you will give yourself over to me."

A long time passed with Crystal tense and afraid. Finally, she relented, but under one condition.

"Fine, but I want a safe word."

That had his brow arching. "And how are you familiar with safe words?" It was a term used for couples who enjoyed bondage, dominance, and submissive-type sex. The idea that she might have done this with someone other than him and Mac, bothered Trent entirely too much. He had no right to inquire of her past relationships. He had a rather checkered past himself, and he would not relish an inquiry by her. Still, he was just chauvinistic enough to wish that he had been the only man to try such things with her.

But her next words had him sighing a little too vigorously in relief.

"I read about them in a romance book. The heroine was experimenting and wanted to be a slave to a master. They used a safe word, which meant that if she spoke it, the lovemaking stopped instantly," she explained, and then calmly demanded, "So, I want a safe word."

"You read some very interesting books, Crystal," he murmured, amused and turned on at the same time. "What word would you like to be your safe word, baby?" His dick swelled painfully as they talked and images bombarded his head, making him want to flip her over to her stomach and slide into her tight, puckered opening.

"Bambi."

Surely, Trent had not heard her correctly.

"Huh?"

She laughed, her body relaxing visibly as she grew increasingly more comfortable with their conversation. "It was the first thing that came to mind, don't ask me why."

At that point, she could have said just about anything; it would not have mattered in the slightest.

"Bambi it is," Trent whispered, then he locked his gaze with hers, slowly lowered his head, and kissed her gently between the legs. She moaned beautifully for him. Trent lifted off of her completely, knowing that she stared at his every movement, her anxious expression cutting through his haze of lust the way nothing else could.

Tenderly, Trent slipped his hands beneath her and turned her over to her belly, careful to keep her as comfortable as possible. He arranged her legs wider and made sure her wrists weren't bound too tight. He looked at her, lying in the center of the rumpled bed, the low light of the bedside lamp turning her skin golden. She was all spread out for his pleasure, her luscious body and plump bottom mere inches away from his eager fingers and cock, and he nearly whimpered like a whipped pup.

"You're a feast for my starving libido, Crystal."

She turned her head to speak, and Trent helped her by moving her long dark hair away from her face.

"You've been with other women, Trent," she said, her voice small and unsure. "Probably a lot of them were more exciting, prettier, and definitely with a bigger sense of adventure than me."

"I won't deny that I've been with other women, but none could compare to you," he told her as candidly as he knew how. "All I want is you. All I need is this." And then he touched her, right where he'd wanted to touch her since they'd begun this wild back-and-forth dance.

The sleek skin of her ass was softer than any silk he'd ever touched. So round and firm and kissable.

So far away from his mouth.

On his knees between her legs, Trent leaned down and licked one smooth cheek from the crook of her leg to the small of her back. The startled sound that came from Crystal was not so much from fear, but from sexual hunger. He recognized her sounds already, her needy little whimpers and anxious groans. He wanted to make her scream with a satisfaction that only he could give her.

Moving off the bed completely, Trent asked, "Oil. Where do you keep your body oil?"

"Bathroom, underneath the sink, there's a bottle of massage oil."

"Sit tight, baby, I'll be right back."

"Hurry, Trent, before I lose my nerve."

He touched the cleft of her ass and stroked her intimately. "Only desire at my hands, never pain, my pretty Crystal."

She did not speak, but her body told him all that he needed. She believed him, and her total acceptance of him was something he'd never felt before—not even from his own family.

She was a treasure, and he meant to keep her.

Quickly, Trent retrieved the body oil and started out of the bathroom, but the words etched in a flowing calligraphy script across the blue bottle caught his attention. The label read, *Touch of Love Aromatherapy. Strawberry-Scented.*

Interesting, even if he was dangerously close to feeling seriously jealous as to the reason Crystal might have such a thing in her possession.

He left the bathroom and wasted no time in resuming his position between the silky thighs of the woman he loved. He popped the top of the bottle, watching for any signs of fear or worry from Crystal, but as he poured a small amount into his palm and smoothed his hands together to warm the slippery liquid, he could almost see Crystal's heart pick up speed. Her body went rigid at once. What did she think? That he would simply shove himself inside of her?

His aim was to prove to her that nothing between a man and woman should be dirty or wrong, so long as both parties agreed.

He touched her shoulders first, and he could tell she was surprised. Crystal had expected him to delve right in, but that was not his way. He savored and enjoyed.

Trent began moving his hands over her collarbone next, and

then her neck got some of his attention. She had a long, elegant neck. He wanted to bite her elegant neck.

But not quite yet.

Then, as he skated his palms down her arms to her bound wrists, he could feel the hum of pleasure emanating from Crystal. He massaged the oil into the skin of her wrists, easing the restraint even more, so that her arms were now barely tied at all. For him it wasn't about the binding. The binding was only for enhanced stimulation. Pleasure and fulfillment came from her total submission. That was what turned Trent's blood to molten lava. And if she was able to get away, but chose to give all control to him instead, then he had not only her body but her trust, as well.

Once Trent was satisfied that he'd made her as comfortable as possible, he poured more oil into his palms and touched her spine. He took utmost care in massaging each vertebrae, feeling her body slump as she relaxed even more. Only then did he lean down to place a small kiss to a spot that he'd already massaged.

"Strawberry, huh?" he asked against her slippery skin, his curiosity over why she might have sensual body oil getting the better of him.

"I, well, I thought maybe I'd try something different with Richard. I thought that maybe if I put more effort into our sex life, he'd be more interested in me."

"Richard," Trent grumbled, "was an ass."

Crystal laughed and said, "Pretty much."

He smoothed his fingertips over her lower back then, and growled, "You're spice enough for any man, Crystal. Props are unnecessary."

"Mm, I don't think I can talk with you doing that. Oh my, that feels so incredible. You're one talented man, Trent. I think I've died and gone to heaven."

He smiled, cocky and turned on all at once.

He let his fingers drift over the small indentations above her bottom, and then murmured, "You're being a very good little sex slave, Crystal. Shall I reward you?"

"Oh yeah, please reward me, Trent."

Trent let his slick fingers slide between her ass cheeks, and then slid one finger up and down. Over and over again, making certain she was completely slick with the massage oil before he slipped it into her a bare inch. He felt her startled intake of breath at the slight invasion. Still, she didn't use the safe word.

"Will you beg for me?" he asked in a heated command, as the need to fill her with his cock instead of his finger began to ride him hard.

Her body, once gone pliant, was now strung tight, and her quiet voice pleaded with him. "Anything, Trent, just please give me my reward."

"Mm, in just a little bit. For now, I want to lube you up so that when my cock slides in it will feel so incredibly warm and full. You will crave this type of lovemaking once I'm through, I promise you."

"Yes, yes! Oh God, it just feels so . . . I don't know how to describe it."

"It feels forbidden," he answered wickedly. "You're my forbidden pleasure, Crystal Shaw."

She mumbled something that he could not quite make out, and then he went on explaining the way it would feel when his cock was thrusting into her tight ass.

"The warmth from my finger and the oil, mixing with the sensitive nerve endings just inside of your tight opening, it's making you want my cock there, isn't it? You'll love me filling you. Spreading you open and pumping into you. Tell me. Admit it, slave! You want more, don't you?"

"Yes, Trent, I do want more. I want you there very badly."

Just what he wanted to hear.

He leaned over her and whispered into her ear, "You will be

able to feel every throb. Every inch will feel like another taste of paradise. Then, when I come, you will feel the heat of it shooting through you. Would you like me to come inside of you? Right here"—he wiggled his finger for emphasis—"in this tight little ass?"

"Oh yes. You make me want it, Trent. I've never felt so ready to come and you've not even touched my clit. Please don't make me wait any longer!" she cried, her eager passion equal to his own.

"No. Not yet. First, I want to make sure you're ready for me. Two fingers now."

Slowly, allowing her body to adjust to the invasion, Trent slid two fingers into Crystal. She moaned and spread her legs further, pushing backward against his hand, as if it weren't enough. As if it would never be enough. It was just the way he wanted her.

"Now you're ready," he ground out. Trent's body was on fire and his dick was aching for release. He couldn't wait another second to be inside this woman.

He reached for the bottle of oil once more and slicked some over his throbbing shaft, already swollen and dripping with precome at the thought of being buried deep. Gently, Trent separated the round globes of Crystal's backside and touched the head of his cock to her entrance, then slowly moved a mere inch inside. It was such sweet torture to hold back from thrusting deep. From fucking her hard and fast, the way his body so desperately craved.

"Oh Trent."

Her quivery voice saying his name as if a caress made Trent want to howl in triumph. Her body vibrated beneath his, and as he slipped in another inch, she whimpered and bucked wildly.

"Easy, baby. Let me take you there slowly. I want to build the pleasure for you, so you will always feel me there, even when I'm not."

Then another inch more and she was thrusting herself backward, taking control of their lovemaking in such a way that

both surprised and pleased him. Her body bowed and he had to
clutch her hips to keep from going in too far too fast.

"Gently, Crystal," he commanded in a tone that brooked no
argument.

She was new to the things Trent and Mac were introducing
her to, and she didn't understand that they needed to go slow.
He refused to hurt her—despite the way his primal instincts
kept battering at him to fill her completely. He ached to show
her every possible way a man could make love to a woman.

Holding her firmly by the hips to keep her body still for his
slow invasion, Trent heard Crystal let loose a needy whimper.
The yearning-filled, delicate sound turned his heart to mush,
and he gave her yet another heated inch of hard flesh, unable to
deny her. In the same instant, he took his right hand from her
hip and toyed with the lovely little bud of her clitoris. Fascinated, as she became a slave to her body's delicious sensations.
She moaned and pushed against him as her orgasm took her. It
was sheer ecstasy to bring her to new heights of pleasure. She
was ten thousand more times the woman than any other.

"Now, Crystal," he whispered. "All of me. Do you want me
to fill your pretty little ass?"

"Yes, damn it!"

A rumbling growl escaped him at her feral response. He
pushed himself the rest of the way inside her tightest opening,
as her muscles sucked him in and her flesh immediately tensed.

Trent swore in two languages. The pleasure/pain of her body's
clutch was both glorious and torment.

"Ease up, baby."

"I—I can't," she cried.

Trent reached up, tore the scarf from her wrists, and flung it
away. At once, she threw her arms out to her sides and grabbed
hold of the blanket. He stroked her sweat-soaked hair away
from her face, and then covered her body with his own much-
larger frame, folding himself around her protectively. He kissed

her upturned cheek and felt her muscles relax the slightest bit. He thanked the heavens above. Much more of her clenching and he would have embarrassed himself.

"Good girl," he praised her. Then he did what he had wanted to do earlier, and bit the smooth line of her neck. He got an eager response for more from Crystal. Her wish was his command.

He licked and suckled at her neck, knowing how wild it made her, and then began a gentle rhythm with his hips. Leisurely he built the pace until his hot flesh was slapping against hers.

"Crystal," he groaned, "you belong to me."

She didn't speak, only licked her lips and pushed against him, joining in the rhythm of their beautiful dance. Soon he felt himself swell and his balls draw up tight. One more thrust and he was there, his cock erupting inside of her, hot fluid filling her. She shouted his name, joining him with her own climactic finish.

Long minutes passed with Trent still buried deep, until Crystal mumbled something he couldn't quite make out.

He kissed her cheek and her forehead, then asked, "What did you say, baby?"

"I said we are *so* late for dinner."

He couldn't help it. He laughed.

12

The meal consisted of perfectly cooked steaks; crisp, steamed vegetables; and then cannoli for desert. She'd never had cannoli before. She'd seen the tubular-shaped dessert on television, but to see and to taste were not at all the same. The flaky pastry shells were filled with sweetened ricotta. Mixed in were bits of chocolate. What more could a woman want out of life? There was no way she'd ever be able to live without the tasty treats now. Then again, she was beginning to think she'd never be able to live without Trent and Mac, either. Not good. Really not good. Her thoughts scattered as Trent's father spoke, his deep voice commanding the attention of everyone at the table.

"I have an announcement to make."

Everyone grew silent. Mrs. Dailey seemed surprised, and if Crystal didn't miss her guess, she also seemed a little worried.

"Carmela will be taking over the winery."

A winery, so that's what the "family business" was. There was an audible gasp at the table from both brothers, and their mother's face had leached of color. Crystal wasn't a detective, but even she could see that the news wasn't what any of them had expected. And she was more curious than ever as to just who Carmela was.

"It's the right decision. Any objections?"

As if right on cue, a beautiful woman came striding into the nightclub, her vivid blue eyes zeroing in on their table. Both brothers and Mr. Dailey stood. The woman smiled when she saw Trent's father; both brothers simply frowned. She spared them each a quick nod as Mr. Dailey kissed both of her cheeks and helped her to sit. They spoke in hushed tones, but Crystal heard her name mentioned and was curious what was being said. The woman finally turned her attention toward Crystal and smiled.

"I'm very pleased to meet you, Crystal. Dad was just singing your praises. I'm Carmela, the sister they both wished did not exist." She grinned and waved a hand toward Josh and Trent.

Trent spoke immediately, not giving Crystal a chance to greet Carmela in return.

"Don't put words into my mouth, sister," Trent said. "I never wished such a thing."

"Maybe not you, but Josh certainly."

"Ah, such an intuitive woman," Josh said, all teasing smiles gone, replaced by a stern mask. Suddenly he looked every bit as intimidating as Trent.

"It is very nice to meet you, Carmela, but maybe I should be going. This seems to be a private matter."

Trent's arm came around her shoulders instantly, his warm palm cupping the nape of her neck in a show of possession. "You need not leave, Crystal. If my father felt it inappropriate to discuss this in front of you, he would have made other arrangements."

"Trent is correct," Mr. Dailey said, his smile kind. "You're more than welcome at this table." As he looked over at his youngest son, however, he nearly growled. "Though I do wish for Josh to behave himself."

Josh said nothing, his eyes never once leaving Carmela, as if he was keeping a very close eye on a cobra.

"Crystal, perhaps we should fill you in just a bit," Carmela said, her shrewd eyes sweeping the lot of them. "I'm their sister and the eldest sibling. However, my mother died during childbirth, before Papa met and married Trent and Josh's mother."

Ah, so there was still some murky water under the bridge, Crystal thought. She felt immensely guilty for being privy to their family secrets. And the stricken look on Mrs. Dailey's face showed clearly that Carmela's words had struck a chord. Did Carmela truly not see that Mrs. Dailey would be hurt by denying her parentage? How could anyone so clearly intelligent be so obtuse?

On a whim, Crystal laid her hand over Mrs. Dailey's, hoping to soothe the older woman, and she was surprised when Mrs. Dailey turned her hand over and squeezed her fingers, smiling gently at her.

Unfortunately, Josh had already seen his mother's pain, pain that Carmela had caused. His frown grew angry and fierce. His words had the entire table gasping in surprise.

"The winery goes to a male heir. It has always been that way in the Dailey family. And since Trent does not wish to see to the day-to-day running of the business, I think I shall." He paused, seeing that his words had done more than shocked Carmela; he'd also hurt her, as was his intention, no doubt. "You're not needed here, Carmela. Go back to . . . where is it this month?" he asked, sneering at her. "London? Is that your latest hangout?"

"Dad has already decided," Carmela spit out, her voice quivering just the slightest bit. "You have no say in the winery, not anymore. What's more, you might want to be careful where you throw those rocks. You might just hit your own glass house."

Josh stood abruptly and leaned across the table, so close to Carmela that Crystal could see his angry breath blowing the woman's dark hair. "You may have convinced Dad that you're an upstanding, moral woman, ready to run a million-dollar company, but I know you for who you really are. If you insist on taking over the winery, know this: I will fight you every step of the way. By the time I'm through, you will beg for mercy!"

"Josh!" Mr. Dailey shouted as he, too, stood. Then Trent stood and they were all shouting at each other. Crystal looked over at Carmela, who stayed seated, her hand clutching the stem of her water glass so hard Crystal was surprised it didn't shatter. Mrs. Dailey had come out of her seat, as well, and was grasping on to the front of Josh's shirt, clearly pleading with him, though Crystal didn't understand the mash of words the elderly woman spoke. Josh calmed a measure, looked down at his mother, and gave her a kind smile.

"Carmela," he said, over his mother's head, "I have a wish to speak to you in private."

"Fine," Carmela gritted out, and then she rose to her feet, seemed to stiffen her spine, and strode off toward the swinging kitchen doors.

Trent helped his mother back into her chair, and Mr. Dailey pulled her in close, giving her his strength. When they were all quiet once more, Mrs. Dailey spoke, attempting to apologize for the unseemly outburst.

"I wish that hadn't happened in front of you, Crystal. I'm afraid Carmela and Josh have always rubbed each other the wrong way. He seems to think she is unworthy of the Dailey name, simply because she lives her life as a modern, independent woman. I don't agree with my son, but he has strong convictions."

"What about me? I'm not exactly old-fashioned, either, and I don't see him acting that way toward me," Crystal asked, wondering if there was more to the antagonism between the two siblings.

"Yes, Crystal, but you're not a Dailey."

The words hit her square in the chest. It hadn't been Mrs. Dailey's intention to hurt her, and yet Crystal felt her world swing out of focus for a second. The very pathetic part of it all was that Trent's mother was correct. Crystal wasn't a Dailey, and she had absolutely no right to be discussing private matters with them. Their meal was done, her time with Trent finished. It was moments like this when reality didn't merely seep in; it gushed.

Crystal rose from the table and leaned down to place a gentle kiss against Mrs. Dailey's cheek. "Thank you for a lovely time, but I'm afraid it's time for me to leave."

Trent stood up slowly, his face a stern mask as he glared down at her. "What is this?"

"I had a lovely time with your family, Trent, but I have to work in the morning and I need to get home."

"No."

Crystal's eyes grew huge, surprised by the finality of that single word, as well as the vehemence behind it. "What do you mean, 'no'?"

"There is no need for you to leave here. You can stay. With me."

Crystal turned a dark shade of red, and she felt like she was going to pass out. "Trent!" she admonished. "This is neither the time nor the place to talk about this."

Trent's eyes bored into hers, a muscle in his hard, masculine jaw twitching angrily. Suddenly he looked at his parents and said, "Sorry." Then, as if she were so much baggage, he was hauling her off.

Soon they were back in the dark confines of his car. It wasn't until he'd driven her back to Mollie's apartment that Crystal came to her senses. "How dare you embarrass me that way!"

Trent stared at her for several long seconds, then he cursed a blue streak—loud enough that she was sure everyone in the next county heard. He shoved a hand through his hair and then spoke so softly she very nearly missed his words. "Jesus! I'm sorry. I was taken by surprise when you announced that you were leaving and I simply acted on impulse. But that doesn't mean you have to go. I want you here, Crystal, with me."

"What do you mean?"

"Move in with me," he gritted out. "You haven't found a place yet, and I have more than enough room."

Crystal's face softened. Damn, this would be a lot easier if she hadn't already fallen head over heels for him. She reached her hand up and stroked a finger over his lips. He grabbed her wrist and placed several small kisses in her palm, melting her heart further. "That's sweet, Trent, but it's not right. I can't just . . . live with you. I need my own place. My own life. Besides, I need to know a man for a long while before I take such a huge step like moving in together."

He released her hand and looked out the windshield. His face shut down so fast he looked like a complete stranger to her. "I can provide for you," he said, his voice soft, but no less insistent for it. "I'm a wealthy man, as you no doubt have figured out by now. You will want for nothing."

She couldn't believe what she was hearing. "You'll 'provide for' me? What exactly are you proposing here?"

His gaze landed on her once more. "All your bills, your clothes, everything. I will take care of you. I want you to stay with me."

Shattered. With a few well-chosen words, he'd managed to shatter her heart and soul. "I can't believe you just offered that to me." She shook her head and opened the door. "You're a fool, Trent." Crystal started to get out, but he wasn't quite through digging at her heart.

"You care about me, damn it," he muttered. "Don't deny it."

He'd just offered to keep her, as if she were a high-priced whore, and she was supposed to just swoon? But something about his tone made her think that he was purposely pushing her away. Crystal hadn't expected that. She'd thought he would

182 / Anne Rainey

fight the issue a little harder. He didn't seem the type to give in so easily. Unless, of course, he really didn't care for her. Had it all been about sex to him? That's when the truth struck Crystal, as if it were a fist in the gut. She really had been nothing but a good time for him.

"Yeah, I care about you. But I care about myself, too. I won't be a doormat for any man. Not anymore," she muttered. With that, Crystal fled from the car, determined to be out of his sight before the dam broke. She wanted to turn around. She really did. She ached to hurl a few insults right back at him. To slap him for doing this to her. For making her fall for him. But she knew that if she started, she wouldn't be able to stop until she was empty. Moreover, she'd regret it later. So instead, she turned, entered the apartment, and waited until he'd driven away before letting the tears fall.

When she reached her bedroom, it took three tries before she managed to open the door. Once inside, she dropped onto the bed and let go completely. She'd never cried so hard in her life. It was as if a vital part of her had just been taken away by the cruel hand of fate. Sometimes life really did suck.

She had no idea how long she'd lain there. Twenty minutes, maybe longer. When she finally stood, Crystal looked in her mirror and saw her swollen eyes and red, blotchy cheeks. She pictured Trent's large form filling the car, anger filling his normally kind eyes.

Crystal pried her eyes away from the mirror and headed to the bathroom. When Richard had served her with the divorce papers, it'd been like she'd been handed a new lease on life. She'd invested time in the relationship. Energy. Only to have two years of her life wasted on Richard.

Trent was a far different story. Being with him made her feel like a woman. Vibrant and adventurous. Scared and happy. She'd wanted to experience things with him, the good and the bad. She'd let her defenses down. Now she was left a bleeding mess. She wouldn't make the same mistake again.

An hour later, Mollie came home. When she saw Crystal on the couch scarfing down a tub of ice cream she said, "Oh no, that can't be good."

"Men suck."

Mollie sighed and sat down beside her, then plucked the ice cream out of her hand. "Some men do, yes. But not all of them."

"I'm convinced your Alex was the last good one left on this earth."

Mollie cocked her head to the side. "Wait, are we mad at Trent or Mac? Or both?"

"Trent. Mac didn't do anything wrong. He's been wonderful, actually."

"But Trent stuck his foot in it, huh?"

"He offered to have me move in with him. He seemed to think it was a good solution to my lack of a permanent home."

"Okay, so far that doesn't sound horrible."

"When I told him I wanted my own space, he added the kicker. He offered to pay to keep me."

"Oh snap, he did not," Mollie gritted out. "What the hell was he thinking?"

"I suspect he wasn't thinking with the right head," Crystal replied. "The jerk."

Mollie handed her back the ice cream. "Go ahead, you need it."

Crystal smiled as she went to work on the double fudge. "I'm going to hate myself later, but to hell with it."

"Crystal?"

"Yeah?" she said around a mouthful of creamy deliciousness.

"Are you in love with Trent?"

"I'm ninety-nine percent sure I'm head over heels for both of them," she said, admitting it for the first time. "I'm sorry for being such a Grumpy Gus. I'm lucky to have a friend like you. I really mean that, Mollie."

"We're lucky to have each other," Mollie said as she patted

her on the shoulder. "Now, what are you going to do about this little quandary?"

Crystal frowned. "Eat myself into a sugar coma?"

She chuckled. "You could do that, but you need to think about something else before you head down that depressing road."

"What?"

"Look, I've seen the way Trent looks at you. The way Mac looks at you."

Crystal wrapped her hands around the cold cardboard carton. This was one of those moments that was sort of like ripping off a bandage: she needed to get it over with fast and with as little pain as possible. "I've made love to both Mac and Trent. At the same time. More than once. And it was fan-freaking-tastic. But that doesn't mean Trent wants more than sex from me. I'm convenient, that's all."

Mollie blushed. "Okay, that sure does paint a picture. Still, I don't think Trent thinks of you that way. If he only wanted a convenient sex partner, he could have his pick at Kinks."

Crystal slumped, feeling awful as she thought of Trent moving on to someone else. "Yeah, there'd be a line of women if he snapped his fingers. Damn it."

"So, do something about it, then. Get that man back," Mollie said as she swatted Crystal on the thigh.

Crystal wondered if she even should. Did Trent truly care about her, or had it just been a fun time for him? "What do you propose?"

"I don't know, but I'm sure if we put our heads together we'll think of something."

"Damn, this is all so complicated. It was supposed to be one night. Something wild and fun. But now I think I'm in love with them. How crazy, right?"

Mollie squinted at her. "Ah, so that's what's bothering you. It's unconventional to love them both at once."

Crystal shrugged and toyed with her spoon. "I've always imagined falling in love and having kids, then living all happily ever after."

"You can have that with both Mac and Trent. It'll be difficult, but what relationship is easy?"

Crystal frowned. "This isn't just difficult. This is a mess."

"What's the alternative? Walk away and miss out on something amazing? I know what it's like to be lonely, Crystal. It's no fun, believe me."

"You mean because of Alex passing away?"

"Alex left me devastated. I didn't think I'd get through it. With the help of friends like you, I did. But it's still painful at times." She took a deep breath and said, "Don't let some old-school idea of what love and marriage should be ruin a good chance here. Talk to Trent. In fact, you should tell them both how you feel."

Crystal stared at her melting ice cream. "I'm so scared, though."

"You're letting Richard influence you, sweetie. You need to take a chance on these guys. They aren't cut from the same cloth as your ex."

Crystal bit her lip, still unsure. "But what will people think? What will my mom think?"

Mollie waved the words away. "I've met your mom. She might have a hard time with it at first, but she'll get over it. She loves you."

"You're right," Crystal said with a smile. "Thanks."

"You're welcome," Mollie said, a naughty grin coming over her face. "And I have an idea."

Crystal snorted. "Should I be concerned?"

"You and I are going to go to Kinks. And we're going to flirt."

"Jealousy?" she asked. "Isn't that a little juvenile?"

She shrugged. "Maybe, but it never fails."

"And if it does fail?"

"We'll buy more ice cream," Mollie promised. "Lots of it."

She laughed. "Thanks, Mollie. I love you."

"Back atcha, sweetie." Mollie stood and pulled Crystal to her feet. "Now, go shower. You look like shit." She snagged the ice cream out of her hands and headed toward the kitchen.

Crystal snorted. "Gee, thanks."

"What are friends for?" she called over her shoulder as she left the room.

Crystal headed for the bathroom, her steps a little lighter now that she had something of a plan. If it failed, well, it wouldn't. She'd see to it, because losing Trent was too suckish to consider.

13

For hours, Trent had sat at the small round table in the kitchen of Kinks while Mac grumbled about decisions they were making over the new club they planned to open. Frankly, Trent didn't see what the problem was. Everything was going according to plan. They'd made good, solid choices as to the building they planned to lease and the renovations that would need to be done before they could move forward. Mac should be in a good mood, instead of bitching at every turn.

"What gives with you today? You're in a shitty mood. Did you have a fight with Crystal?" Trent asked.

Mac stood abruptly and paced around the room. His agitation puzzled Trent. It worried him that Mac was so obviously bothered. He'd thought Mac and Crystal had been getting along great—unlike the way he'd bungled everything with her. But if that was the case, then what was up Mac's craw today?

"Okay, spit it out. What is it you aren't telling me?" The instant Mac turned around, Trent knew he'd hit a nerve. There *was* something Mac was not sharing.

"What the hell is going on?" Trent prompted further.

Mac came back to the table and sat, then shoved his fingers through his hair. He'd never seen his good-natured friend so stressed. His own words to Crystal came back to haunt him. Damn, he hoped they hadn't both fucked up with her. Wouldn't that just be a kick in the teeth?

"I told her I love her," Mac muttered as he stared at the tabletop.

Trent was dumbfounded as to why that would put Mac in a foul mood. "That's great, right?"

"She never said it back. Now I feel like an idiot." He paused then added, "I mean, I know she cares, but that asshole of an ex-husband of hers has really done a number on her. I'm worried she may never let herself be that vulnerable again."

Trent shot to his feet, every muscle in his body pumped and ready for a fight. "That bastard deserves to bleed for the way he treated Crystal."

"You'll get no arguments from me." Mac shook his head. "He's called her a couple of times, did you know that? It's really pissing me off."

"He showed up at Mollie's apartment one day, too. If I hadn't been stopping by, Crystal would've been alone with him." Trent balled his fists at his sides, wishing he'd knocked some sense into the guy when he'd had the chance. "Exactly when were the phone calls?" When Mac told him the dates, Trent cursed. "That means he's contacted her even after I sent him away. Persistent bastard, isn't he?"

"Yeah. It worries me. I don't think he's just going to disappear," Mac answered.

Trent willed himself to stay calm. Nothing would happen to Crystal. It couldn't. "We need to keep an eye on her."

Mac's jaw went rigid, and his eyes grew cold. "I'm not letting him within spitting distance of Crystal. Hell, now I'm thankful she didn't find an apartment yet. At least she's not alone at night."

"I may have a minor problem keeping an eye on Crystal."

Mac frowned. "Why?"

"She's pissed at me," he grumbled.

"What the hell did you do?" Mac asked as he glared at him.

Trent threw up his hands in surrender. "Look, I love Crystal, too. I'd make her my wife if I could."

Mac's eyes lit with amusement. "Since you tend to bury your emotions under a ton of concrete on a good day, I take it she doesn't know how you feel, am I right?"

"Pretty much," Trent admitted, wishing he could undo all the damage he'd done between him and Crystal. "Right now she would rather I stick my head in the nearest toilet."

"Damn, what'd you do?"

"I asked her to live with me."

"I'm not following you. What is so wrong in that? A lot of couples live together."

"Yeah, but when I did it, I offered her money. Offered to pay her expenses and shit."

Mac's eyes shot wide. "Like a mistress? Shit, Trent, it's a wonder you can still walk!"

"I didn't mean for it to come out like that. She was leaving and I panicked."

Mac arched a brow at him. "Gee, you think?"

"I want her back," he said, his voice rough with emotion. "She's everything I could ever want in a woman. I can't imagine my life without her."

"I know the feeling, but what if she decides she doesn't want either one of us?"

"I still need to try," he replied. "I knew it the instant she walked into Kinks, that she was different. Somehow the three of us . . . it works. I never thought it would, but it does."

Mac smiled. "She really is something. This type of relationship is always tough, but she fits us. Like the piece we've been missing." Mac's eyebrows pulled together as he asked, "So, you're certain you'll be content never sampling another woman?"

The answer to that was easy. "My desire is only for Crystal. I imagine her pregnant with my child and the image doesn't send a shiver of fear through me like it once did."

"The very idea of becoming a father would've caused my manhood to shrivel at one time, but not now," Mac confessed.

Trent cocked his head and looked at Mac. "We both love her. Did you think that would ever happen?"

"No, I didn't," he admitted. "But if you want to keep our trio intact, then you need to do some serious apologizing."

"Yeah, that's what I figured. Got any ideas for me?"

Mac stroked his chin and grinned. "Not really."

Trent wanted to strangle him. "You're enjoying this too much."

Mac chuckled. "Hey, she might decide we're both too much damn trouble. I wouldn't blame her, either." They were both silent a moment before Mac finally said, "Maybe you should send her a big bunch of flowers, then get on your knees and tell her what a fool you've been. Don't women sort of dig that kind of romantic crap?"

"Am I a fool for loving a woman who would rather see me strung up by my ears?"

"Yes, but men have been making fools of themselves since Adam and Eve. Why stop now?"

"True." Besides, if she laughed in his face, then he'd think of something else to do to win her back. If he knew one thing about himself, it was that he had a stubborn streak a mile wide. One way or the other he'd get her back.

By the time Crystal and Mollie had arrived at Kinks, she was having some serious second thoughts. "What the hell was I thinking wearing this thing?" Crystal hissed as she and Mollie walked into the club. "I feel like I'm wearing a freaking tube sock."

Mollie winked as she looked her friend over from head to toe. "Yeah, but you look really hot. He'll have to drag his tongue off the floor once he gets a load of you. You'll see."

Crystal groaned, suddenly not so sure about anything. "And what about you, huh? I didn't even know you owned a dress like that."

"I have a wild side, girlfriend. I just don't let it out to play very often."

"I can see that." Crystal looked at Mollie again. The dress she wore was black, strapless, and short enough to stop traffic. She could see Mollie's cleavage, though she didn't realize her friend even had cleavage until tonight. Mollie looked sexy and wild with her hair piled on top of her head and little tendrils falling down around her shoulders. With Mollie's large, almond-shaped eyes and full, ruby-red lips, she could have passed for a gorgeous starlet. Crystal hadn't realized Mollie could look so incredible.

Not that what Crystal wore was anything less than drop-dead gorgeous. The narrow strip of cream silk that wrapped around her body was the most lethal thing she'd ever worn. It left her feeling exposed, as if she were on display in a department store window. It was disconcerting, to say the least.

After searching her closet for what had seemed like hours, they'd both agreed to do lunch together and go dress shopping. Crystal needed something devastating to suit the occasion. Mollie had taken her under her wing by escorting her to one of her favorite boutiques. Crystal hadn't even realized Mollie had a favorite boutique. The woman had been holding out on her, that much was as plain as day.

Side by side, Mollie and Crystal strode up to the bar and grabbed a stool. The bartender came over straightaway. "Nice to have you ladies back. What will it be this time? Two club sodas?"

Crystal was surprised he'd remembered her at all. She didn't think she'd made that much of an impression on him the last time, considering he'd been swamped with customers and she hadn't stayed around any longer than it took to take a few sips of her drink. Apparently, she'd been wrong.

"Yep, works for me. Mollie?"

"The same, thank you," Mollie said, giving the man a beaming smile.

"Coming right up." The bartender's eyes lit with warmth and lingered on Mollie's cleavage for an extra few seconds before he sauntered off to fill their order.

After he left, Crystal leaned in and said, "Girl, you are just full of surprises tonight."

Mollie looked at her, puzzled. "Why?"

"Just look at you. You're gorgeous, and every man in this place is staring. Heck, I wouldn't be surprised if our drinks were free, and all the ones after that."

"You know, it's sort of good to have a guy look at me with desire in his eyes," Mollie said, sounding entirely too sad for Crystal's peace of mind. "After Alex passed away, it was hard to get used to. I felt like I was cheating on him if I encouraged a man."

Crystal linked her arm with Mollie's and said, "Alex would want you to be happy. You need to remember that."

She smiled, but it didn't quite reach her eyes. "Let's leave him out of this tonight. Right now it's all about having fun, right? You and me and getting a little something for ourselves."

Crystal sat up a little straighter. "Right you are."

When the bartender returned with their drinks, he said, "Drinks are on that gentleman over there." He placed their glasses down in front of them and pointed to a man at the far end of the bar.

He was good-looking, but he wasn't Trent or Mac. Crystal

smiled and brought the drink to her lips. When she put it down, she saw a movement out of the corner of her eye. She turned her head and saw Josh walking through the door. Immediately, his eyes sought out Mollie, as if they'd been drawn to her. Mollie looked at Crystal, followed her line of vision, and fell so incredibly silent she didn't think her friend was even breathing. The chemistry arcing back and forth between the two was something for the record books. He started toward them, and Mollie stiffened.

"Hello, Crystal, care to introduce me to your companion?"

"Mollie Alexander, meet Josh Dailey, Trent's brother."

Josh took Mollie's hand in the same old world way he'd taken Crystal's upon meeting her for the first time, then he kissed the back of it. He had a decidedly devilish gleam of arousal in his eyes. Now, *that* wasn't there the first time he'd met Crystal. She wasn't sure what to make of Josh. He seemed like a huge flirt, and Crystal wasn't too keen on the idea of him getting all hot and bothered for Mollie. Mollie was a little raw tonight; she didn't need a guy to mess with her head. Crystal was about to say just that, when Josh broke her train of thought.

"I assume you're here for Trent?"

"Actually, I'm just here with Mollie," she said, then added, "Trent and I didn't have plans tonight."

Josh frowned at her dress. "I see," he said. He looked back over at Mollie as if she were a tall glass of water and he'd just come in from the desert. When Josh glanced at his cell phone, his brows drew together. "Would you two care to join me at a table, then?"

"Sounds good," Mollie chimed in, a little too quickly for Crystal's peace of mind.

"Mollie, I thought we were here to, ah, mingle. Remember?"

"We are mingling—with Josh," Mollie said as she eyeballed the man.

"Yes, great idea, mingle with me, ladies." He held out both

arms and grinned as Crystal gave in with a sigh and took one, while Mollie took the other with a rather beaming smile. He led them to a table in the corner, then looked the two of them over from head to toe before remarking, "You two sure are turning a lot of heads tonight." He looked back and forth between them both. As his gaze landed on Mollie, he lingered. "Beautiful." He seated them, politely holding each of their chairs. They no sooner got their tushes planted than someone was tapping Crystal on the shoulder. She turned and saw a handsome man staring at her with a wide grin.

"You here alone, darlin'?"

Crystal very nearly gave him the brush-off, then remembered her plan and changed her frown to a smile. "Yep."

She started to get up, only to have Josh stop her with a large hand on her shoulder. "Are you sure you don't want to wait for Trent? He'll be along any minute."

"No, but thank you," she said, turning down Josh's offer. Crystal let the stranger lead her to the dance floor.

He pulled her into his arms and whispered against her ear, "Name's Brad."

"I'm Crystal," she said, wishing she wasn't aware of how different and wrong it felt to be in the man's arms. She wanted to be in Trent's arms. Or Mac's. No one else would do.

"So, Crystal, what's a beautiful woman like you doing alone at Kinks?"

"What's a handsome man like you doing alone at Kinks?" she tossed right back. He chuckled, but the timbre of his voice wasn't the same deep, intoxicating sound as Trent's.

"It must be our lucky day, that's the only thing I can figure," he drawled, then pulled her in tight as he moved along with the slow beat of the music.

Brad's body was big and muscular. He was handsome and polite. His voice was as silky and as deep as crushed velvet. Still, there were only two men she wanted pressed up against her. Two men who could make her body hum with desire in ten seconds flat. Brad was neither of those men. And she was just so damn pissed that Mac and Trent weren't there, watching her dance with a gorgeous guy right at that moment. So they could see that she'd moved on. That she wasn't going to wallow in self-pity. That she wasn't going to sit around and wish for something that could never be.

Oh, who the hell was she kidding? She wanted Mac and Trent there so they would get insanely jealous and rip her out of Brad's strong arms and . . . was that a tattoo?

"What is that?"

Brad followed her line of vision. His grin turned rather ornery as he answered, "It means good fortune. I believe it's an Asian symbol." He shrugged. "It was an impulse thing."

Crystal laughed. "Does it work? Have you had good fortune?"

He winked and pulled her close again. "Seems to be working for me tonight," he whispered into her ear.

Whoa. Now this was getting to be too much. The fact that a gorgeous man was holding her in his arms and whispering in her ear and she felt not one iota of interest was enough for Crystal to freeze up a bit. Maybe give Brad a hint or two.

Crystal pushed back just the slightest, grateful that he didn't protest, and she tried to sound kind as she let him down flat. "You're a very . . . interesting man, Brad. But I'm afraid we'll have to keep the dirty dancing out of it for the time being."

Brad stared down at her for long seconds, then glanced back over to where Mollie and Josh sat. "I know you're not with that big fella sitting at the table you just vacated, because he's all over your girlfriend. So, who is it that's keeping me from my fortune tonight?"

Crystal tried not to feel the kick in her gut as she thought of Trent. She looked away from Brad's suddenly very serious brown eyes and answered his question. "His brother. But he's

not interested in me any longer. I only came here tonight to . . .
I don't know why I came."

Brad pulled her back into his embrace, only this time he
seemed to keep it on a more platonic level. The intensity that
had been radiating from him was gone, replaced by a man who
admitted defeat with rather remarkable aplomb. "If you wanted
to rile him up, don't look now, but I think you've accomplished
that particular goal. In fact, I'd hazard a guess that he's none too
pleased with either of us right now."

Crystal started to swivel her head around to see if Trent was
there—it had been too long since she'd seen his gorgeous, chiseled face—but Brad stopped her.

"Ah, now hold up there, darlin'. You want him to come
after you, don't you?"

"Yes," Crystal replied, all the while wishing she could just
go to Trent and smack some sense into him.

Brad winked. "Then just follow my lead and he won't be
able to resist."

"He probably could care less if I'm dancing with another
man. This whole thing was a mistake, I just knew it. I should
just go home and put on my pj's," Crystal ground out, feeling
more the fool every minute.

Brad chuckled low and bent to whisper into her ear, "Don't
bet on it, darlin', it's eating him up watching me tell you all my
dirty little fantasies right now. Hell, he never even made it past
the front door. He's just standing there, looking for all the
world like a raging bull ready to charge."

Oh, now didn't that just give a girl a grin? "So, you think if
I whisper back in your ear he'll maybe get the lead out?"

"I guarantee it."

Crystal grinned, a bit of the naughty vixen surfacing, and
she rose up on tiptoe, her breasts flattening against Brad's chest
as she did. She spoke in a low whisper for Brad's ears alone,
"There's no way I'll ever tell you my dirty secrets, Brad, but I

don't mind making that man a bit nuts, since I've been going insane ever since I met him."

"Mm, you can tell me anything, so long as you keep that sweet body of yours pressed tight."

Crystal pulled back and slapped Brad's chest playfully. "You really are a flirt. And trouble, if I had to guess."

"Right on both counts," Brad said, as he straightened a bit. "Here he comes now."

Crystal shook with nerves, but Brad's strong arms around her kept her from falling on her face. Thank God for small favors.

"Whoa, he's a mean-looking one," Brad bit out.

"Crystal."

The deep, dark voice was barely recognizable, it was so cold and remote. Where was the warm, cajoling tone she remembered?

She turned her head and pretended to just now notice him, even though she knew she was a lousy ass liar. "Trent! I didn't realize you were here."

"Just arrived," Trent answered as he pinned Brad with a steely look. "Care to introduce me to your friend?"

Crystal looked back at Brad and saw the mischievous glint in his eyes. She knew two things in that moment. One, Brad was probably one hell of an ornery child. His mother deserved a medal. Second, there was about to be lots of bloodshed, because it was clear that her plan to get Trent to realize he'd made a huge mistake in offering her money for services rendered was about to blow sky-high. She'd seriously miscalculated just how jealous the man could be.

Damn and double damn.

"I'm Trent Dailey, and I own this nightclub. You are?"

Brad dropped his arms from around her, and Crystal suddenly felt very afraid. While Brad had been holding her, she'd had a false sense of security—sort of like having a cell phone handy when you're driving down a lonely, deserted street, even though you know that, should something happen, the cell phone would probably be out of range and rendered useless. That was how she felt at that moment—rendered useless.

"Name's Brad Mayes." The two men shook hands as if they were greeting a new pal. As if you couldn't cut the tension between them with a knife.

Trent nodded and then zeroed his powerful gaze on her. He looked at her from head to toe, and she watched as a muscle twitched in his jaw. He never said a word about her outfit. "I didn't know you were coming here tonight," he gritted out.

"I know," she said, unable to say more for the lump in her throat.

His gaze seemed to devour her, and Crystal shivered from head to toe. "You don't own a single dress like this," he said in a low voice. "Your clothes are classy. This is—is something a call girl would wear."

His angry voice shook her to her bones, but she was still too furious with him over his offer to "keep her" to stay on the side of caution. "Isn't that what you wanted me to be? Actually, this dress ought to fit the image you have of me much better."

He shoved a hand through his hair. "Will you never forget about that? You're the most stubborn woman!"

Her anger drained away at his description. Was she truly that stubborn? She had no retort. Nothing at all came to mind.

Trent cupped her face in his large, calloused palms. "I don't want to keep picking at this wound. You're here now, and I want to show you something."

Crystal looked around and realized Brad had disappeared. "Yes, I'm here. I'm not sure why I haven't walked out yet, though."

"Come with me," he said as he led her to the private apartment upstairs. Once inside, he flipped on the light and said, "I've missed you."

"Trent," she said his name in warning as she crossed her arms over her chest.

His expression was one of comfort, as if he was trying to let her know that everything would be okay. His anger dissipated, and he was once again in control of his emotions. She wished she was so quick to bounce back. But then his heart wasn't breaking with every sliver of time she spent with him. He didn't know that she was deeply, madly, helplessly in love.

Trent reached out for her hand, and Crystal stared at it a moment as if in a daze, then finally she took it. He held it tight and pulled her over to the bed. He gently sat her down on the side of the bed, then to her utter shock, he knelt in front of her and said, "I'm sorry for what I said. I've been slowly dying since you left me."

In that moment, Crystal saw a vulnerable side to Trent. He'd seemed so confident and in control. Watching him now, she knew she wasn't the only one with their emotions in overdrive. It went a long way to soothe her ravaged heart.

"You don't want any other men except Mac and me," he whispered. "You sure as hell don't want Brad."

It wasn't a question, but she answered him anyway. "No, and it's frustrating, believe me."

He frowned. "Why does this bother you, baby?"

"Because you're no good for me, Trent. You insulted me, and still here I sit." She covered her face in her hands and groaned.

Trent pried her fingers away and brought them to his lips, where he kissed each fingertip with relish. Crystal opened her eyes to see Trent staring at her hands.

"You were slipping through my fingers, like water. I thought to capture you before you were gone completely."

"I don't understand."

"I reacted badly with you," he explained as he looked back up at her. "I wanted you to stay and you made me feel . . . needy. I'm not real good at feeling needy. It goes against my very nature."

He stroked her cheek with his thumb and murmured, "You send me out of control every time you're near me."

She understood because she felt the same way. "This may come as a shock, but you aren't the only one who hates that feeling."

Trent's eyes held hers captive as he wrapped his hand around the nape of her neck and drew her close. "Mm, so I'm beginning to see," he murmured, then he kissed her. It was so brief and soft, she barely had time to take in his scent before he pulled away. "This evening is for you."

She had no idea what he meant by that, but when he released her and pushed her backward until she was sprawled atop the cool blankets, she forgot everything she was thinking. Her worries flew out the window as erotic images of her gorgeous lover filled her head.

Trent, in all his bronzed and dark-haired glory, stripped out of his clothes and spread out on the bed next to her. His well-muscled body and the intensity in his eyes were enough to have any woman drooling, but the heavy weight between his legs made her face burn. He was hard and ready, and he was all hers.

Crystal tore her eyes away from his erection and searched his face for answers. He didn't wear his heart on his sleeve the way she did, but Crystal could still make out his thoughts. It was as if he was trying to reassure her, even encourage her to take the lead. She was lost to this new type of lovemaking.

Trent wrapped his arm around her shoulders and pulled her stiff body in tight. She was as rigid as a wooden plank, every muscle strung tight with nerves and fear.

"Relax. Leave all the big questions for later. For now, just feel my body against yours," Trent softly commanded, his voice so rich and smooth, sliding over her skin, soothing and firing her blood at the same time.

"It all feels different now. I'm scared," she confessed and buried her nose into his side.

"I know, but it will be okay," Trent promised.

She didn't move. Her intense emotions for him had her feeling like an open wound.

"You aren't relaxing. I need you to leave everything for later and simply take joy in our bodies. Think only of the two of us and how good we are together."

Crystal wanted to strangle Trent. *He wants relaxed, I'll give him relaxed,* she thought with venom. With the single-minded purpose of making Trent squirm, Crystal began touching him. She moved her right hand first, smoothing it over his pectorals, running her fingers through the coarse curls that littered his chest. Then she inched her leg up and over his, letting her sex slide along the side of his muscular thigh. Trent groaned and she continued, encouraged by the hungry sounds coming from him.

She teased her fingers down the front of him, giving herself free rein, as in some dark part of her soul, Crystal enjoyed having Trent at her mercy. Evidently, she had a bit of the dominatrix in her. Who knew?

"You are so sweet, Crystal, so soft," Trent complimented. His hands skated over her overheated skin, as his lips pressed into her hair.

Crystal brushed her fingers over the head of his cock, rubbing the pearl of moisture all around, then brought her fingers to her lips and sucked the sticky fluid off them one by one. Trent groaned and pulled her on top of his huge body. He grinned wickedly up at her, then drew her down for a kiss. His lips, so warm and eager, tasted her as if he wanted to spend a good long time pleasuring each and every part of her with his mouth. Lips parted and tongues met in a wild mating dance, and all the while his hands massaged and caressed. When his fingers came so close to her clitoris, she broke the kiss and opened her eyes.

"Let me."

"I'm still mad at you. I'm only a challenge to you. You saw

me walking away and you wanted me all the more." Even as she said it, she knew it was a lie.

Trent stroked her nether lips. Crystal's body vibrated at his touch. "I love you. My life without you is like a day without sun," Trent murmured. "You are a challenge, yes, but that is only one of the things I love about you, not the only thing. You should know better, baby. I do not play such childish games."

"But I—"

Trent stopped her torrent of questions with a lingering kiss. Afterward, he raised his head a mere inch. "No more talking," Trent ordered. "Just feel. Drop your guard and give yourself to this moment."

He loved her. Trent was in love with her. Crystal's heart soared to the clouds and beyond as his words sank in. Here she was, lying atop the wild and rugged man, his hands all over her, stroking and touching and driving her crazy with need, and all she could think was, *He loves me.*

"Will you let me make you feel good?" Trent asked. That's when she noticed he hadn't gone beyond touching her. He was waiting for her consent. The decision was an easy one.

"Only if I can do the same for you," she answered, grinning down at him. Trent gave her a sexy hum of approval. He seemed to need no other incentive.

In another heartbeat, Crystal found herself flat on her back with Trent leaving the bed. She waited, unsure what he would do next. He went to the closet again and retrieved a small wooden box. She frowned. "What is that?"

"Something for your pleasure."

Feeling naughty, she whispered, "I thought that's what *you* were for."

"Mm, you're in a mood, aren't you?"

She couldn't deny it. It'd been too long since she'd had him inside her. She was desperate for the connection. "Yes, so hurry."

"Impatient little thing," he crooned, then came to sit on the bed beside her. She rolled to her side and propped her head on her hand to watch as he opened the box. She let out a startled squeak when he raised the lid. Enfolded in red velvet lay a dildo.

"Uh, I don't know about this, Trent."

"You wish Mac were here with us, don't you?"

She bit her lip and nodded.

He winked. "That's what I thought. I can't give you that right now, so this will have to do."

When he lifted the flesh-toned tool from its bed of velvet and brought it between her legs, she stiffened. With tender care, Trent stroked her clit with it. Crystal was amazed to note its warmth. She'd thought it'd feel cold and unnatural.

It didn't.

It wasn't as if she'd never seen or felt a dildo before. After all, what single woman wasn't familiar with one of those babies? Still, it was the first time she'd ever had a man use one on her during sex.

"Get up on all fours for me, baby."

Crystal obeyed, her blood racing, her body wild with anticipation. Moving behind her, now on his knees, Trent stroked the seam between her buttocks with his index finger. A moan erupted from deep within her as he let his finger drift back and forth over her puckered opening. She wanted him there and she knew he wanted to be there just as badly.

He leaned over her and kissed the base of her spine. "You like your ass fucked, huh? Remember how sweet and tight it feels?"

"Yes, Trent. Oh yes, I could never forget." Her voice had gone hoarse with need long ago.

"Would you like me there now, while the dildo fucks your wet pussy? Do you think you can handle both at the same time, baby?"

"Trent, please."

"I love the sound of my name on your lips," Trent urged, then he let his finger penetrate her, little by little, until he was buried deep inside her anus. She shuddered and pushed against him. His finger moved in and out, fucking her with slow precision.

Just as Crystal started to think she could take no more of his teasing, one of Trent's big, warm hands clutched her hips. He told her to hold still and she obeyed. Then his hand was holding the dildo. She felt him caressing her clit with the large toy. Crystal writhed and moved in time to his strokes. When she squeezed her bottom, Trent growled.

"I thought I told you to hold still." Crystal couldn't concentrate on Trent's words. Thankfully he didn't wait for a reply. "Such sweet torture you are."

She moaned and wriggled. Her breasts swelled and her sex grew damp. His finger pumped her ass, while the dildo slid back and forth over her swollen nub. Crystal felt every heated touch. He was slow at first, then faster, and soon a second finger joined the first and Crystal went wild, her inhibitions dropped as need rushed in and took command. She gyrated against Trent while he tormented her with the toy. When he leaned down and bit her hip, she lost it.

Her climax came from somewhere deep inside. Crystal screamed hard and loud, her back arching as her body flew apart. Everything she thought she knew about sexual pleasure seemed to pale in the wake of what she was experiencing. Trent's rough voice just barely broke through the quagmire of her mind.

"I want this ass, Crystal," Trent hissed, then he moved his fingers out of her and cupped her dripping mound. "Look at me, baby."

She turned her head, already limp and sweating from her orgasm, but when she saw the intensity, the insane yearning etched into his not-so-perfect features, her body went from sated to hungry all over again.

"You are mine. From this moment forward, you are mine."

No words sprang to mind over such a bold claim so she stayed silent. When the heavy weight of Trent's cock entered her bottom and the thick toy nudged into her sex, her inner muscles clenched. She automatically attempted to close her legs, panicked and scared. It was too much, too soon.

"Trent, I can't!" she cried out, her body tensing further.

Trent pulled out instantly. "Shh, it's okay. No need to hurry, baby."

Crystal relaxed a little, relieved by Trent's words. He slowly slid the toy deep inside her vagina and held it there, then leaned down and kissed her shoulder. She rocked against him when his tongue flicked over the sensitive spot behind her ear. Her panic disappeared and her body hummed back to life.

"You will enjoy this," he whispered into her ear, "but I know you're still mad at me. Give me a second chance. I'm not like Richard. I would never hurt you the way he did. I might make mistakes, but I'd never intentionally cause you pain, I promise."

He never waited for a reply, only began stroking her hair and smoothing a palm down her arm to her hip, where he cupped her bottom and kneaded the plump flesh. She melted, giving them both what they needed in that moment. Trent felt it instantly and began a slow glide into her ass, filling her. She felt a delicious sort of pressure and friction. Fullness, oh God, so full, but not so much that it hurt. It was like nothing she'd ever experienced before. The silky inner walls of her vagina were caressed with gentle thrusts from the toy. The taboo nature of what they were doing sent a rush of rapture through her.

With each inward stroke from Trent, the dildo was pulled outward. Her muscles held them both tight, and she squeezed her ass, giving Trent the pleasure and pain that he craved.

Trent shouted her name and pushed against her hips one last time, spilling his seed deep. Crystal felt his every spasm, and it spurred her own orgasm.

Trent pulled the toy free and tossed it aside, then they both collapsed onto the bed. He brushed her damp hair from her face and kissed her cheek. "I love you, baby."

"Wait," she blurted out. She hadn't even known she was going to say it. But now that it was out, she knew it was the right thing to say.

His head shot back as if she'd slapped him. "What?"

She pushed out of his arms and stood up. "I need time to think, Trent," she said as she began getting into her clothes. "About everything. You. Mac. Me. I feel like I've been on a roller-coaster ride and I need to stop and get off. Even if it's only for a day or two."

He stared at her for several intense seconds, then got off the bed and went to her. "Fine. Take your time and think things through. But while you're doing that, remember what I said. I may make mistakes with you, but my love is true."

He dipped his head and kissed her, leaving her breathless. As Crystal walked away from him, her mind focused on keeping her head high and her legs moving, she knew that there was no way she would ever be whole without Trent and Mac in her life. They'd stolen her heart, and that was that.

Crystal hadn't seen Trent or Mac for a full week. She'd asked them for time to think, and they'd granted it. But each day away from them had caused her heart to ache. Now, as she stood on the porch of Trent's home, shaking with nerves and her stomach in knots, Crystal thought again about how much time she'd wasted, all because of her own insecurities. Richard had done a lot of damage, but it wasn't irreparable. She wasn't going to give up on love. And she loved both Trent and Mac. Who cared if it wasn't a traditional relationship? She knew with the two of them, she would always be cherished. Now she aimed to set things right. If Trent slammed the door in her face, so be it, but at least she had to try.

She took a deep breath and rang the bell. Out of her peripheral vision, she noticed a man striding up the sidewalk. When she turned and saw Richard, her mind stuttered to a halt and her heart seemed to stop beating. The look in his eyes was something out of her nightmares. She suddenly felt as if she'd been tossed into a bad horror movie. She started to move backward, but then her ex struck her across the face so hard she fell to the porch. Time seemed to stand still as she watched the scene unfold around her. The fear of him killing her had her attempting to crawl away. When she heard him whisper her name, it spurred her on. But he was bigger and stronger, and the last thing she thought of before the world went black was how close she'd come to finding her happily-ever-after with the men of her dreams.

14

Mac had waited a week to hear from Crystal. They'd exchanged texts, but nothing in the last twenty-four hours. He'd sent several messages to her with no reply. Finally, he'd called Mollie, and she'd said the last time she'd talked to Crystal was when she was heading out to talk to Trent. But Trent hadn't seen her, either. The hair on the back of Mac's neck rose. Something was wrong, he could feel it.

As he stood at the door to Mollie's apartment, his impatience had him knocking louder and longer than he'd intended. Of course Crystal didn't answer because she was most likely already in bed by now, but the only thing that mattered was seeing her, at home and safe. When no one answered the door, Mac became edgy. "Crystal!" he called out as he looked in the front window. Instinctively he knew he wouldn't get an answer. She wasn't there.

Mac began to run through his options. It was late, and something told him she wasn't out partying. The idea that something could've happened to her sent fear and anger traveling through his body. Had Richard come around again? God help the man if she suffered even an ounce of pain because of her ex.

Later. He would think about revenge later. Now he had to keep his head and consider where she could be. Mac got in his car and started searching, his eyes watching out for any sign of her dark hair. He took his cell phone out of his jacket pocket and called Trent.

"Did you find her?" Trent asked.

"No, have you talked to her?"

"No, damn it." He paused. "Could it be that prick of an ex?"

Mac sighed. "Fuck, I don't know, but I hope not."

"Where are you now?"

"I just left her place," Mac answered. "I've called her cell, but there was no answer. I'm going to try Mollie again."

"Should we call the police?"

"Hell, it hasn't been long enough for them to do anything."

"I'll go looking, too," Trent said. "That bastard better not touch her."

Mac could hear the barely suppressed rage in his friend's voice. "No shit."

They hung up and Mac called Mollie next. "Hey, Mollie, I can't find Crystal and I was wondering if you've heard from her yet."

"I haven't heard from her," she said with worry in her voice. "I tried to call a little bit ago, but I got her voice mail." A few beats later and Mollie's frantic voice came over the line. "Where could she be, Mac?"

His hopes took a nosedive. Even as he held the phone to his ear, his eyes scanned the sidewalks on both sides of the street. It was already ten o'clock on a Wednesday evening, and there weren't that many people out.

"I honestly don't know," Mac groaned. "I'll call you the minute I find her. Don't worry, sweetie."

"Did you two argue or anything?" Mollie rushed to ask before he could sever the connection.

"No, nothing like that. I don't think she'd ignore my calls, though, even if she was pissed."

"No, it's not like Crystal to be so thoughtless."

Mac thought the same thing. That left only her ex. "I'll find her," he vowed. There was no other option.

"Of course you will," Mollie said adamantly. "Call me the minute you do."

"I will."

They hung up, and Mac searched for another hour with no luck. He finally turned around and went back to his own place, hoping she'd shown up there while he was gone. He'd left her a note in case she did, asking her to call his cell. His mind imagined her safe and sound inside his apartment. Maybe she just hadn't spotted the note?

Mac pulled up next to the curb and killed the engine. He sprinted to the door and sent up a silent prayer that she was safe. He had visions of her lying in some gutter, cold, hurt, alone. It made him feel sick to his stomach. He pushed the door open and was met with dead silence again. She was nowhere to be found. It was as if she'd dropped off the planet.

As he turned to leave, Mac's phone dinged, signaling a text. He looked at the screen.

WANT HER? COME AND GET HER.

"Richard," Mac bit out. The address the bastard gave him wasn't far away, either. Mac quickly dialed Trent. "Son of a bitch just texted me." He told Trent where to meet him, then shoved the phone back into his pocket.

Within minutes he and Trent were standing in front of a big, run-down old two-story. As they entered the house, Trent asked, "What game is he playing, Mac?"

"I don't know, but if she's here we'll find her."

"I'll kill him if he—"

"Don't even go there," Mac interrupted. He couldn't let himself think of Crystal hurt.

After they searched the main floor and found it empty, they took to the stairs. When they reached the upper landing, Mac swiftly scanned the hallway. No one was around, or at least there didn't appear to be anyone around. He noted several doors, all closed. They'd have to open each one to find Crystal. Maybe they'd get lucky and she'd be in the first room they came to.

Mac went to the closest door on the right and turned the knob. It opened easily, probably because it was empty. Completely empty. Not even a stick of furniture, just a white-walled room. The upstairs was just like the downstairs, all modern with solid marble flooring. There wasn't a single hint of color; everything was either white or gray—like a crypt. Jesus. He closed the door and went to the one to their immediate left. Like the first, this room was also devoid of life. Okay, so maybe they weren't going to get lucky.

"This place is fucked up," Trent gritted out. "I'm not getting a good vibe here."

That was the understatement of the year. The house Richard had sent them to had very little furniture. There were piles of trash and empty beer bottles all over, and the smell of rotting meat made him gag. If this was the way Richard lived, it was weird as shit. Mac felt as if he'd just walked into the filthy den of a wild animal. Crystal had put up with a lot more than abuse during her marriage. Hell, the man wasn't playing with a full deck. Jesus, no wonder she'd been so slow to trust.

Mac moved down the hall, passing door after door until he reached the last one on the left. He stopped and listened. He heard a rustling sound. "This is the one." He could feel it in his bones. *Please, God, let her be okay.*

Without waiting another second, Mac turned the knob and the door opened easily. Inside he found Crystal tied to a chair, her mouth duct-taped shut. Her clothes were still intact, and he thanked the heavens for that much at least. The wild tangle of her hair hung around her face, and she was too damn pale. When she looked up, the fear and vulnerability in her gaze tore a hole in his heart. His rage boiled out of control.

With single-minded purpose, he and Trent practically leapt across the room. Trent yanked at the binds that held her to the chair, while Mac worked the tape loose. Mac looked around, but he didn't see Richard anywhere. This setup was too easy. Why would Richard allow them to rescue Crystal without even the slightest resistance? "Where is he?"

Her eyes widened. "Behind you!"

Mac didn't have time to think, only react. He swiveled around just as Richard jumped toward him, a machete in his hand. Mac ducked as Richard swung. Richard snarled like a rabid animal. Mac had never heard a human make such a crazed sound. Trent quickly moved behind Richard and wrapped his arms around him, giving Mac an opening. Mac knocked the machete out of Richard's hands, then delivered an uppercut to the bastard's jaw, sending him crumpling to the floor.

Trent picked up the ropes he'd removed from Crystal. "I've got him. Get Crystal."

With Richard unconscious and Trent busy tying up his hands, Mac bent down and pulled Crystal into the cradled warmth of his arms. He got pissed all over again when he felt her body shaking like a leaf. He needed to get her out of there. He wanted her home, where she belonged. Safe.

He forced his voice to sound soft and soothing, belying the

way his mind still screamed for vengeance. "Shh, it's okay now. You're safe."

"Mac?"

The sound of her voice was all it took. Relief swamped him. "Yeah, angel, you're safe now."

She seemed to hesitate, as if trying desperately to comprehend his words, then she nodded. She wouldn't look directly at him, and that bothered him. She just kept her face snuggled against the safe haven of his chest and held on tight. Mac was anxious to whisk her away from that horrid house.

"Good girl. Now just relax and soon we will be far away from this place," he said in a soothing voice. She seemed to obey, albeit reluctantly. He speared Trent with a look that conveyed his sense of urgency.

The sounds of sirens rent the air. Soon the place was filled with police officers, and Richard was taken into custody, while Crystal was loaded into an ambulance.

Several hours later, Mac and Trent had Crystal safely tucked in bed. Their statements had seemed to take forever. The only thing on Mac's mind now was the fact that he'd failed to keep her safe. Hell, he'd be lucky if she spared him a glance when this was all over.

When the doorbell rang, Mac rushed to answer it. Mollie stood on the doorstep, her gaze filled with worry. "She's okay," he murmured as he took her into his arms. "And Richard is in custody."

Mac desperately wanted to be alone with Crystal and Trent, but Mollie needed to see her friend for herself—to see that Crystal was really safe. And he knew Crystal needed to see Mollie right now, too.

"Thank you for finding her," Mollie said, her voice wobbly.

Mac put his finger under her chin and tipped her face up. Her sad expression hit him first, but underlying that was the love she had for Crystal. It went deeper than friendship. They were more like sisters. "She'll be glad to see you."

When they entered the bedroom, Trent was sitting on the side of the bed, his hand resting on Crystal's blanket-covered thigh. Crystal looked over at Mollie, and while the two women stared at one another, something seemed to shift and change. Finally, Crystal smiled. Relief swept through Mac in an instant. It was the first smile he'd seen from her since her ordeal. It was a damn good sign.

As much as he wanted to be alone with the two people he loved most in the world, it was still his first priority to aid Crystal in any way he could. Mac was grateful for Mollie in that moment.

"Mac," Mollie said, gaining his attention. "She's going to need a few things if you're up to getting them for her."

He turned and nodded. "Anything, just name it."

"I'm sure she'd be grateful for some of her own clothes, as well as a few toiletries." Mollie crossed the room then and asked, "You okay, baby?"

Crystal's lower lip quivered. "I—I couldn't do anything. I felt so . . . oh God, I felt so helpless."

In an instant, Mac and Trent were on either side of her. They wrapped her in an embrace as Trent said, "Shh, you're safe now, baby. Don't think about it anymore."

Mac smoothed his hand down her hair and whispered softly, "Trent's right. Richard can't hurt you. Not ever again."

After a short bout of tears, Crystal appeared to gather herself. She nodded. "I'm glad he's in jail. It's where he should've been ages ago."

"No argument here," Mac gritted out. He didn't move away, didn't let go of her hand. He needed that small connection with her to know she was really and truly safe.

"I'm sorry for being such a baby," Crystal said. She smiled, but it didn't quite reach her eyes. "Thanks for . . . everything, you guys."

Mollie smoothed Crystal's hair back with a compassionate hand. "From where I'm sitting, you look more like a survivor," she replied. "Some TLC and a good night's rest, and you'll be good as new. You'll see."

Crystal smiled slightly, and whispered a thank-you. Then she quickly rattled off a list of things she would need from her apartment, as if drawing on the last vestiges of strength she had. Grudgingly Mac left to get the things she'd asked for. The sooner he left to go retrieve them, the sooner he could be back with her again. She would be safe for the few minutes it would take to drive to her place and back.

After Mac left the room, Trent stood and said, "I'll go make some tea."

Crystal nodded. "That sounds wonderful." After both men were gone, she let out a breath. "God, it's all like a strange nightmare."

"Now that it's just us girls, do you want to talk about it?" Mollie asked. "It might help."

Crystal was amazed at Mollie's sharp observation. "How did you know I didn't want to talk about it in front of them?"

Mollie shrugged. "I'd have a hard time sharing something so traumatic with those two guys. They're pretty intense."

Crystal's heart did a little flip as she realized how lucky she was to have both Trent and Mac come to her aid. "I don't know what I would've done if they hadn't been there." She shuddered. "I don't know what Richard would've done."

Mollie frowned. "But they *were* there, and that's all that matters."

Already Crystal felt better with Mollie there. She closed her eyes and rested against the pillow as she went over the evening's events. "Richard showed up at Trent's house and knocked me on the back of the head. I didn't even see it coming." She shook her head at her own stupidity. "Like an idiot, I thought that if he knew I didn't love him anymore, he'd get the hint and let me go. I pleaded with him, but it only made him angrier." She hesitated, trying to put Richard's strange demeanor in proper perspective. "He's always been abusive, both physically and emotionally. But this time he didn't appear to want to harm me. It was almost like he'd convinced himself that he couldn't live without me or something." She swiped a hand across her face, pushing back strands of hair that clung to her cheek. "I've never seen him like that before. As if he'd lost all grasp on reality."

"God, you must have been so scared," Mollie said, her voice full of concern.

"When we got to that awful house, he took me upstairs and put me in the chair. He told me he'd rented it a few months ago. He's been living so close and I didn't even know." She shuddered. "Anyway, I tried to get up, to get away, but he was ready. He tied my wrists, my ankles. He started questioning me about Trent and Mac. About our relationship. He said a lot of ugly things." She looked up at Mollie, seeing her concern, and quickly finished her account. "He must have gotten Mac's number from my cell phone. I don't know, but after that he left me alone." To her complete horror she started crying again, and through trembling lips she said, "I was so scared. I really thought he was going to kill Mac and Trent."

Mollie hugged her, soothing her the way only a best friend could. "They're both way too tough to be brought down by a guy like Richard."

Crystal forced back the tears and nodded. "Yes, they are, thank God." She remembered the moment Mac and Trent had stormed through the door, looking for all the world like conquering heroes. And she knew they'd always be her heroes.

Mollie laughed. "And right about now, Mac is probably

breaking all the speed limits trying to get back here. He's been worried sick for you. He cares about you a great deal, honey. Trent, too."

"I hope so, because I think I love them—both of them."

"Damn right you do." Both women jumped when they heard Mac's deep-timbered voice.

Mollie crossed her arms over her chest and gave Mac a stern look. "Just how long have you been standing there?"

Mac strode to the bed and dropped all the things Crystal had asked for onto the end of it. "Long enough to know that Crystal loves me."

"I'd tell you how incredibly rude it is to eavesdrop, but it'll have to wait until the room stops spinning."

Right away Mac was contrite. "Tell us what to do to make you feel better."

"Love me," she whispered, taking a leap of faith. "Just love me."

"Always and forever, angel."

"Yeah, what Mac said," Trent replied as he strode into the room, carrying a tray laden with tea. He placed the tray on the bedside table, then sat down beside her. "We've loved you from the first moment we saw you."

Crystal's heart filled, and tears sprang to her eyes. "I feel like the luckiest woman in the world right about now."

Mac cocked his head to the side. "And why is that?"

She reached up and kissed his cheek, then did the same to Trent. "Because I have the two of you. Almost makes me feel like a glutton." She winked and let a small grin escape. "But not quite enough to give you up."

Mac took her face in his hands. "You're amazing and the only woman we've ever wanted to share our lives with."

"Mac's right," Trent said as he wrapped an arm around her shoulders and hugged her into his side. "You're the only one, baby."

Crystal settled against Trent and realized how right it was to be there. "So, how about we go to Hawaii for my *recovery?*"

Mac and Trent both chuckled. "Anything you want, baby," Trent said, "it's yours."

"Ditto," Mac murmured.

Oh God, she truly was the luckiest woman alive.

EPILOGUE

One month later . . .

Crystal stood on the balcony, staring out at the clear blue water. Hawaii was simply beautiful. And so much more romantic than she'd imagined. She'd been beyond pleased when Trent and Mac had offered to take her on a weeklong trip to the tropical islands. It was exactly what she'd needed to recoup from Richard's *Fatal Attraction* episode. And although it had taken a ton of work to get Kinks 2 up and running, Mac and Trent had made it happen. God, they were amazing when they put their heads together. They'd designed the new club to bring in maximum profits, while still keeping a private club feel. Mac had agreed to take on the job of running the new club, while Trent handled the first Kinks. It worked out perfectly.

The warm weather in Hawaii was perfect for sunning and boating. Now, as the cool night breeze off the water sent a chill down her body, Crystal watched the dark waves slowly rolling in, then back out again. It was their first night there. She wondered whether Trent and Mac would even let her out of bed to enjoy the sights. Or whether *she'd* let *them* out. She grinned at the thought, then heard a shuffling from behind. Turning her head, Crystal watched Mac and Trent striding toward her. They were dark, strong, and mostly naked. Her body stirred to life.

"Why are you out here when we're in there?" Trent asked.

Crystal barely suppressed the need to moan. Trent's deep voice always had the power to turn her on. Of course, his bare chest and sexy black boxer-briefs didn't hurt, either. "I'm enjoying this beautiful evening. It's amazing here, Trent. Thank you for this."

Trent took her in his arms and held her tight. "You're welcome, baby."

Crystal pushed backward and peered to the left of Trent to see Mac in a pair of navy blue pajama pants, a sexy grin on his handsome face. "Why are you over there?" she asked.

He leaned close and pressed his lips to her temple. "Because I want you back inside."

She stepped out of Trent's arms and followed Mac into their suite. The hotel was beautiful, the room ridiculously expensive, and yet it could be a hole-in-the-wall for all she cared. Her sole concentration was on Mac and Trent in that moment as he tossed his pj's on a chair and headed toward her, a gleam of wicked intent lighting his eyes.

As if they'd done this a thousand times, Crystal walked backward until her knees bumped up against the end of the bed. Mac gently pushed at the center of her chest, knocking her back onto the gorgeous, ivory-colored comforter. She scooted up the mattress so that she lay in the center. Trent, in all his bronzed and dark-haired glory, stripped out of his clothes and spread out on the bed next to her, while Mac lowered himself on top of her. Their well-muscled bodies and the intensity in their deep eyes was enough to have any woman drooling, but the heavy weight between Mac's legs had her aching and wet. She peeked over at Trent and realized he was every bit as hard.

Mac pushed his pelvis against her, gaining her attention. With the single-minded purpose of making him squirm, Crystal began smoothing her right hand over his pectorals. She ran her fingers through the coarse dark curls that covered his chest, then inched her legs upward until they were wrapped around his lean waist. She let her sex slide along the length of his cock, luxuriating in his deep groan of satisfaction.

"You make me crazy, angel," Mac confessed as he teased his fingers down the front of her, setting off several little fires along the way. "Ah, soft as flower petals," he groaned as he kissed her. His lips, so warm and firm, tasted hers with luxurious thoroughness, as if he wanted to spend a good long time pleasuring each and every part of her body with his mouth. When he flipped them both over, putting her on top, she started to protest. His pleasurable torture continued, distracting her. By slow degrees, he took playful licks of her tongue and nipped her lower lip with his teeth. When she felt a pair of masculine hands cupping and caressing her bottom, Crystal broke the kiss and looked beside her to see Trent propped up on his elbow. The intensity in his silver gaze scorched a path clear to her core. His fingers dipped into the cleft and touched her clitoris. Crystal moaned. He stroked her swollen pussy lips, and her body vibrated at the touch. "I love you."

"I love you," she finally admitted, unable to contain the glorious feelings rioting inside her any longer. "Both of you."

Trent dipped his finger into her pussy, sinking deep, then murmured, "I fucking love hearing you say that, baby."

"Damn, me too," Mac said, his voice a low rumble of sound in the quiet room.

With Trent's finger thrusting in and out, Crystal was having a hard time concentrating. Her body was on fire. "I didn't think it was possible to love two men at the same time—until now."

"As long as we're the *only* two men," Trent said teasingly as a second finger joined the first. "And we're going to want to hear you say those three little words a lot. Like, at least ten times a day."

"I have a little something for you," Mac interjected.

"You and Trent are all I need," she said, meaning every word.

In another heartbeat, Trent pulled his fingers free. She let out an unhappy whimper. "Come over here and I'll give you more," Trent invited as he moved to his back and held out his hand. Yeah, like she could say no to the dark-haired devil. Crystal slid off Mac and moved on top of Trent. True to his words, Trent's fingers found their way between her legs. Soon he was pushing two of them deep inside her and driving her body higher and higher. When Mac reappeared on the bed, he was holding a small red gift bag. She might be turned inside out by Trent's talented fingers, but even that couldn't completely kill her curiosity. "What is it?" she asked.

"Open it and see, angel," Mac murmured.

Crystal propped her head on her elbow on Trent's chest and took the bag from Mac. She peered inside and her breath caught. "Oh Mac, it's beautiful." Her voice caught, and tears stung the backs of her eyes. She tugged it out and held it up. It was a diamond-encrusted sub collar with a heart dangling from it.

"You have our heart, angel," Mac whispered tenderly. "Always."

"Always," Trent confirmed.

Mac took the bag and collar from her trembling hand and gently placed them on the table next to the bed. "Later, we'll put it on you. For now, there's still the little matter of your pleasure." She watched as he picked up a tube of lubricant and popped the top.

With tender care, Trent pulled his fingers free of her pussy, then drove back in, harder and deeper. Crystal threw her head back and moaned. He stroked her clit and she trembled. Out of the corner of her eye, she saw Mac move behind her. Large hands caressed her buttocks. A moan erupted from deep within Crystal as Mac let his lubricated finger drift back and forth over her puckered opening. She wanted him there. She was so hungry to feel both men buried deep inside her that she started pleading.

Trent lifted and sucked one hard nipple, setting off a maelstrom of need inside her. Mac lowered his body over hers and kissed the base of her spine. "You want to be fucked, angel?"

"Yes, Mac. God, yes!" she cried, pushing her ass backward to take more of his exploring finger.

"Mm, that's right," Mac urged. "Take it."

A second slick finger joined the first, and little by little he stretched her, preparing her ass for the invasion of his cock. Crystal shuddered as Trent's fingers moved in and out of her wet cunt, fucking her with slow precision, as if he had all the time in the world. Trent's thumb pressed against her clit, his tongue licking and playing with her nipples. Mac's warm, firm hand took hold of her hip and held her still while he pressed a third finger inside her ass. Crystal dropped her head to Trent's shoulder as her body began to spiral out of control. When she squeezed her bottom, Mac cursed.

"Goddamn. You make me crazy. So fucking crazy."

Crystal couldn't concentrate on Mac's words as sensation after sensation bombarded her.

Trent flicked and teased her nubbin and whispered sweet words of encouragment as he suckled one needy breast, then the other. Mac kissed an arousing trail down her spine, and Trent rammed his fingers deep inside her pussy. Crystal lost it.

Her climax came out of nowhere, hitting like a tidal wave and knocking her into another realm. She screamed, her back arching as her body flew apart. She collapsed on top of Trent, exhausted, every nerve ending humming.

Mac's rough voice just barely broke through the erotic fog coating her mind. "My dick is going to feel so damn good inside this tight little ass."

Trent slipped his fingers free of her dripping mound and cupped her chin, lifting her gaze to his. She watched, transfixed, as he licked each digit clean. "Delicious," he breathed out. Trent pushed upward, and Crystal felt the heavy weight of his cock pressing against her pussy. Her body went from sated to famished in a heartbeat.

With slow, deliberate movements, Trent tucked the head of his cock between her swollen folds, then pulled her down to press a kiss to her lips. She rocked against him when his tongue flicked over her lower lip, nipping and driving her into a horny stupor. A few inches of his rock-hard erection slipped deeper as he vowed, "I swear I'd live forever like this if I could. My dick all snug and warm inside your pussy, hell, yeah."

Good thing he didn't wait for a reply because Crystal was utterly incapable of speech. She felt another hand smoothing over her back to her bottom. She turned her head to look at Mac. In one hand he held a tube of lubricant, and in the other he cupped a handful of her plump flesh. She watched as he squirted a portion of it onto his dick and smoothed it up and down his shaft. Her vision blurred as he began a slow glide inside her ass, filling her. She felt the familiar sense of fullness as his cock stretched her inner muscles. Trent flexed his hips and buried the rest of his cock inside her throbbing pussy.

"Please," she cried.

Mac picked up the pace, fucking her a little faster, while Trent seemed content to take his time. Crystal's body held both men tight. Mac's hips slammed against hers as he pumped her ass with his cock. Trent let loose a low growl and began moving in time with Mac. Soon both men were dancing to the same rhythm. Trent's fingers dug into her hips as he thrust hard. Mac shouted her name and hammered her ass. Once. Twice. Suddenly both men erupted, jets of hot come spilling inside. Crystal felt every pump, every spasm of their cocks, and it spurred on her own orgasm. She flew over the edge, barely aware of Trent's strong arms surrounding her and Mac's gentle hands petting her hair and back. She collasped on top of Trent, her breathing ragged, their sweat mingling.

Mac carefully slid out of her body, then plopped down on the bed beside them. He reached out and brushed a lock of hair off her face as Trent kissed the top of her head and whispered, "Thank you."

Crystal blinked away some of her lethargy. "For what?"

"For not giving up on us."

She forced her limp neck muscles to lift her head and realized he was staring at Mac. Both men turned their gazes toward her and grinned. "I love you," she blurted out, again, as her watery gaze took in the sight of them. They were totally sex-crazed and wildly inappropriate. And she wouldn't have them any other way.

"Damn," Mac groaned, "I'll never get tired of hearing you say that, angel."

"Ditto," Trent agreed before swatting her bottom. "Now, who's up for round two?"

Crystal let out a deep sigh. "I think I've died and gone to heaven."

If you enjoyed *Body Shots*, turn the page for a
sizzling sample of Anne Rainey's

BODY RUSH

A Kensington trade paperback and e-book on sale now!

PROLOGUE

The loud music hit her the instant she stepped through the doors. Lydia loved it. Going to Charlie's, her favorite hangout, after work on Friday night always helped her forget about the lawyers she worked for. There were three of them and they were all exasperating. Working at a law firm sucked in ways that most people couldn't grasp. Her only escape from the stress came when she met up with her two best friends, Roni and Jeanette. They'd known each other since grade school. While everyone else had moved on and forgotten about their school pals, the three of them had stayed in touch. Sometimes she thought they were closer now than ever. Maturity maybe. Who knew the reason, all Lydia knew for sure was that she'd be lost without them.

As she moved through the crowded room, Lydia felt someone's hand on her ass. She turned and glared at the man sitting with a group of men, all grinning like idiots. The hateful look she tossed his way must have worked because he pulled his hand back and started to scope out his next victim. Lydia spotted her friends sitting at a high round table at the back of the bar. Roni waved her over. Lydia smiled and headed toward her.

As she reached them she noticed her favorite drink, a fuzzy navel, ready and waiting. Roni moved to another chair, giving her the one on the end. "Why is it men think it's cute to grab a woman's ass? Do they really think it's going to get them laid?" Lydia shouted in an attempt to be heard over the noise. She slid onto the chair and grabbed her drink, wondering if she'd look like an alcoholic if she downed half the glass in one gulp.

"I'll never understand why men do half the things they do," Roni tossed back with an angry edge to her voice. "Trying to figure them out is a waste of time."

Jeanette leaned close and said, "There is one particular guy I wouldn't mind grabbing my ass. The only problem is I don't think he even knows I exist."

Lydia and Roni both moved closer, their attention rapt. Lydia spoke up first. "Are you still hot for that motorcycle dude coming into your café?"

Jeanette's gaze filled with unbridled lust. "If you saw him, you'd be drooling too. I'm telling you, he's the yummiest thing I've seen yet."

"You've lusted after this guy for what, a year?" Roni asked.

Jeanette laughed. "It feels that way sometimes, but it's only been about six months."

Lydia took a sip of her drink. Already she could feel herself relaxing, as if the last several days were a distant blur. She looked across the table at Roni and shook her head. She still couldn't picture her sharp-tongued friend as a psychologist. On a good day she was hard to get along with. On the other hand, Jeanette's job seemed to fit her to a T. Owning a quant little coffee shop seemed the perfect choice for her introverted friend.

"If you don't ask him out, someone else will," Lydia taunted, hoping to push her friend into making a move.

Jeanette bit her lip. "I'm so damn shy around him. He comes in with this black leather jacket and tight, faded jeans and I just want to jump him. All that dark hair and those dark eyes." She sighed. "Every time I see him I think, this is it. I'm going to ask him out. Or at least find out if he has a damned girlfriend. But I just get all tongue-tied. Like I'm in high school again." She clenched her fist around the longneck bottle of light beer she'd ordered. "It's frustrating as hell."

Roni piped up with her usual bit of sensitive logic. "He rides a motorcycle, he's gorgeous as hell and he comes to your shop every morning. Get a clue, girl; he wants to fuck you!"

Jeanette rolled her eyes. "What makes you think he wants me at all? He comes for the coffee, not the owner."

"Bullshit. He comes because you're hot and he wants to lay you across the counter. He could get coffee anywhere. Hell, he probably doesn't even live near your shop."

Lydia could see her friend's spirits perking up. "You really think so?" Jeanette asked.

Roni laughed and swallowed the last of her sex on the beach before waving the waitress over and ordering another. After the waitress had hurried off to fill their order, Roni said, "He's just watching you squirm a little. Enjoying the way you blush and stammer. It's a game. He's wondering how long you can hold out."

Jeanette started to peel the label off the beer. "I've never asked a guy out before. Usually they ask me. I'm not shy exactly, but I am a little old fashioned, I guess."

Lydia spoke up this time. "I think Roni's right. It's a new world these days. Men like it when a woman is sure of herself. You should definitely ask him out."

Jeanette's eyes grew round. "This coming from the shyest one of all?"

Lydia shrugged. "I've been doing some thinking. It's time we livened up our lives a little, don't you think?"

Roni narrowed her gaze, as if suspicious all of a sudden. "In what way?"

"I don't know," Lydia admitted as she looked down at her half-empty drink. "It's just that we come here every Friday and nothing is ever any different. We work all week, date boring men and then come here to bitch about it. I'm getting sick of it. I'm ready for a change."

"*You* might date boring men, but that doesn't mean we all do."

Lydia knew that tone. Roni always got her back up when someone pointed out that she wasn't perfect. "Oh, really? What about that guy you went out with last weekend? You said he took you to the opera and you wanted to sleep through the whole thing it was so boring."

Roni slumped. "Men always think they're going to impress me by bringing me to some expensive restaurant or some fancy theater. Or they go the opposite route and attempt to please me by playing on my kinkier side. Just once I'd like to go out with a real man. Someone who isn't trying to impress."

"See? That's exactly what I mean. We all have these secret desires, but we don't act on them." Lydia looked at Jeanette, who'd remained silent throughout the exchange. "Just once wouldn't you like to toss caution to the wind and do something . . . wicked?"

Jeanette sat back in her chair and crossed her arms over her chest. "Yes, I would. I can't tell you how many times I've wanted to strip naked and just offer myself to Mr. Motorcycle Man. But how can I possibly do that when I don't know a thing about him? These days it pays to err on the side of caution."

Lydia nodded. "I agree we should be cautious, but that doesn't mean we can't, just this once, do something completely out of character." When Roni and Jeanette both started talking at once, Lydia held up her hand. "Hear me out. If you don't like my idea, then we'll forget I ever mentioned it. Agreed?" Both women looked at each other before giving her the floor. "Roni is ready to get down and dirty with an honest, blue-collar kind of guy. Jeanette, you're so hot for Motorcycle Man I can practically see steam coming off you. I have my own little fantasy in mind too. I say we make a bet to see who can make their fantasy come true first."

Roni snorted. "Are you serious? We're going to bet to see who can get laid faster?"

"Not just laid, dork. The bet is to see who can make their fantasy become reality."

Jeanette gasped. "I cannot believe you're suggesting this. I can see Roni suggesting something like this, she's half crazy, but you? I've never even seen you loosen the top button of your blouse, yet you're sitting there proposing we make our wildest fantasies come to life?"

Lydia's face heated. Jeanette was right. It was insane to think she could actually make her own fantasy a reality. If her friends had half a clue what she wanted to do, they'd commit her to a sanitarium. She was about to call the whole thing off when Roni spoke up

"What's the winner get?"

Jeanette's gaze swung to Roni. Lydia couldn't speak.

"You're actually considering this ludicrous bet?" Jeanette squeaked.

Roni grinned. "Why the hell not? It sounds like fun. And Lydia's right, our lives are boring as shit. While I admit I do have some pretty wild sex, there's still something missing. I want more, damn it."

Lydia wished she could be more like Roni. She took life by the horns. All Lydia could ever control was her cat, Socrates. "I haven't thought that far. What *should* the winner get? While we're at it, what does the loser have to do?"

Jeanette held up her hand. "Wait, I'm already confused. How does one lose?"

"By not making your fantasy real," Roni answered.

"So in order to win, I need to ask Mr. Motorcycle Man out?"

"Not just ask him out, but you have to do the very thing

you've been dreaming of," Lydia said, already wondering what she'd gotten herself into.

"I've had a lot of dreams about that man."

"Make one of them happen and you're safe from losing," Roni said as she finished off her second sex on the beach.

Lydia took a deep breath and went for broke. "So, back to the question. What does the winner get and what does the loser have to do?"

"The winner gets to have her fantasy come to life, obviously," Roni chimed in. "The loser . . . buys the rest a round of drinks?"

"No, that's not incentive enough," Jeanette said, as if she were beginning to warm up to the idea. "The loser has to . . . strip naked and walk down main street."

Lydia shook her head. "Illegal. It can't be against the law."

"Then the loser has to clean my car," Roni tossed out.

Lydia and Jeanette both shuddered. "That's cruel and unusual punishment, Roni," Lydia said. "Damn."

Roni rubbed her hands together. "But it's legal and it's incentive enough to get you two busy."

"What makes you so sure you're going to win?" Jeanette shot right back, her back stiffening in pride.

Roni winked. "Because I never lose, honey."

Lydia sucked down the last of her fuzzy navel, then ordered another. "Okay, now for the next part of this wager. We each have to reveal our fantasy."

Jeanette shrugged. "Mine's already been revealed. I want to have wild and crazy sex with Mr. Motorcycle Man."

Roni frowned. "I want a man who wants me for me. A man who isn't out to impress."

Both women looked at Lydia. "I want to have sex with a stranger, no strings, no names, just sex." *Or maybe with two,* she thought, but she wasn't ready to admit that.

Jeanette's jaw dropped and Roni's eyes filled with awe. "Damn, I've never admired you more than I do right now," Roni mused.

Jeanette laughed and soon they were all cracking up. Deep down Lydia shook like a teenager on prom night. *What the hell did I just get myself into?*

1

"Good morning, Mr. Gentry," Lydia said as Dane Gentry of the Gentry, Anderson & Dailey Law Firm strode through the door, a scowl marring his handsome face.

A grunt seemed to sum up what he thought of her chipper greeting. One thing Lydia had learned over the two years since coming to work for Dane, the man hated mornings. "Coffee's on your desk and here's your schedule for the day." She handed him the printout. If it were possible, his frown deepened as he looked her over.

"What time did you get here?"

She pushed her glasses higher on her nose and said, "Uh, five, Mr. Gentry. I had a few things to catch up on."

He rubbed his jaw. "Do I pay you overtime?"

Lydia was so confused by his question she just sat there, staring at him as if he'd lost his mind.

"Lydia, answer the question. It wasn't that hard."

"No, sir, you don't. I'm salary."

"Then it makes no sense to work overtime, now does it?"

"I suppose not, but I needed to finish up some research."

Dane shook his head. "You work too much."

Lydia was beginning to feel a spark of anger. She liked her job, but there were days when working for three lawyers really was a joke. "Are you complaining about my performance, Mr. Gentry?"

He frowned. "Of course not, but you put in way too many hours."

"Someone had to finish the research. I don't have a magic wand here . . . sir," she said, allowing a hint of sarcasm to seep into her voice.

Her boss leaned across the desk, coming way too close for comfort, and whispered, "You have a very smart mouth, Lydia. One of these days it'll get you into trouble."

Lydia tamped down the urge to move her chair closer, to inhale his clean masculine scent. She'd always had a weakness for Dane. He was so tall and broad shouldered. His messy dark hair with the little curl at the collar always made her want to reach out and play with it. Deep brown eyes watched her with an intensity that had her feeling as if someone had jacked up the temperature. It was no wonder he had so many female clients. She thought of his statement and answered, "There are times when I find my quick wit to be rather helpful, Mr. Gentry."

"Dane," he gritted out. "Will you ever call me Dane?"

"I see no reason to, no." This was an old argument between them. She stood on formalities and it drove him crazy, which was partly why she did it, of course.

"I can make it mandatory."

She laughed. "That can't be legal."

"Who gives a damn if it's legal or not?"

She was about to remind him that he was a lawyer when another voice intruded. "Is he giving you a hard way to go, sugar?"

Dane straightened and turned around. Lydia peered around Dane's massive body to see Mac Anderson striding through the door, a bagel in one hand and his briefcase in the other. Lydia went back to work mode. "Good morning, Mr. Anderson. Your schedule," she explained as she handed it over. "Don't forget you said you'd have lunch with your mom today at one."

Mac grinned and looked at Dane. "Think she'll ever call us by our first name?"

Dane snorted and crossed his arms over his chest. "Unlikely."

Mac was Dane's polar opposite. He walked around with a perpetual grin and everyone was a friend. In fact, she wasn't sure she'd ever seen the man grumpy. With his sandy blond hair and pale blue eyes, he looked more like a laidback surfer than a lawyer. His easy charm was merely a veneer though. He was every bit as sharp as Dane and just as cunning in the courtroom.

"This subject has been beaten into the ground," she replied as she pretended an interest in the e-mail she'd been going through. "You both might as well get used to the fact that I'm never going to call you by your first names. It's not professional and that's the end of it."

"Mouthy, isn't she?" Mac noted.

Out of the corner of her eye she saw Dane frown, again. "Someone needs to teach *Ms. Burke* a lesson, if you ask me."

"Someone has a meeting in half an hour and shouldn't be wasting time chatting."

"She has a point," another voice chimed in. They all three looked at the door to the office just as Trent Dailey marched through it, his movements precise, his expression serious. Lydia straightened in her chair. Trent had a way of making people check themselves. He wasn't exactly a drill sergeant, but she secretly thought he would have made an exemplary one if he ever chose to change professions. Ever the serious one, with his amber eyes, neatly trimmed black hair and powerful build, Trent rarely cracked a smile, and he always did everything with efficiency. She often felt like a slacker around him, and for a workaholic like her, that was saying something.

"If you two can find it in you to break away from the charming Ms. Burke, I have something I need to discuss with you."

Mac looked back at her and winked. "He's at it already. Look out, sugar, you could be next."

Dane didn't say another word, just growled something about coffee and stomped into his office, Trent and Mac hot on his heels.

The phone rang and she had the feeling her day was about to turn chaotic. "I just love Mondays," she mumbled, before picking it up.

Lydia had started the day with a smile, but that was well before Dane turned her world upside down. There wasn't a moment's peace. The minute she finished one task, she'd end up having fifty more dumped on her desk. And it was only noon!

"Lydia, I need you to get Gordon Michelson on the phone," Dane said. "I want to set up a meeting right away concerning his personal injury case."

"Yes, Mr. Gentry," she replied, barely containing a groan. As she closed the document she'd been working on for Mac and searched through her list of contacts for Michelson's phone number, Dane popped his head out of his office once more. "Lydia, did you do that research for the Wilson case?"

"It's not quite finished. I'll have it to you by the end of the day, sir."

"That's fine. By the way, don't forget to interview that potential client, Sam MacKenzie."

Lydia had finally reached the end of her rope. "Okay, you know what? This is too much for one person. I get a few things done and you drop a hundred more on me. I'm not a robot!"

She grabbed her purse and started for the door, aware she'd attracted the attention of her fellow coworkers. Dane was quick to intercept her. She tried to move around him, but he only grabbed her arm, halting her forward progress.

"Where are you going?"

"I need a break," she gritted out.

"I'm sorry. Don't quit, please."

She put her hand on her hip and glared up at him. "Well, of course I'm not quitting! But I am taking the rest of the afternoon off. You can get along without me that long, can't you?"

Dane leaned down and whispered into her ear, "If you don't come back tomorrow I'll come looking for you, sweetheart. I won't let you get away from me so easily."

Lydia shuddered at the sensual tone. All the time she'd worked for Dane, he'd never used that dark, mysterious tone on her. Or endearments for that matter. He wasn't like Mac, where every woman he met was either sugar or darlin', an influence of his Texas upbringing. Dane had just crossed a line, and despite warning bells going off inside her head, his wicked threat tantalized her.

As he released her arm and stepped to the side to let her pass, Lydia watched his lips tilt to one side. He was flirting with her and she was woefully unequipped to handle a man like Dane Gentry.

Lydia forced her feet to move, her entire body suddenly too warm for comfort. As she left the office building, she could swear all three men stared at her, and she had a sneaking suspicion it wasn't professional concern they had on their minds.

As soon as the office door closed, Dane let out a breath. Jesus, that was close. He'd been a heartbeat away from kissing her. That would be the wrong thing to do. Way wrong. But if that was the case, then why did he feel as if he'd lost a golden opportunity? What would she have done if he'd closed that little distance? Damn, Lydia Burke had been a fire in his blood for too long already. If he didn't do something about his fascination with her, he was going to lose it.

As he'd watched her get all authoritative and demanding, he'd been tempted to push her to her knees and force her to submit. There was a chemistry between them. Hell, there'd always been a spark. Though he had a feeling she liked to pretend it wasn't there, Dane knew the truth. Lust, craving, obsession; whatever the label it didn't matter. It wasn't going away, not until they did something about it.

"Shit, that was close," Mac groaned. "I thought she was leaving you for good this time."

"She won't leave," Dane stated. "She knows I'd find her and bring her back."

"We've got another problem," Trent grumbled as he motioned them into his office. After he closed the door, he said, "Clyde just put in his two weeks' notice and we need to replace him."

As Dane glanced at Trent across the room, the throbbing in Dane's head gained momentum. Trent referred to the manager at Kinks, the bondage and submission club they owned. "Damn, he was the best we had so far. No one stepped out of line as long as Clyde was around," Mac said.

Dane moved toward Trent's desk and sat on the edge. "What happened?"

Trent pushed his fingers through his hair in agitation. "Hell, he always did say it wouldn't be a permanent thing for him," Trent explained. "He's getting married and his fiancée wants him to concentrate full time on the landscaping business they've set up. Being our manager wasn't really part of his five-year plan."

Dane crossed his legs at the ankles. "I met the fiancée once. She's such a damned prude, I'm surprised Clyde lasted this long."

Trent's eyes widened. "She came into Kinks?"

"No, she picked him up at the door one night; his car was in the shop. She took one look at me and went pale as a damn sheet." His lips twitched. "I think it was my leather dom hood that did it."

Mac laughed. "It's wrong for us to find amusement in that."

Dane laughed, though it felt hollow. The rest of his day would be shit because Lydia wasn't there. He never quite understood his fascination with her, which was one reason he'd kept his distance. He didn't like going into a relationship blind.

"Back to the problem at hand," Trent insisted. "We need to replace Clyde. I asked him if he knew anyone he could recommend. Of course, he didn't; that would've been too fucking easy. I thought maybe we could bump Ralph up. He's been there the longest and knows the ropes. We put him on as manager and replace his spot on the floor. It's bound to be easier to find someone to replace him, rather than taking the time to train someone new to take Clyde's position, agreed?"

Dane and Mac both nodded. Dane was the first to speak. "Fine by me."

Trent moved toward his office. "Done then. We can take care of it tonight."

Dane suddenly felt exhausted. "Did either of you think it'd be this much work to run that damned club?"

Mac arched a brow at him. "Having second thoughts?"

Dane shrugged and sat back. They'd taken over the running of the club a little over a year ago, after the previous owner had found out he had cancer. They'd grown close to Leo, so when he confided in them that he wanted the club to go to someone he knew and trusted, someone who would take care of it, they'd stepped in and made it happen. The place now made them a hefty profit. It was never about the money though, not for any of them. It was their home away from home. The only place they could truly be free to explore the darker nature of their souls. The three of them had gone to college together. It had been there that they'd discovered they shared a common passion for the kinkier side of sex. When the club had practically been dropped into their laps, it'd seemed perfect. But Dane hadn't counted on how much work was involved. Trent liked having a club to run, Mac just plain enjoyed sex, but he'd been

244 / Anne Rainey

drawn to the dom role. Still, being a club dom was fast losing its appeal.

"I don't know. I think I'm getting worn down from burning the candle at both ends."

Trent moved toward Lydia's chair and sat down. "I've been feeling the same way, but now that it's turning a profit we can start thinking of hiring more help."

Mac's usual grin was replaced by a scowl. "That could be tricky as hell, considering what we do during the day. We have to protect our interests."

"That's why we have the employees sign a confidentiality agreement and it's also why we never go out to the floor without our hoods." Trent reminded him.

The members of the club thought they wore the hoods for effect; never allowing anyone to see their faces lent to the dark mystery. The truth wasn't nearly as enticing. Dane knew the legal end was secure, but society didn't always care about laws and regulations. In the end, the general population would still view the club as a place that catered to sexual deviants. "Can you imagine if someone found out we run a BDSM club? We'd be finished as lawyers."

"It's not illegal, Dane," Trent growled. "You make it sound like we're drug lords or pimps."

"Our clients wouldn't give a damn about legalities, Trent, and you know it. They'd find a new law firm quicker than any of us could blink."

"You're forgetting one important factor here, buddy," Mac said, a mischievous gleam lighting his eyes.

"What?"

"Some of our clients are also members at Kinks. They want their privacy protected just as much as we do."

Dane nodded. "No shit. And they're way more connected than we are. We give them a place to play in safety. They'll damn near kill to keep that little privilege."

"Besides, it's not like anyone at Kinks is beyond reproach," Trent said. "I've yet to see a single goody-goody come near the place."

Trent's words brought Dane back to his talk with Lydia that morning. "Speaking of goody-goody. I'm about fed up with Lydia's constant refusal to call me by my first name. The woman's been my paralegal for two years."

"It'll never happen," Trent said, his voice resigned. "I don't know why you even bother. Lydia is way too professional. In her mind it's inappropriate. End of story."

"Damn, can you imagine her coming into Kinks?"

Mac's question tore straight through him. Hell yeah, Dane could imagine it. He'd done so a hundred different times, usually while he jacked off. "She'd faint dead away," he mused.

"There's just something sexy about that librarian getup she wears though," Trent added. "It makes me want to tear it off her and see what she keeps hidden."

"Paradise," Mac assured them. "I can feel it in my bones. That woman is built."

"Then I'm not the only one who's fantasized about my delectable paralegal?" Dane asked. Trent and Mac both shook their heads. Somehow that made Dane feel better, like less of a debaucher of virgins. "If she ever does venture into our lair, she'll be in for one helluva ride."

They all three grunted in agreement.